THE MAN WHO LOVED TOO MUCH

Book 3: Oxymoron

by John Rachel

Published by
Literary Vagabond Books
Los Angeles • Osaka
literaryvagabond.com

The Man Who Loved Too Much,
Book 3: Oxymoron
Copyright © 2014
by John Rachel

Trade Book ISBN: 978-0-692-47688-8

Cover Art by Thelonius Fotochop

Table of Contents

Acknowledgements

Special appreciation goes out to Justin Beardsell for helping me bridge enormous generation gaps and connecting me with contemporary youth culture. Also to Ryan Paul Burke and Max Coldham Brewer for bringing me up to speed on currently popular traditional and designer recreational drugs.

As has become my custom, I of course want to thank my best friend and wife, Masumi Nishida, for her encouragement and faith in me, and her magnificent ongoing role as my teacher and guide in discovering the wonders of Japan and Japanese culture, despite my resistance to achieving even a rudimentary grasp of the Japanese language.

For their inestimable contributions to my literary and intellectual development, and my tentative, fleeting grasp on reality, I also wish to express my appreciation and awe shucks to: Tom Robbins, Kurt Vonnegut, John Irving, Stanislaw Lem, Studs Terkel, E. L. Doctorow, Jerzy Kosinski, Ken Kesey, Sinclair Lewis, Ralph Ellison, Bertrand Russell, Ludwig Wittgenstein, Ralph Nader, Noam Chomsky, Naomi Klein, Chris Hedges, Howard Zinn, Bill Moyers, Malcolm X, Martin Luther King, Buddha, Jesus of Nazareth, the Dalai Lama, Nelson Mandela, Mahatma Gandhi, George Carlin, Cornell West, Thomas Kuhn, Aldous Huxley, Neil Postman, and Jared Diamond.

Inspiration ... Masumi Nishida, Rebecca Jones, Randy Calligan, Julia Isabel, Nic Penrake, Gerald Everett Jones, and Lance Collins.

Perspiration ... Gary Cambra, Alexa Wiley, Megan Stonic, Chelsea Nouvelle, Sabrina Nagel, Kamaria Wilson, Chad and Rachel Hamar, Shannon McAllister, Kate Mann, Keary Kase, my adopted mother and father (may they rest in peace), my natural mother (may she be reincarnated as a sane human being for another go at it).

Conversation ... Travis Rood, Mickey Finn, Mansur and Neelofar Langoo, Sigismund and Ursula Hadelich, Ron Ruiz, Gilly Atkins, Oliver Lamm, Russell Swider, Gary Clark, Judy Rachel, Kristi Cobb, and Alex Malherbe.

Lastly, for their belief in me and their unwavering enthusiasm, thanks and butterfly kisses go out to my unapologetic publisher Literary Vagabond Books, specifically the svelte and droll head of that organization, Sybil Fairbanks, and my latest editor there, Penelope Kastenbach. Both of you are studies in and witness to the irrepressible power of the human imagination.

Chapter One

THE DAZE OF OUR LIVES
Late Autumn 2007 Winter 2008

Planet Oblivion

A week had gone by. Halloween had come and gone.

Still no word from Candy.

Maybe she had written him off.

Life in the big city.

Billy was sitting in Planet Hollywood on Broadway, in the heart of the *new* Times Square.

This area at one time had been the unofficial strip mall for all of the depravity, decadence, vice, and almost every commodifiable form of affliction and death, available from the slimy lowlife of New York City. You name it. You could buy it there. Drugs, sex, stolen goods, guns, a gangland assassination.

At night, so concentrated were the bottom-dwelling scum on 42nd Street between Broadway and 8th Avenue, spilling out onto the contiguous streets for several city blocks in every direction, the *selling* public — hookers, hustlers, pimps, fences, hit men, drug dealers, con men, and other illicit entrepreneurs — often outnumbered the *buying* public.

All of that changed in the 90s. Using coercive police sweeps and sanitizing enforcement of zoning laws and business licensing, under the direction of then mayor Rudolph Giuliani, the area became a miracle of urban renewal. The massage parlors, peep shows, strip clubs, pawn shops, hooker bars, triple-X movie theaters, adult book stores, and scummy fast food joints were forced out. Planet Hollywood and scores of other multi-national restaurant, tavern and clothing chains moved in and made the Times Square enterprise zone their base for spreading consumerist homogeneity throughout the Big Apple, eventually turning the entire area into a family-friendly tourist trap — a Universal Studios City Walk with a New York accent.

Billy ordered the Spaghetti Pomodoro, sipped on a glass of ice water with a slice of lemon hanging on the lip, and watched people stroll leisurely by. They had to be from out of state. They were smiling.

Several booths away and behind him, a boisterous group of six was arguing and causing such a ruckus, Billy's curiosity got the best of him and he turned around to see what was going on. The manager of the restaurant was standing there, partially blocking Billy's view. But it looked like they were members of a rock band, some local act he didn't think he recognized. All musicians wore the same uniform anyway, so it was hard to tell them apart. The manager was trying to keep his cool, but was becoming more animated and appeared to be on the verge of throwing them out. Then the person directly behind the manager stood up. Billy recognized her at once.

Amethyst Reigns. That must be her band.

There was one extra guy with them who stood out only because he didn't. Unlike the other boys, he had on an ordinary button-down shirt over a white cotton undershirt, and a haircut he couldn't have paid more than six bucks for. Maybe he was the band's manager. Amethyst had mentioned something about a manager at the Mercury Lounge gig.

She spotted Billy, winked and gave him a peculiar but not unfriendly smile, then flipped off everyone at her booth and walked over to him.

"Can you help me out?"

"Why me?"

She nodded towards a fat, balding man across the aisle in a three-piece suit with the juice from a BBQ Bacon Cheeseburger running down his chin, trying look up the skirt of a waitress at the next table. She was immodestly bending over to serve another customer.

"Because fat fuck there is busy."

She gave him the address and directions for her studio loft in Soho — in an area that had so far been spared being gentrified into million-dollar warehouse spaces and store fronts — and asked him to be there day after tomorrow.

"Say around 6 pm."

"What's the favor?"

Amethyst laid her hand on the table palm up.

"Press the center of my palm with your index finger."

He did.

She held up three fingers.

"How many?"

"Three."

"Perfect. You can handle this. You may be overqualified."

Amethyst then reached down the front of her low rider pants and pulled out a small medicinal locket. She showed it to him.

"Used to belong to my grandmother."

She took out a tiny pill and handed it to Billy.

"What's this?"

"2Cb."

"What's that?"

"Trust me. Just take it."

Billy spent the rest of that evening and the entire night sitting on a bench in a large, popular park near Cooper Union. He wanted to move but at the same time didn't.

On a scrim that seemed to cover the entire range of his vision, projected from the occipital lobe of his brain like smoky filaments onto the shimmering fabric wherever he looked, were images from the last five or so years. If proper billing were to be had, he and Natalie were co-stars of what appeared to be both a comedy and tragedy, though a myriad of other major and minor characters made their appearances.

It was a plotless montage. Or maybe an experimental cinema nouveau piece, ignoring the need for clear exposition and narrative continuity. It was a long dark movie, in the end making it clear that the comedy was only there to mock the tragedy, ultimately pointing to the pointlessness and futility of everything.

The sun came up, as much as it ever came up on the murky eastern horizon over Brooklyn.

He watched as the pace of the city picked up. Never fully asleep, it quickly returned to its normal adrenalin-raging tempo, horns blaring, tires squealing, pedestrians hurrying to their daily destinations.

Billy sat motionless but alert.

He had thought with making new acquaintances — Candy and Amethyst featuring prominently — and the change of scene, he would beat the grinning Grim Reaper of the living dead, the orchestrator of his nightmares, choreographer of the ghosts of his past, that demon dervish who with the sinister twirling of his mustache and arrogant flicking of his fingers, played Billy like a puppet jester, jerking and twisting him into impossible and agonizing shapes, torturing him with the worst suffering of all, the self-inflicted pain of his own self-loathing.

Billy stood up, exhausted and drained. He felt foamy and spent. Eviscerated.

Marginally confident now that he could distinguish the navigable elements of reality from the hallucinations, he started making his way back to his apartment.

It was fully light now. The street lamps had all been turned off. He walked across 6th Street, down 2nd Avenue, across 3rd Street, cut through a small park. Behind the only bench in the park was the body of an old man, probably a bum, judging from the state of his clothing, his lack of shoes, and the layer of grime on his feet, hands and face. The old man's head was bashed in and a large pool of blood spread out around him. He was obviously dead.

Billy stared at the corpse for some time, intrigued by the amoeba-shaped hematological puddle that in slow motion was pooling on the cement walkway. His emotional stasis felt curious. He was not in the least concerned about the loss of the man's life, or even what his own role as an innocent bystander might entail. He felt nothing.

Finally he exited the park.

He continued along 2nd Avenue and spotted some graffiti on an abandoned building. Primitive and Spartan. Nothing to distract from the message.

Art imitates life.
Life imitates art.

Okay. But what if there was no art?
Would that be the end of life?
Ah! That's what happened.
Art disappeared. Everyone died.
Metaphorically speaking, of course.

He stopped at a liquor store. How could you not love a town where the liquor stores open for business at eight in the morning? A few minutes later, he was back to the dismal torpor, the sheer ugliness of what he called home.

In less time than it would have taken him to eat the bowl of cereal he should have had, Billy finished two bottles of pre-mixed margaritas.

He slept for 14 hours straight. Then he smoked a joint. Slept 9 more hours.

When he finally woke up, he saw that someone had thrown a brick through his window. There was no note attached, so it wasn't a secret admirer.

He carefully picked up the large shards of glass, whisk-broomed the splinters into a dustpan.

Maybe he should read a book. He still had those same two staring back at him bedside.

Naw! Too much work. He might learn something. Or worse, find out things he didn't want to know. He had already had too much of that.

Billy lay down. Not that much different than sitting up. Except he had a better view of the water-stained, yellowed, peeling paint on his ceiling.

He wished he lived by a beach.

That way he could stick his head in the sand.

Up his ass would have to do for now.

A Small Favor

If he was nothing else, Billy was dependable. A man of his word.

He had one item on his calendar.

A small favor.

When Billy arrived at her loft, Amethyst was no where in sight. But the other members of Machines of Melanoma were hanging about. Billy cornered one of them. He was only three or four years younger than Billy, but looked at Billy like he was some elderly relative who had flown in from Kansas to check up on his runaway niece.

"Where's Amethyst?"

Nodding to a closed door at the other end of the room.

"In there probably getting her brains fucked out."

"What am I doing here?"

"Our fucking tyrant lead singer doesn't think any of us is capable of handling a camera. You're supposed to take pictures. Not make it too obvious. Us and him. Her and him. Him. It's for publicity purposes. Like we hang with the big stars. It's total bullshit."

"Who is this *him*?"

"Some fucking pseudo-legend from the 90s. A big wank from California. She met him during a video shoot the other day at the Roseland."

"She's in a music video?"

"As an extra. They needed New York's finest sluts as a backdrop for a burnout hair band. She just played herself."

"Do you have anything nice to say about her? She's your lead singer."

"She's got a nice ass. Standing behind her makes the gigs almost tolerable."

"So where's the camera?"

He yelled across the room. "Hey numbnuts! Bring me that camera. Right there on the table."

Numbnuts or whatever his real name started across the room toward Billy with a small Canon digital camera in hand.

Suddenly, the door at the other end of the room burst open and a tall, dark, creepy dude came striding out. He was throwing a leather vest on over his hairy chest. His boots thudded heavily on the wood floor as he bolted for the door and went running out.

"Who *was* that? He did look a little familiar."

"Famous author, man. Wrote the *Better Homes and Gardens Book of Etiquette*."

"And *Jonathan Livingston Seagull*."

"What are you stupid? You don't know who that is?"

"He married that famous blond chick. Big Hollywood star. Giant tits."

"Oh right. The blond Hollywood star with big tits. That pins it down."

Amethyst staggered through the door. Everyone turned to look.

Blood was dripping from her nose. Her face was badly bruised, one eye swollen almost shut. One of her lips was split and her teeth appeared to be bloody. She was naked from the waist down, except for a pair of gaudy purple platform pumps.

The guy Billy had been talking to was first on his feet and running toward her. Billy was right behind him. The other band members gathered around her as badmouth grabbed her by the shoulders.

"Am! What happened? Holy shit! I'm gonna kill that motherfucker!"

She fell into his arms and collapsed. He lowered her to the floor.

"Come on, guys! Don't just stand there. Get some towels. A washcloth. Wet. Make it wet. Bring a pan of water. You. Get a blanket."

Billy wanted to help. But he had no idea what he should do.

"Should we call the police? How about an ambulance?"

Amethyst was still conscious, though she kept her eyes closed.

"No no. Please. No police. I'll be alright. Do I look bad?"

"You need to go to emergency. Let's get you dressed."

The guy who had had nothing nice to say about Amethyst, obviously cared about her a lot. Maybe with the comments before, it was all some sort of nihilist tough-guy show he put on for strangers. But now he really took charge.

Within fifteen minutes, he had her cleaned up the best he could, instructed her to hold a couple of improvised sandwich bag ice packs against the swelling areas of her face, got her dressed into a complete change of clothes, and with the assistance of Billy was taking her down to street level. He had sent one of the other band members ahead to hail a taxi.

Amethyst sat in the middle between Billy and badmouth on the way to the hospital. She was kind of drowsy — Billy smelled alcohol on her breath — and several times slumped over onto his shoulder, unsuccessfully trying to hold the ice pack on her face as her arms grew limp. Several splotches of blood accumulated on his shirt.

Badmouth leaned over to see how she was doing. Then he looked at Billy.

"I'm Kevin, by the way. But everyone calls me Hypo."

"I'm Billy."

"Yeah I know."

They waited forever in the emergency waiting room. Many of the others being treated at that time of night made Amethyst's condition look like she had come by to get one of her acrylic nails glued back on. Fire victims, gunshot victims, car crash victims. One guy had been bludgeoned with a baseball bat by a rival gang. A drunk had been hit and dragged two entire city blocks by a bus. A young girl had been gang raped, then stabbed and left to die next to a bridge abutment. A delirious man, weeping and pleading for help, was holding in his arms the bloody corpse of a newborn baby.

This wasn't some crime scene or ER reality show. There were no commercial breaks. Just a steady stream of real life horror stories on a Saturday night in New York City.

When Amethyst was finally admitted to a treatment room, she was only gone for 20 minutes. Her injuries relatively speaking were not that serious. No broken bones or even any chipped teeth.

She returned to the waiting area with a few bandages, smears of antiseptic cream on various abrasions, four stitches in her eyebrow, and a prescription for painkillers in her hand.

She held the prescription up between her healthy thumb and bandaged index finger as she approached the five guys slumped over in the uncomfortable plastic chairs waiting for her.

"Anyone want to get high?"

"You better keep them. You'll probably need them later."

They caught a taxi back to the loft. It had been a long night. The sun would be up soon.

Amethyst was in good spirits. Especially considering how she looked. The hospital must have shot her up with some painkillers. She definitely had an icy glaze in her eyes and her pupils were so dilated, her irises looked like the thin decorative line on the edge of a black candy dish.

When they got back to the loft, she lay down on a dirty futon mattress toward one side of the big room, which doubled as the band's rehearsal space. All of their equipment was pushed up against the opposite wall, below several industrial-type steel and glass windows, which were just beginning to admit the light of the new dawn.

The four band members, yawning and making no effort to hide the signs of weariness, started gathering their stuff, each to head to back to his own place to catch some sleep.

Billy sat down beside Amethyst. She was starting to wind down, gliding from the initial euphoric rush of the anesthetic into a mellow chill, and appeared to almost be asleep.

She opened her eyes and looked at Billy.

"I'm glad you came."

"I think I've let you down."

"How's that?"

"I didn't get any pictures."

"It's a damn good thing. This is a bad hair day for me."

11

"I think I saw a 24-hour hair salon on Broadway."

"I'm going to sleep."

And she did.

Meet Me in St. Louis

Billy never went back to the Tunnel of Love or Planet Hollywood. In fact, for two months he hardly went anywhere. It just didn't seem worth the effort.

He was low on energy. Low on curiosity. Low on inspiration. Low on imagination.

And he was running low on money.

Candy wasn't back. Amethyst called a couple times but he had trouble taking very seriously her invitation to come out to see her band. He couldn't imagine she had any real interest in seeing him and figured he would just be another body stuffed in a club.

His phone never rang.

He never called anyone.

He sat at home counting his money — he had withdrawn all but $200 from his account — calculating and recalculating, trying to figure out how he could make what he had left last for as long as he needed it to last. Which was the big question mark. How long that would be he had no way of knowing. He had faith that Natalie was doing what she could and would call him when the house sold. Since he was on the title, she would have to ask him to come to Newburgh and sign the papers for the closing. There was no way around that. But so far no call.

He was tempted to ring her, maybe to check on progress, maybe to offer advice and some encouragement for what it was worth. Probably little if nothing. But each time he reached for the phone, he couldn't gather the strength to actually pick it up.

Or was it the courage?

New York was a fuck of an expensive place to live. Even as modestly as he lived. The price of everything was off the map.

Maybe he should get a job. Doing what?

Never mind.

Stupid idea! Work was a four-letter word. At least for now.

This malaise, this detachment, this conundrum, this languor, it wasn't just Billy's problem.

Frankly, after 9/11 New York never quite got its groove back.

It was still the center of the Universe. But a center that was worn and sloppy. A loose fit. Drunk and wobbly like a worn old wheel. Or a button hanging by a single frayed thread.

No one seemed to acknowledge it. Not consciously. Not even Billy.

The whole of New York City was in massive denial.

Billy just kept his head down and waited for the inevitable. He wasn't quite sure what the inevitable consisted of. Maybe it was the other shoe. The tax bill. A fat lady singing. A death certificate.

Whatever it was, it didn't matter. It would come at a good time or a bad time. But it would eventually come. That was inevitable.

His phone rang.

"Happy Thanksgiving!! Are you eating turkey?"

It was Thanksgiving?

"Hi mom. Is it Thanksgiving already?"

"I know you New Yorkers are busy. But you could slow down for one day and celebrate the ...whatever it is we celebrate on Thanksgiving. Being thankful, I guess."

"The Pilgrims setting up shop. Having a friendly meal with the natives so that they could kill them off later."

"Billy Billy! What am I going to do with you? Such a bitter view of American history. Anyway, I called to see how you are and invite you to spend Christmas with me. How about it? You want to spend the holidays with an old lady?"

"Gosh, mom. I'd love too. But I'm pretty broke."

"Listen, my stubborn and proud baby. First of all, if you need money I can send you some."

"I'll pay it back."

"I know you will. So don't worry about it. Besides, this is my treat. A very special Christmas holiday. You and I are going to St. Louis."

"St. Louis? What's in St. Louis?"

"Red Wing hockey! That's what!"

His mom never ceased to amaze him. He had no idea she liked hockey. And maybe she hadn't always. But at least for now, she had become a doting, adoring fan of the Detroit home team hockey club. They were scheduled to play St. Louis five days before Christmas, then the day after. She wanted to make a week-long vacation of it, just the two of them.

"They are kickin' ass this year, Billy. They're 15, 5 and 1. Can you believe it? 15 wins, 5 losses and a tie. People have already got Stanley Cup fever. The games are a huge party!"

"What about dad?"

"The usual. Vegas. It's become his yearly ritual. It's like going to Mecca."

"Are you sure? I mean—"

"I'm absolutely sure! We're gonna have a good time. Meet me in St. Louis, Billy Boy."

And so they did.

First she sent him $3000 out of her "secret savings account", then he received a FedEx containing an airline ticket just a couple days before he was to board the plane for St. Louis.

While the destination would have probably been 149th on his list of places to go, it was just what he needed. He had dug himself so deeply in a rut in New York and no one was there to take away the shovel.

There was a game the first night they arrived. After checking into a Holiday Inn, they headed to the Scottrade Center Stadium to yell and scream like a couple high school kids. Unfortunately, the Red Wings went down 2-3 to the Blues.

"They were off tonight, Billy. Osgood must have forgotten to wear his contacts. He's such a good goalie. He's only had three goals scored against him. Three times all year! And two of those games we won anyway."

"Wow! You're really into this."

"For some reason, hockey reminds me of being married."

"I can understand that. I would think it's something you might not want to be reminded of."

"Yeah. Except we get to kick the other guy's butt!"

"Mom. You are one of a kind."

The next game was in six days. Billy and his mom spent the time seeing the sights in St. Louis, which turned out to be a more interesting city than Billy would have imagined.

Of course, they saw the Gateway Arch, which is hard *not* to see, since it towers more than six stories in a majestic parabolic arch over the Mississippi River.

Since his mom had rented a car, they drove out to Forest Park and nearly froze to death walking around the lakes and hiking paths. They went to Grant's Farm, then next day did a tour of the Anheuser-Busch Brewery, where Billy learned what an exotic art and precise science it was to turn out some of the blandest beer on the planet.

And since it was Christmas, they went shopping. They agreed to not spend more than $20 on one another, a pact which they both broke, then made all sorts of excuses why. Billy really got the best end of the deal, since it had just been his birthday and his mom decided to give him a belated b-day present as well. She bought him a top-of-the-line iPod and a $99 gift certificate to buy music at the Apple Online music store.

"But mom. Nobody pays for music anymore. They steal it."

"If everyone filled their underwear with sardines, would you do it?"

"If it made me sexy I would."

Billy bought his mom beautiful soft furry earmuffs for Christmas. She was ecstatic.

"These are perfect, Billy. So fluffy and cuddly. These can double as a pet, since your father won't allow animals in the house."

"They're already housebroken. It was the first thing I asked."

They spent Christmas evening in their room listening to carols on the radio and eating room service food. They even toasted the holiday with a bottle of champagne.

The Red Wings came through in style on the second match up. Osgood was back in the net, made some spectacular saves, and didn't give up a single goal. Detroit shut out St. Louis 5-0. The way she carried on, Billy thought his mom was going to burst a blood vessel. He had bruises on him from all of the surrogate body checks she landed on him from the next seat. He told her that her bony elbows should be registered as lethal weapons with law enforcement agencies wherever she went.

Parting at the airport with good old mom would presumably be sad under any circumstances. But this time was especially poignant. While there was no turning back for Billy — certainly he didn't want to ever live in Detroit again, nor could he consider, especially as an adult, ever living under the same roof with his father — his mom still provided him with a kind of mom-shield against the random harshness of the world, as she had done from his earliest days as a child. There was some unique comfort being held in those thin, frail arms, pressed against her breastless body, as they hugged and said their good-byes in the airport. It was a comfort he only experienced with her.

Maybe that's why it is almost universally reported that on the battlefield, dying men in their last desperate cries before the life drains out of their bodies, yell out for their mothers.

"Thanks, mom. You saved my life. This has been great."

"It's always so good seeing my big grown-up boy. We had fun now, didn't we?"

She reached in her purse and pulled out a small gift-wrapped package.

"If you ever are feeling like you're missing your old mom, here's a little something I wanted you to have to remind you of me."

He excitedly tore it open. It was a Red Wings souvenir hockey-jersey.

Billy smiled from ear-to-ear and hugged her tightly. She couldn't see the boulder-size tears in his eyes.

The public address system blared the announcement for the boarding of his plane. His flight was leaving first, hers about an our later from a nearby gate.

"There's your plane. Be nice to the stewardesses now. Some of them are very pretty girls, have you noticed?"

"Yeah, mom. I noticed. I'll try to be a *good boy*."

"You took the words right out of my mouth. I love you, Billy Boy."

"Love you too, mom."

Billy waved one last good-bye before disappearing down the passageway to board the plane.

He had no way of knowing. But this would be the last time he would ever see his mom alive.

Running on Empty

It felt good to get out of New York, even if it was just for a week.

Being gone for the last-minute Christmas shopping frenzy was especially fortuitous timing. Admittedly he saw some of the panic and desperation in the eyes of the St. Louis shoppers, as they frantically worked their way down their gift lists, the Christmas Eve deadline looming only a few days away. But holiday shopping in St. Louis was like a game of touch football, whereas in New York it was more like Wrestlemania.

Unfortunately, it was not even an hour after Billy got back into the city — literally right after he completed the subway ride from the airport and was popping back up to street level at 2nd Avenue — that the Big Apple funk again shrouded him in the monastic gloom of his misery.

He just couldn't deal with it, the faceless people, the callous anonymity, the hustle-bustle busywork of surviving, the rush-rush hurry-up-and-wait. All he could think about was getting into his flat, locking the door, pulling the drapes, and shutting it all out.

When he flipped on the lights, as if somehow they were attached directly to the switch, he was flooded with thoughts of Natalie. The good, the bad, the beautiful, the ugly.

Like dominoes falling, one memory triggered the next and the next, and he was whipsawed through a montage of his nearly four years with her. He was tickled and punched at the same time, regaled then bludgeoned. The aggregate mauling causing him to choke on the stale air of his flat. His breathing became a shallow panting. He felt like an overheated dog with emphysema.

He stood up and tried to shake it off, as if he were trying to lose cockroaches which inexplicably were crawling all over him.

A hollow lump of deadness opened up inside of him, as he ached for what he had lost, despaired that it would never be regained. This had become an all too familiar feeling for quite some time, a wistful dull presence. But rebounding from the trip to St. Louis, it was back with a vengeance.

Billy was also feeling something else. Something which had never reared its ugly head before.

Billy was feeling rage. It was a rage not directed at Natalie herself. It was diffused through the entirety of the situation he found himself in. In fact, if it was directed at any one person, that person was himself.

Like a junkie long overdue for a fix, he rolled a joint. The baggie of sedatives sat in his drawer next to his bag of reefer, so in one smooth motion he popped a couple of Valiums.

The next four days he spent reading the same chapter of *The Da Vinci Code* over and over. Each time he got to the end, he concluded that it made no sense and he must have missed something. So he would start the same chapter again, with slightly less enthusiasm and greater impatience at the whole enterprise of reading a book.

New Years Eve, he spent watching the red ball over Times Square descend, as the countdown ushered in the new year, Eastern Standard Time. It had been a very brutal December, but the mass of warm bodies which numbered in the tens of thousands, kept all but his ears and nose from feeling the bitter midnight cold.

Being there was everything he had imagined it would be, but less. The less was him. He was a numb observer in a rowdy herd of dancing, shuffling, prodding, laughing, freezing loonies.

People were drunk, crazy, wild, loud, boisterous, full of the arbitrary cheer that comes with an institutionalized occasion for yelling down the frustrations, defeats, agonies, and general hopelessness of their lives, while believing for an evening that things were going turn around and be amazing from now on.

Billy didn't yell, scream, wave his hands in the air, or sing *Auld Lang Syne* with the largely tone deaf crowd, didn't even hug any of those in his immediate proximity in a random act of euphoric love.

He greeted the new year with the calm one would, on seeing a bus arrive on time. Then he went back to his apartment, flipped over his mattress, tossed the sheets and blankets haphazardly back on the bed, and went to sleep.

Candy reappeared on Billy's doorstep a month later. Friday February 1st, to be exact. In an eerie déjà vu, she showed up and took him to see Machines of Melanoma at the very same club he had first seen them, the Mercury Lounge.

At first glance, she was exactly the same. But something was different. Though she tried her best to hide it, Billy sensed as the evening went on, that under her layers of Candyesque flippancy and quirky fun, some body of pain now resided in her.

He knew better than to ask.

Just as they had on their original date, at the end of the evening they went their separate ways. No kiss. No hug. Just awkward good-byes.

There was one thing that struck Billy as particularly odd, simply because it was so mundane and Candy never seemed to have time for the silly particulars of life that monopolized most conversations everyone else had. It was something she said on their way out of the club.

"I'll be moving soon."

"Out of New York."

"No. Just to a new apartment. Time for a change."

Billy had never been to Candy's place. For all he knew, she lived in an barracks full of Mongolian gypsies. It seemed like an odd thing to mention.

"Let me know. I like to keep all of my records right up to date."

"I will. I know you're as punctilious as they come."

Candy came over two days later. Never one to let randomness wield the baton for very long, as soon as she walked through the door, she took control. She was all over Billy and they made love like they hadn't been alone together for several months. Of course, they hadn't.

With a rare but highly amenable nod to convention, they actually made it to his bed for their three-minute leap into the volcano of frenzied eroticism.

When they were done, she leaned up on one elbow and pressed the bed with her free hand.

"Did you flip the mattress?"

Billy laughed so hard, his stomach hurt.

"You are the most unique human being I have ever met."

"And you're not boring. So far anyway. How are you set for money?"

"You want to borrow five bucks?"

"At your interest rates? I don't think so. I just thought that if you needed some extra money, you might want to join Amethyst and I next week. She came up with a job at NYU but we need a guy. If you can't do it, I can always ask that bum who's taken up residence on the stairs outside."

"Which one works best for you? Just because we're friends, you don't have to give me preferential treatment."

"It's a close call. But you have a slight edge."

"Why is that?"

"You don't smell like a sewer."

After Candy left in the morning, something occurred to Billy.

It was astonishing how dramatically things abruptly flipped. When he was with Candy, things were suddenly pretty okay. Decent. Adequate. Tolerable.

When he wasn't … it was what it unfortunately was.

The thing that always amazed him was how open and accepting she was.

Sure. She cut him no slack. Nothing got past her. She was forgivingly unforgiving.

But she was there. Truly there *for* him. Totally right there *with* him.

Of course, sometimes she confused him. She seemed to blow hot and cold with no predictable pattern, rhyme or reason. Was that the way she was?

Or maybe that was just the way he read her. Or couldn't read her.

Really difficult to say. She was a wild card.

Right … *he* was one to talk!

That poor girl. Being around him had to be a constant 40 G whiplash, given *his* mood swings, temper tantrums, rocketing ascents to manic heights of autism, his plummeting dives into the abyss of dumb stupor, his hiding within the crazed but fleeting euphoria of the drugs and the booze, his suffering the ego-battering he too often subjected himself to.

But through it all, she was there.

Candy was a rock.

Very rarely would she get caught up in the siphoning asphyxiation of his backdraft. She never played into or fed his manic-depressive swings. Usually, she rode him right down the center, only bending to whatever self-generated breezes gently blew her along her own independent path.

Billy didn't know if he loved her.

He didn't know if she loved him.

It didn't seem relevant.

Are those things people really need to know? Why would someone want to know something like that? Why would anyone dare risk asking the question? They might not like the answer.

All that was certain was that when they were together, they were together.

Somehow it felt right. At least for now it did.

That could all change.

It probably would.

Which sucks.

But it was great to have her back.

Blood Simple

Billy took the job with Candy and Amethyst. They assured him it was easy money. Easy money was something he never turned away. With the money his mom had loaned him, he had enough to live for a couple months, maybe three if he stretched it. But this was $100 for an hour's work.

Not bad.

He showed up right on time. Candy and Amethyst were waiting for him.

They stepped out of their clothes and up onto a small stage. More than forty eyes examined them from head to toe.

15 minutes passed. Only 45 more to go. He had to admit. This certainly was easy money.

He could just barely hear Amethyst and Candy, catching words and phrases. They were whispering.

Amethyst: "Ohmigod … happened?"

Candy: "My brother …"

Amethyst: "How? … Christmas?"

Candy: "… hemophiliac. Internal bleeding."

The instructor cleared his throat loudly. "Quiet please."

Billy: "What are you saying?"

Candy: "Not now."

Amethyst: "… so sorry, Candy."

Candy: "It's weird … eventually …"

The instructor was at the back of the room but was getting impatient. "Shhhh!!"

Billy: "This instructor is a tyrant."

Amethyst: "… your mom … other brothers?"

Candy: "… hard to believe … 27 … it was …"

Amethyst: "… anything? … hospital …?"

Billy: "Anytime you want to let me in on this is fine with me."

The instructor finally scurried over to them, folded his arms, and glared. "PLEASE! Please be silent. We can hear you."

The voice of authority. Amazing who gets to be in charge these days. What a twerp.

What Billy had signed on to was a modeling job. They were at the NYU Art Department's sculpture lab, offering themselves for preliminary sketches of what would ultimately be a larger-than-life bronze sculpture, a collective project of the twenty some students in the room at the time, all apparently in the advanced Fine Arts graduate program.

The three of them were completely naked. Thankfully, the room was a warm 72° Fahrenheit.

While Candy and Amethyst apparently couldn't care less, this was not especially comfortable for Billy. As a result of his priggish upbringing in the Midwest, he was still rather self-conscious about his body in general. And here he was exposing his reproductive organs! A little more than half of the students in the room were girls. It was small consolation that they seemed no more interested in him personally, than if they were looking at a window display at Macy's or a life-size cardboard cutout of a polar bear.

The working title for the sculpture was *The Genesis of Jealousy*. The diminutive instructor, who apparently was the mastermind of this particular group project, pretentiously referred to it as "the piece" — short for masterpiece.

After posing, Billy, Candy and Amethyst got dressed and lingered in the adjacent room within earshot, while the instructor explained that the inspiration for the work was complex. They heard something about an Ethan and Joel Coen movie, the Joni Mitchell song "Sex Kills", a reference to a rabbit boiling in a stew pot in the 80s film *Fatal Attraction*, and a perfume ad for some popular women's fragrance Billy had never heard of. There was no doubt in Billy's mind that, genius or not, the half-runt was full of shit.

Finally the instructor finished his pomposifying and as the class filed out, came over to them and handed them the vouchers they had been waiting for. They were each $100 richer.

He offered one haughty parting shot.

"You were noisy and rude. You really don't deserve this money, you know. We didn't need to hear about your petty little personal problems."

Billy wanted to kill the little rodent just to put him out of his self-important misery.

Candy just turned and quickly got out the door with Amethyst right behind her.

They got a ten-second head start. Billy finished tying his shoes and power-walked after them. As he turned the corner at the end of the hall, he found them sitting down on a bench. Candy was putting something back in her purse, maybe her cell phone. She looked up.

"Let's eat."

Food was the last thing on Billy's mind.

"Are you two going to tell me what you were talking about back there?"

Amethyst just glanced away, then looked to Candy to answer him.

"Not right now, Billy. I don't feel like talking about it."

Amethyst jumped in and ran interference for Candy.

"Hey Billy! Were you getting a boner back there? Your thingy looked to me like it was starting to point at that fat chick over by the two gay dudes. Or maybe it was pointing at them. They *were* kinda cute."

He knew when he was outgunned.

"Pizza? Chinese take-out?"

"I have been dying for some good goulash."

"Yeah! And a big plate of boiled cabbage with tons of salt."

"Candy. Amethyst. You are both freaks."

They caught the E train uptown and parked themselves at a very pricey Eastern European restaurant on East 53rd called Caterina's. Cokes were $6, entrees $20 and up. Billy was at risk of spending a good chunk of the money he had just earned, except Candy picked up the entire tab. The food was great but the three of them were about 1/3 the age of anyone else in the place, except for the waiters.

When they finished eating, Amethyst headed back to Soho in a taxi, Billy and Candy took the subway back to the East Village, then walked the few blocks to his flat.

Neither had much to say. Candy was especially quiet.

"Is anything bothering you, Candy?"

He was sitting on the bed. She came over next to him and looked intently into his eyes.

"Cabbage is a serotonin-enhancer."

Candy then took off Billy's socks, pants and underwear. She remained completely dressed.

She took him in her mouth and he climaxed almost instantly.

Candy pulled a blanket up from the lower part of the bed and lay down next to him, cuddling in his arms, shrouded by the warmth of his body and softness of the wool cover.

"Did you steal this blanket from the guy out front?"

"The Mayor of Avenue C? He gave it to me as a political bribe."

"Shrewd politician."

"He knows power when he sees it."

"Listen. Something horrible happened at home. I'm not ready to talk about it. But I will. When I'm up to it."

"You can talk to Am but you can't talk to me?"

"You have enough to deal with. You are too important to me. This isn't idle chit chat."

"I have no doubt about that. It never is with you."

She curled up closer. She couldn't have gotten any closer.

Soon Billy could hear the slow shallow breathing of her immersion in the world of dreams.

For the brief moment before sleep took him to a parallel place, he wouldn't have traded for anything or anybody in the entire world, the feeling of this strange girl curled in his arms.

Next morning, Candy was very upfront with him. She wouldn't be around for a few days. She had a lot of things to take care of.

It ended up being nearly two weeks. She called a couple times but the conversations were matter-of-fact and very succinct. None of the usual flights of fancy and barrelhouse banter.

The third time she called, Candy seemed more relaxed and asked Billy if he could meet her at the Paradiso Café, a coffee house and deli that had recently become her favorite hang. It was in the West Village.

When Billy got there, she was waiting at a table in the furthest corner. Once Billy's espresso and cheese croissant arrived at the table, she started right in on her story.

"While I was at home my older brother died. He had been dating a girl in town for about two months and her ex-boyfriend was jealous. He and a couple of his buddies decided to scare Travis — that's my brother. I don't think they meant to kill him. Travis was coming out of a movie theater with his new girlfriend. Her name is Diane and she is a very sweet girl, totally perfect for him. I really like her."

Candy stopped for a minute and looked away. She fished some Kleenex out of her handbag. She was having difficulty keeping from completely losing it. Billy put his hand on hers and just kept quiet.

"They roughed Travis up. Nothing all that serious, if he had been like anyone else. What the assholes didn't know is that he is a hemophiliac. To make a long story short, Travis had some serious internal bleeding, and before anything could be done about it, he died."

The cheese croissant sat untouched and both of their coffee drinks were at room temperature before Billy broke the silence.

"You were really close to him? Your brother, I mean?"

"Close but far away. I haven't lived there for over five years. But when we saw each other, it was always good. He was a great guy. He was great as an older brother. He always took care of me, even when he didn't have to. I was his kid sister and he thought it was his duty. It wasn't an easy job."

"I believe that."

They sat in silence again for quite a while. He had never seen Candy like this. Not even close. She hung her head and couldn't look Billy in the eyes. Her shoulders slumped from the enormous weight of her loss. She looked drained of all of the wild energy that was the Candy he had known until this moment.

"Are you … I mean, it's hereditary, right? So do you have hemophilia?"

"Think about it, Billy. With all of these tattoos, if I did have it I'd look like a lawn sprinkler."

He tried not to laugh. It was a very Candy piece of imagery.

"You can laugh. It was supposed to be funny. Listen, Billy. I don't want to talk about this anymore. I don't even want to think about it. I mean, there's all of this obligation and these ridiculous expectations about mourning and working through your grief. I guess I'm supposed to show the world how lousy I feel. But the simple fact is that none of that will bring him back to life. So I am done with it. But you wanted to know. So now you know."

They paid and left.

A panhandler approached them as they stepped through the door.

"There are two cups of coffee and a croissant inside, if you get there before the busboy."

Light late-winter snow flurries started to fall. The weather was beginning to warm, so the flakes melted as soon as they touched the ground.

Billy was not one to be generous with his affection these days, but he took Candy's hand. It felt both strong and fragile. Maybe it was a reflection of the whole.

She looked pensive but some sixth sense told him she was not thinking of her brother.

Everyone deals with loss differently.

Billy sure had a lot to learn.

Maybe everything.

Spider Man

Billy and Candy were heading back to the East Village along Houston. She hadn't been to his flat for over a week. She was a very busy lady.

Doing what he didn't know. But then again, he never bothered to ask.

Though it was getting late in the afternoon, it was still light out. It had been a cloudless day, brisk but holding the promise of spring.

They headed up Bowery and went east on 2nd Street.

Right after turning the corner, as they came up to some steps beside a secured metal-grated garage door with giant padlocks at the base, they heard a gnarly old voice.

"Are you here for a spider?"

Beside the cement steps was a bum. He appeared to be sober and was sitting in the midst of several fishbowls. One of them sat directly in front of him on a cement block. It was so dirty it was impossible to see through the glass, the lip had a large chunk broken off, and a crack went down one side almost to the base. A good bump would probably cleave it in half.

Leaning against the cement block under this bowl was a handwritten sign.

Save the planet!

Free Spiders

Only 50¢.

Billy's curiosity got the best of him. He walked over and tried to look into the bowl.

The old man quickly covered it with his hands, which looked as though they hadn't seen soap and water since Ronald Reagan was president.

"Your sign says the spiders are free. How can you charge 50 cents for them?"

"These spiders ... these spiders are freer than you and me. Freedom is never having to say you're sorry. Besides, the 50 cents is not for the spider. It's packaging and handling, shipping and taxation without representation. Some goes to the United Nations and MOMA to keep the dream alive."

"I see." Billy turned to Candy with a mock-enthusiastic grin. "What do you think, sweetie? Is this something we could use?"

The old man whipped his moth-eaten filthy wool hat off and shook it at Billy like it was a scepter or a sword.

"I'm on to you! You're just a smart-mouth punk who thinks he's smarter than an old man just because you floss your teeth and have no ring around the collar. But let me tell you something. Are you listening? Because you might learn a thing or two they didn't get around to teaching you at girls boarding school. You can't buy a spider any more than you can by a snowflake or a breath of air."

He put his hat back on and glared at Billy in disgust.

Candy sat down next to the old man. He didn't smell as bad as he looked.

"I want to meet one of your spiders."

The old man reached into a bowl behind him and took out two beautifully red, ripe Roma tomatoes. He held one up and handed the other one to her.

"Spiders are colorblind. These are like beach balls or small planets. They don't watch TV."

"So can I see one?"

Billy was glancing into all of the bowls, including the one right in front of the old man.

"I don't see any. Where are they?"

"They're not here. Home stays. Time shares. Adopt-a-spider-go-to-jail. Three strikes and you're out. I told you. I'm on to you! You can't have everything your way." He turned to Candy. "Why do you want a spider anyway? Are you lonely? Did your cat run away? You're not a Satanist, are you?"

"No, I'm not a Satanist."

The old man smiled at her sympathetically. His rheumy eyes seemed on the verge of spilling yellow mucous-laden tears.

"I'm sorry, sweetheart. We can't disturb them now. They're on break. IWW union rules. Even Roosevelt didn't see that one coming." He started laughing raucously, then shook his head as he let it hang against his chest, grinning away at the irony of his being an insider on all of the political machinations of the spider world.

He pointed at Billy.

"That's something else you don't understand." Pointing to all of the empty bowls around him. "They know I won't fuck with them. I won't turn them in just for the lousy reward money. We took the same loyalty oath, see. It's about love thy neighbor and don't fuck thy neighbor's wife. The Golden Rule. In case you didn't know."

The old man was silent for a long time.

All of a sudden, he perked up and noticed them, as if for the first time.

"I'm sorry. I didn't see you. Do you want some spiders? I can give you recipes. You're not vegetarian, are you?"

Candy stood up and came around next to Billy.

"Thanks, old man. We're all set. We better be going."

Billy reached in his pocket and held out a ten dollar bill. The old man just held up his hands and shook his head.

"I'm set for life. Money won't mean anything anyway. You can't take it with you."

Billy and Candy headed east across 1st Avenue. He finally spoke up.

"There but for the grace of God go I."

"Don't push your luck."

It had just gotten dark. As they approached Billy's Avenue C apartment, the caterwaul of two cats across the street announced some unresolved territorial dispute.

"I really love my loft."

"But you live in a basement."

"Can't I have my utopian fantasies?"

"You mean dystopian delusions. Am I the only sane person in this bloody city?" She held out her hand, palm up, empty. "How many spiders do you see?"

"I'm just trying to see the glass as half full."

"I'm seeing your cranium as half empty."

They entered. The stale air and some undefined stench caught in Candy's throat.

"Jesus, Billy, do you ever clean this place? It smells like the graveyard shift at a meatpacking house in Bosnia."

"Light some incense."

"How about lighting a drum of kerosene with a six-pack of heavy-duty highway flares and a flamethrower."

"You are OCD."

"If I were OCD, I wouldn't be anywhere near you. You are anathema to order, cleanliness, coherence, balance and sanity."

"But what about my bad points?"

"It's one thing to rise above the hungry addiction of consumerism, but to abandon all standards of hygiene and embrace chaos and filth with messianic devotion is pathological."

"Sounds to me like you want to fool around."

"Alright alright. I admit it. The smell of rotting carcasses always puts me in a sexy mood. But take a shower first. Please!"

Billy came out with a towel wrapped around him. Candy was laying on the bed, naked as a newborn child, except for a few dozen tattoos. He dropped the towel and got onto the bed, savoring the view.

She put her arms up and raised her legs high. He would need no instruments to land this one. He aimed for the thin pink line below the Brazilian.

"The eagle has landed."

"Oh my God! That feels *sooooo good*."

Then it was over. It took two minutes tops.

"We're getting good at this."

"Did something happen?"

"You're right. Hit the rewind button. I think I missed something."

Billy started poking and tweaking her nipples and she curled into a ball giggling hysterically. When he got tired of tickling her, they both fell into a deep imperturbable sleep.

At some point late into the night the phone rang.

And rang and rang and rang.

Candy dreamed it was raining tiny Hindu prayer bells and they played melodically as they rippled through a shimmering glassine force field which held her body gracefully suspended.

Billy dreamed he was in a commercial jet which had lost power and was tumbling earthward towards total annihilation, with emergency alarms and passenger screams creating a cacophony of fear.

Just as the phone finally stopped ringing, they both woke up.

It was either a wrong number or a right number at the wrong time.

They lay quietly for a while. Faint echoes of bells trailed off in their shared subconscious.

When they eventually got up, Billy made coffee. Candy made breakfast. After the quick meal, Billy spent an inordinate amount of time in the bathroom trying to deal with the disfiguring effects of bed head. When he finally came out, he found Candy looking at a leaflet that came with his phone bill from Verizon Bell Atlantic, which listed the cornucopia of wonderful extra services he was being charged for, whether he knew it or not.

"You've got all sorts of features on this thing, Billy. Call waiting. Caller ID. Call ID block. Speed dialing. Call forwarding."

"What's Call ID block?"

"It's so that people with caller ID can't see who's calling them." She punched some numbers into the keypad. "There. That's activated. Now you can make obscene calls without fear of prosecution. Let's see. What else? Call waiting is already working. You don't need call forwarding, since you don't have a cell phone."

Candy showed him how to enter phone numbers so that just pressing * and a digit, he could dial a call. She put her own number in as *1. Billy had her enter his mom as *2.

"There you go. Welcome to the modern world."

"I feel positively futuristic."

Candy stood up, then leaned over and licked Billy's right eye like she was getting the last dollop of whip cream from a spoon. He laughed and buried his face in both of his arms to avoid any more dog kisses. When he looked up, she was gone.

All morning he stared at the phone. Then shortly after 1 pm, he picked it up.

He entered Natalie's private office line into the speed dialing menu as *666.

*666. *"Natalie Diamond. May I help you?"* Click. He hung up.

*666. *"Natalie Diamond. May I help you?"* Click.

*666. *"Natalie Diamond. May I help you?"* Click.

*666. *"Natalie Diamond. May I help you?"* Click.

*666. *"Natalie Diamond. May I help you?"* Click.

All afternoon. Every fifteen or twenty minutes.

At the end of the day, her phone just rang and rang.

The next morning, shortly after 9 am, he started again.

*666. *"Natalie Diamond. May I help you?"* Click.

*666. *"Natalie Diamond. May I help you?"* Click.

The fifth time, she was obviously angry. *"Who is this? This is pissing me off. Stop it!"*

He waited a while. After lunch, he started up again.

*666. *"Natalie Diamond. May I help you?"* Click.

*666. *"Natalie Diamond. May I help you?"* Click.

*666. *"Is this you, Billy? You childish fucking moron!"* Click.

That's nice. She's still thinking of him.

The next day he got a recorded message. *We're sorry but this number is no longer in service. Please check the number and dial again. If you need further assistance ...* blah blah blah.

Billy lit a joint and sat looking at the blank wall across from him.

He couldn't remember. Was Natalie afraid of spiders?

Chapter Two

LIVING IN A MOSH PIT
Late Winter Spring Summer 2008

The Tea Lady of Kashmir

Billy and Candy were heading from SoHo walking through the West Village. It was an atypical March winter day, quite warm and comfortable — low 70s — heralding the early onset of spring. Fortunately, the muggy swamp that drown New Yorkers in sweat every summer was still a few months away.

They turned west off Hudson onto Bethune. She was looking for a new place to live. A friend of hers was leaving in two weeks and had not told her landlord yet. Candy's hope was to slip into the place without having to bear some astronomical increase in the rent. Billy was along for the ride.

"Why am I doing this?"

"That's what friends are for."

"I've been promoted from fuck-buddy to friend? Awesome!"

"You should view it as a demotion."

That's when he saw her. Standing on the front edge of a porch. Stretched above her was a shimmering cloth banner.

Readings in the Journey of Life
Please come inside!

She couldn't have been more than fifteen years old. Olive complexion, heavily made up eyes, peering around a gold-trimmed crimson veil, following their progress toward her. She was wearing a full-length sari, also trimmed in gold but with glittering reflective jewels all through the flowing pashmina of her dress. She had lovely delicate toes, the nails of which were painted an iridescent blue. They peeked from under the silver straps of sandals, which glittered with polished stones and sequins.

The girl had a mysterious if ambiguous smile, one which said more about the person viewing it than the inner workings of the person who wore it — maybe it was seductive, possibly pensive or even meditative, or it might reflect the exhaustion of a world-weary traveler, perhaps simple abandon, or the open tabula rasa innocence of newborn child. Her face was a quintessential mirror.

Billy was both mesmerized and a little put off. Something felt strange.

He momentarily thought about turning around but was powerless to resist. He and Candy came even with the steps to the porch where the girl stood.

She remained perfectly erect, almost floating in place.

Billy felt compelled to stop.

He was confused. Try to ignore or deny it as he might, he was excited.

It felt like he had a Japanese radish in his pants.

This was crudely ironic.

Billy glanced over at Candy. She was so beautiful and sexy. Blatantly so. Openly erotic. Today — hardly unusual in terms of how much sex appeal she had on display — she wore tight-fitting safari pants, rolled up high on legs that seemed to go on forever, up top a very loose cotton cross-your-heart halter top which tied around her neck, leaving her back and shoulders bare. It loosely flopped open at the sides giving fleeting glimpses of her flawless breasts.

By contrast, the young Indian girl was covered completely from head to toe, with only her hands, face and neck exposed. Her allure seemed somehow to emanate from what she didn't show, which was practically everything.

Billy continued to study the girl and found himself attracted by a force he couldn't really grasp. He felt a twinge of guilt. She was so young. What was with him? Was he becoming a pedophile? He wanted to believe that his curiosity was something other than — something more noble than — a vulgar, impulsive and indefensible sexual urge. Trouser-mouse hots for a young filly.

Candy could read Billy like a Caswell-Massey catalog.

"Hmm. I see. The allure of the exotic."

Billy just stood there, trying to ignore Candy's amused scrutiny.

He flushed with embarrassment and struggled to decide what to do.

Without for a moment taking her eyes off him, the young girl with a genteel grace that belied her immaturity, folded her right arm across her waist, then raised her left arm, bent sharply at the elbow. With a subtle flick of her index finger, she pointed at Candy. She then brought both hands together directly in front of her face in a gesture of humility and prayer, lowered her eyes, and ever-so-slightly bowed. Then she again looked directly at Billy.

"A serpent slithers lost across familiar terrain and holds in its mouth a well of easy comfort. The milk from this well will sustain others but never satisfy you. Your longing begs real order. There is hope in this confusion. The chart for your journey is in the eyes of the Tea Lady. The Earth is a teabag in the cup of life and you are thirsty. Please come in."

The reference to a serpent disoriented Billy. Candy had a serpent tattoo which ran from her back, "slithering" around her body, with its head culminating at one of her nipples. He had certainly had his share of "easy comfort" there, though having a serpent stare at him while he was sucking on her breast could be a little disconcerting. How in the world did this Indian girl know about the tattoo in such detail? Candy's back was turned away from the girl and the head of the serpent hidden by her halter. His curiosity egged him on, as did an anxious gnawing which he couldn't quite put in perspective. Was he being hypnotized or seduced? Billy had to know.

"You're saying I need help and you can help me?"

"The eyes of Lady Hashpura never close. Follow me."

Candy laughed out loud.

"Go ahead. Good investment of time and money. Really good. Go for it!" She pulled a handful of twenty dollar bills out of her woven hemp handbag. "We're on the same page here, Billy. I'm going to find a Kinko's and see if they have a paper shredder."

"Christ, Candy. Where did you get all that money?"

"Dot com. I invented the internet."

"Seriously."

"I'm still collecting on the 1997 World Series. I had 3 to 1 going for me on the Marlins."

"Right. You were making bets when you were what? Twelve?"

"*Taking* bets. I was making book for the whole school system. I made a ton off of the Board of Education alone. My history teacher had to take a second mortgage on his house."

"So much for getting a straight answer out of you."

"Most answers are orphans, Billy. It's the right questions that are missing. Go with your little Miss Mystical there. Maybe she'll give you the right questions. Meet me at Paradiso Café when you're done. If you don't end up flying to Kabul."

Candy continued down Bethune Street at a power-walker's pace. Pedestrians parted for her like the Red Sea.

Billy didn't even watch her leave but kept his gaze fixed on the young girl. He stepped onto the porch and she led him into the parlor of the house, then directed him to sit in one of the plush over-stuffed love seats.

"Please wait as we prepare. It will only be a few moments."

The room was garish beyond comprehension. A chaotic clashing cacophony of colors and patterns and textures. Yet it seemed to somehow work. There were brass fixtures and lanterns and candelabra, swatches of elaborate cloths, portraits of what Billy assumed were Hindu or Sikh gods, mystical shapes and signs, panels of text in some foreign alphabet — maybe Sanskrit? — several thick hand-woven carpets in bright colors and annoyingly dense patterns and ornamentation. The girl had exited through a pair of shiny gold and turquoise lamé curtains, above which hung a huge gold relief casting of a multi-armed goddess with a naive but haunting grin, not unlike the one the young girl had exhibited standing in the front of the building when he first spotted her.

She came back through the curtains.

"We are ready for you now."

She held back one drape and he entered the reading chamber.

In sharp contrast to the blaze of bright colors and chaotic montage of intricate designs which had assaulted his eyes in the parlor, the reading chamber was completely white. It looked like a big milky womb. The walls billowed with giant seamed panels of white satin. Actually they looked a lot like surplus military parachutes. There was a low table in the center, covered in a diaphanous snowy fabric which spilled over the squared edges in puffy folds, almost like clouds pouring over the escarpment of a mountain range into a valley below. The only light came from a single tiny candle in the center of the table, and five more just like it in candleholders suspended from the ceiling above the table.

It immediately became evident to Billy that he would not be spending the next 5 or 15 or 30 minutes — how long was this supposed to last? — with the sweet young thing who got him in here in the first place. Too bad.

Really too bad.

On the other side of the table opposite him was a massive mountain of a woman, a hybridization of Moms Mabley and Jaba the Hut. Beyond the disparity in size between the petite young girl and this barrelhouse of human lard, who was dressed similar to the girl, but required about eight times as much material to create the revival-tent sari she was wearing, the woman was indescribably ugly. Could this creature and the lovely young girl possibly be related? Were they even the same species?

"Please be seated, Billy."

How did she know his name? He quickly tried to recall if Candy had said it aloud in the brief minutes out in front of the house? He couldn't remember.

"Is Candy your girlfriend?"

Candy! Again he was thrown a bit. Maybe she can read minds or something.

"You tell me."

She looked blankly at Billy. Then she reached under the table and pulled out a fingernail file, which she used to touch up her nails. She would file a bit. Then glance up at him. File a bit. Glance up. File some more.

The silence made him very uncomfortable. He wanted to say something.

But what?

He kept his mouth shut. Maybe to keep from throwing up. There was something extremely repulsive about her. Something which made him think of entrails. He had never had such an adverse reaction to another human being.

She finished with her nails and stared at Billy.

After an eternal minute she again spoke.

"Candy is not your favorite dessert."

"What is my favorite dessert?"

"You tell me."

Billy was starting to get pissed. The fact that she was talking in circles was annoying enough. The fact that he wasn't getting to spend this time with the beautiful young girl was definitely making him testy. The fact that this fortune-telling whale was so fucking ugly it hurt to look at her was grating on him terribly. Then there was the smell. Though the air in the room had the strong lingering bouquet of incense, he was quite sure that he had just gotten a noxious whiff of body odor from her side of the room. It was body odor that had been vintaged over a few days. It made him gag.

"Billy. I can't tell you what to do. But the clock *is* running here."

"As far as I'm concerned, we haven't started yet."

"But we have." She pulled out a stopwatch. "Six minutes thirty-three seconds."

"Just hold on a minute. What is this whatever-it-is supposedly costing me uh … uh … whoever you are?"

"You really don't know who I am? Boy, you are a piece of work! You trust the reading of your transcendental chart, the realignment of your path of destiny to a complete stranger? What, are you stupid?"

He couldn't believe this. What an obnoxious old cow!

"I don't read Sanskrit or Punjab or whatever the fuck all that squiggly mumbo-jumbo says on the wall out there. Just tell me who you are. You do have a name ... maybe?"

"I am Punathan Hashpura, the Tea Lady of Kashmir. I grew up in Sri Lanka but took my spiritual apprenticeship in Jammu and Kashmir under the holy tutelage of Tibetan monks in a monastery at Ladakh."

"Fine. Now back to what I'm coughing up for this ... this thing here, whatever you call it."

"Twenty-five dollars for a basic reading. Fifty dollars for a lifestyle reading. One hundred dollars for cosmological charting and predicting the date of your death. I take Visa and MasterCard. Sorry, no American Express or Discover."

"The date of my death! Why would I want to know that?"

"Estate planning? I don't know. People have different reasons. So what's it going to be?"

"What's what going to be?"

"Which one? $25, $50 or $100."

"Just give me the basic."

"It's your dime. Don't expect a lot."

"Listen, Lady Teabag. If you give me something useful, I mean really useful, I'll pay you whatever you want. Within reason, of course. But the ball's in your court. Impress me."

"You can't be impressed."

"What's that supposed to mean?"

"You've got a crappy attitude. That's what it means."

"I'm paying you for this abuse? I'm forking over $25 so you can insult me?"

"What would you rather have me do?"

"Go for it. Show me what you got. Pull out all of the stops. Give me your best shot."

"Okay ..." She paused, then mumbled some incantation under her breath. Started to tremble. Rocked from side to side with her arms raised high into the air. Suddenly she stopped.

"Could you pay the $25 first, please?"

Billy was really getting angry now. Why had he let himself get suckered into this? Actually, he knew why. There was this amazing little tart on the front porch who enchanted him with some mystical nonsense, while a monstrous woody rendered him completely irrational and vulnerable. Billy had to wonder. *Will I ever learn?*

He fished a twenty and a five out of his wallet and threw them across the table.

She pulled at the top of her sari and stuck them between her breasts. Billy shook his head and thought to himself: *Good luck. Those could get lost for years in there!*

"Okay, where was I? Got it." Her hands shot back into the air. She started rocking from side to side again. At first she moaned, but then it slowly built and built, becoming louder and louder. Then she started doing the tongue-clucking caterwaul women in the Middle East do to express extreme grieving. She became so shrill that Billy brought his index fingers up to plug his ears. Just

31

before he got them fully inserted, she abruptly stopped, leaned forward as far as the table allowed her fat belly to lean, then pointed an accusing finger at Billy.

"You are insecure, plagued by feelings of guilt, and are alienated from the rest of society. You doubt your self-worth, have trouble relating to and communicating with your parents, feel anxious a lot of the time, know that your problems are out of your control but blame yourself anyway. You want a solid long-term relationship with a significant other but doubt that it can happen, feel you are damaged goods, feel everyone else is damaged goods as well. You don't want to think money is important but do anyway, therefore don't believe you ever have enough. You are afraid to cry, are haunted by—"

"Whoa! Whoa! Whoa! Slow down! What are you doing? Trying to demolish me?"

"Just trying to give you your money's worth. You asked for it."

"After you get done with me, I'll feel like jumping off the Brooklyn Bridge."

"That would be bad."

"The other thing is, now that I am thinking about what ... trying to remember all of that abuse you just piled on me. I mean, what's the point? Is this supposed to help? I ... I don't get it."

"I see what you mean. So you want something less ... less difficult."

"Well no. Life is difficult. That's just the way it is. Difficult. Everything is difficult. People are difficult. But I want solutions. Something positive. Something I can build on."

"You are going to go on a long trip. And you will meet someone very special. I see the possibility of love and marriage. You could be very happy."

"I want my fucking $25 back!"

"I don't see how that's possible. In the first place, we have gone overtime. I will have to charge you more if you want more."

"Do I have to rip you apart? This whole thing is a joke. Just give me my money back!"

"Billy, I can see that you are frustrated. I am a woman of special talents. Spiritually gifted. I can see into the heart and soul of people like yourself."

"Then you know I'm going to rip that goddamn sari off of you and look through the tectonic plates of your fat until I find my twenty five bucks!"

"No. I think that next time you will opt for the $50 or $100 dollar reading."

"There won't be a next time!"

"This anger is very bad for your karma. I never want a person to leave without knowing in their heart of hearts that I have shared something with them which will significantly make their lives better. So I am going to do something very special for you."

"Don't even think about it! I'm not going to pay another dime."

"Billy jin, my friend. This will cost you nothing. It is my gift to you as one seeker to another. This rare and priceless gift, by the way, usually only goes to those who engage my most special reading — my exclusive $200 Strings of the Metaphysical reading."

"You never said anything about any $200 reading."

"With the preternatural sensitivities I am gifted with, I knew you were too cheap to consider it. So I didn't mention it."

"You never quit, do you?"

"Billy it is a blessing and a curse to be beholden to helping others as I am. Anyway, here's what I want to tell you. Please pay careful attention."

"I'm hanging on your every syllable."

"Each of us is a traveler on a holy sojourn. We become so preoccupied with the challenges of everyday survival, we lose sight of who we truly are and what we are here to do. You are in your own unique way a holy man, a man responsible for your own deliverance to that place of perfection. Some call it Nirvana, some Heaven. Others say it is the Infinite Oneness of All. Or the Everything of Nothingness. It doesn't matter. I see that your holy vestments are in need of repair. Your prayer shawl is torn, so to speak. This shawl is woven of the stuff of the Universe, the essential thread that is weaved into all that is. To repair your prayer shawl, you must visit an expert in such matters. I know of one such mender here in Manhattan, a man who understands metaphysical strings, the stuff of which destiny is weaved into the fabric of our past, present and future. His name is Apocalypso."

Apocalypso! It was all he could do to refrain from rolling his eyes and laughing in her face. But he maintained a poker face.

She reached back into her sari and fished around for almost a minute.

"Here is his business card. If you are to put yourself back on track, Billy, to proceed properly robed and worthy of your own deliverance, you must visit this holy man and contribute to the support of his Ashram. And Billy, it is crucial that you tell him you have been specially referred to him by me personally, Punathan Hashpura, the Tea Lady of Kashmir."

"Can I have my money back now?"

"No."

"No?"

"Go in peace, young man. Hare Krishna."

Billy was tired of fighting. He looked at the card. Then back at the Tea Lady.

"Thanks from the bottom of my heart."

As he turned to go, the curtain suddenly popped open. There was the little girl. She was wearing a cap sideways on her head. It said *Tupac Lives*. No makeup. Big baggy pants. Loose hooded sweatshirt. Sneakers with metallic turquoise laces.

"Hey grandma. I have my hip hop class. I'll be back at six. Can we see that movie tonight? You promised. Remember?"

"What movie?"

"*The Girl Next Door*."

Billy recognized it. He winked at grandma Tea Lady.

"Oh yeah. That's a really cute movie. Perfect for her age. Make sure you get the unrated director's cut."

As he walked back to Hudson Street, then crossed 8th Avenue to get to Bleecker, the only thing that kept him from feeling like a total moron who had been had by an obese, unscrupulous, and transparently fake soothsayer, was the remote but probably laughable possibility that there was some value in the tip she had given him. The Apocalypso guy.

Billy would much later find out that Apocalypso, master of self-promotion, had made sweet-heart deals with all of the local crystal-gazers and palmists — a ten percent kickback. This was just one small segment of his recruiting base, a grass-roots referral network, a word-of-mouth juggernaut, intended to swell the ranks of his army of believers, and create a potential source of serious funding for his Ashram. He had representatives and agents of all shapes and sizes spreading the word of Manhattan's newest prophet and nascent political activist. Besides those pouring in from a cadre of palm readers and yoga teachers, Apocalypso had referrals coming his way from news stands, hot dog and chestnut vendors, taxi drivers, off-track-betting parlors, sports and concert ticketing agents, peep-shows and gentlemen's clubs, suicide prevention and sexual health counseling centers, substance abuse clinics, even battered women's shelters. Most of the people feeding him recruits had no idea what his agenda was and could care less. It was a good way to make a few extra bucks.

Of course, Billy didn't know any of this at the time. For now he could look at the business card as salve for the flesh wounds which had just been inflicted on his pride by Lady Teabag.

Even so, Billy still couldn't stop the tape that was playing in his head.

What a chump! What a chump! What a sucker! What a chump!

Billy went shamefacedly to the Paradiso, the coffee house and deli on Bleecker, where he had agreed to meet back up with Candy. It had been a little over an hour since they parted. He had briefly considered not going, knowing full well that his ego would be diced up into a bloody mincemeat with the samurai-sword of her sarcasm. He wasn't in the mood for her piling ridicule on his humiliation.

He really didn't have to worry. She was nowhere in sight.

He had ham and gouda cheese on a croissant. And a foamy caramel latte.

He almost stopped feeling like a complete idiot.

Apocalypso

The guy was ubiquitous.

After getting his business card from the Fat Whale of Kashmir — he was still pissed about his $25 — Billy started seeing Apocalypso posters everywhere, some with catchy sayings, some announcing prayer meetings and rallies. He even spotted a small billboard in China Town, written in Chinese characters no less. The guy had his own Public Access TV show. And though Billy didn't bother to read it, he saw a feature article on him in the Village Voice, titled "Guru To The Moral Minority".

Billy finally succumbed to what increasingly appeared to be inevitable.

He was going to go to an Apocalypso function.

Candy was into it. She would be — quirky as she was 99% of the time.

"This must be the place."

"So right you are."

Billy and Candy had just made the short walk from the subway station to a former bank building in Tribeca, which was now rented out for performance art events, concerts, parties.

"You know, I've known about this guy for some time now. His headquarters, the Ashram of the Urban Night, is right near my place. Right on 1st Avenue."

"I can't believe you've been keeping this from me, Billy."

"After this evening, you might wish I had."

As they approached the building, they could hear over loudspeakers what sounded like heavy male monk voices in a rhythmic incantation.

YO - HAMA - HAMA - YAMA - YO
YO - HAMA - HAMA - YAMA - YO
YO - HAMA - HAMA - YAMA - YO
YO - HAMA - HAMA - YAMA - YO

They paid the admission and went inside.

The "temple" was so crowded with chanting, dancing, rapturous bodies, apparently at the peak of spiritual merriment, it was nearly impossible for Billy to squeeze into the main hall. With Candy in tow, he used his scrum legs and mosh pit skills to best advantage, grunting and hurling forward into the tumbling sea of enlightenment seekers, incurring more than once the disdain of someone he had shoved aside with his unenlightened aggressiveness.

As they entered the cavernous main hall, they were assaulted by dazzling display of intense multi-colored lights and a thunderous explosion of sound.

boompa - ta-ta-ta-ta-ta-ta-ta boompa - ta-ta boompa - ta-ta
boompa - ta-ta-ta-ta-ta-ta-ta boompa - ta-ta boompa - ta-ta

Four drummers — bare from the waste up, adorned with Chinese jute hair ties and necklaces of teeth and bones, shells and flowers — thrashed out a driving, infectious rhythm on two sets of congas, prayer bells, a tabla and a djembe. The two conga players were the dark chocolate of the Congo, smooth and taught in their youthful muscularity. Their shiny oiled cornrows spawned long braids which thrashed and bounced about in sync with their histrionic hand chops to the drums. The djembe player was albino but he had shaved his head and eyebrows, and applied red and black war paint to his face and pale torso. He was always laughing at some musical joke only he could hear, and regularly made eye contact either with the other percussionists or members of the audience, encouraging them to laugh along. The man on the prayer bells and tabla was actually a woman, but one who had played down her femininity to the point where her gender was not so much of an issue as was her species. Her tangled, unwashed hair dragged across her snarling face, sticking to her cheeks. She held her mouth open wide and clicked her teeth together in time with the music, creating the impression she was trying to snatch insects out of the air. She was wearing huge farmers overalls and no shirt, offering glimpses nobody wanted, of the flabby udders on her chest. Whenever she played the prayer bells, her eyes rolled back in her head suggesting the urgent need for an exorcism.

Competing for the audience's eye with this malformed menagerie of musicians, were several spontaneous dancers who either possessed by the rhythms or the need for attention, had jumped onstage and were whirling about in a freeform frenzy of euphoria. First there were two, three, then finally four girls, egging one another on to greater heights of improvised showmanship. The floor around them was wet with their perspiration, and their sticky pheromones filled the air.

People watched the drummers and go-go girls, slack-jawed by the visuals and riveted by the sonics, for thirty minutes before the star of this evening's performance made his appearance. Once Apocalypso took the stage, all eyes fixed on him.

It was no celebrity walkway entrance, rather a graceful, understated arrival. Dressed in nothing but a simple white sarong, hair pulled back off of his face in long dreadlocks and tied into a single clump in back, no facial hair other than thick eyebrows which set off his intense brown eyes, he was handsome to the point of causing gasps from the females — and of course the gay men — in any room he entered. He was of medium height but muscular and thick with lean masculinity. He stepped easily and unceremoniously onto the stage.

> *"It is my honor to be here with you, to feel, and absorb, and radiate with you the energy of our shared divinity. We're about to begin a new beginning. A new beginning for each of us here. A new beginning for the spiritually empty people of the nation which once held great promise. A new beginning for a troubled America. A new beginning for the world. Into the great void — the gaping chasm left by the empty pursuit of material wealth, the emptying of all value from the human mind by modern media — into the desolate vacuum the banks and corporations have thrust the souls of good people like ourselves, only to gasp and face extinction, into that frightful, artificially-created black hole of nothingness ... yes, you and I now send the infinite and boundless energy of our shared enlightenment. We each are one, one of many. Thus, we are a many of ones. But individual singularity is an illusion. Each and all is but the Oneness of All. Let us now commune in silence and let the power of our Oneness flood the world with the majesty of our love."*

The entire audience — there had to have been over two thousand people crowded into the building — stopped talking, stopped moving, stopped breathing. The only sounds that could be heard were random city noises bleeding through the thick bank walls from the street.

After about a minute, Apocalypso raised his hands heavenwards as if to invite the approval of invisible onlooking deities. He then lowered his arms and let them hang at his side. With an impish grin, he shrugged his shoulders, smiled broadly showing the full splendor of his even white teeth, then walked off the stage as calmly as he had come on only minutes before.

The crowd went wild, the drummers again started pounding away, and the party to celebrate the coming spiritual revolution was underway again.

Behind all of the flowery, high-sounding phrases and painful mix of metaphors, there really wasn't much message to Apocalypso's message.

It wasn't the words that moved people.

It was the man.

Whether he consciously knew this, or was guided by the gift of solid instincts, Apocalypso used his effect on people to his fullest advantage. He took them where he wanted them to go. He got them to do what he wanted them to do.

There were naturally a few hard-core nay-sayers and hardened skeptics who resisted him, isolated individuals who walked away from his forums, lectures, prayer sessions, rallies, and group meditations, shaking their heads and spouting the same invectives and rejectives they without fail carried with them wherever they went, whatever the occasion.

But most people who experienced Apocalypso came away convinced, infected by his passion and hope-filled vision of personal and societal perfection. Pumped up by the collective enthusiasm of the crowd at the events, they made firm if somewhat ephemeral commitments to promote and spread his world view and spiritual teachings.

Tonight's crowd was no exception. The rally, which consisted of four minutes of inspiration and four hours of celebration, would carry on well into the night.

Billy had a splitting headache, the source of which could have been any number of things. High on the list of possibilities was a new bag of dope he had just scored, which he again suspected was laced with defoliants, compliments of the DEA's helicopters over Hawaii and northern California. The sweat and noise of the crowd at the rally contributed their share to his misery.

They left early. No one seemed to notice.

"So, Candy. What did you think? Are we still friends?"

"Are you rich?"

"Do I look rich?"

"No. But it's the only hope for our continuing friendship. And the price is way up there."

"So, you weren't impressed."

"I'm impressed by results. I hope the guy can get the lard-asses moving. But frankly I have my doubts."

"What do you mean? I didn't see any lard-asses there tonight. I thought it was a tasteful display of body-conscious underground chic."

"Do you write for Fashion Week Magazine?"

"I try to see the good in everyone."

"Right. I was referring to the bulk of Americans."

"Clever pun, girly."

Candy burst out laughing. She laughed all the way to the subway station.

Then she became very quiet.

On the train, she turned to Billy. She looked tormented. Uncharacteristically afraid.

"I think I'm in love."

"Anybody I know."

"I don't think so."

"Oh ... I see."

She closed the gap between them, put her nearest arm inside his, laid her other arm across his stomach and pulled herself as close to him as she could. She appeared anxious, expectant. A nun with wire-rim spectacles seated across from them peered over a Midnight Tattler she was reading, and gave them a fleeting look of disapproval.

Over the noise of the subway car, Billy didn't hear what Candy then softly said.

"Billy, it's you."

Married with Children

The call came none too soon. Billy was running out of money fast. Though he could easily have, he didn't want to lean on his mother for another loan.

"The house sold, Billy. We got a good price. $266,500. You need to be here next week to sign. Can I count on you?"

Strange way to put it. Of course, she could "count on" him. When had he ever let her down?

Bitch.

She would set it up for the following Wednesday.

Billy took the train to Newburgh for the closing. All parties agreed on 10:30 in the morning. This was perfect. He could be back on the southbound shuttle shortly after noon, back to the insanity but to the relative amenability of the city. No way did he want to stay the night in Newburgh.

He got to the office of the escrow company a little early and watched as the players in today's drama filed in. The real estate agent, her assistant, two women in charge of handling the legalities — reams of documents, disclosures, acknowledgements, receipts, warrants and representations —the excited couple who were buying the house, and finally ... Natalie.

She was seven months pregnant and showing it.

Billy could not hide his shock. Nor could he prevent his outrage from violently bursting out of his pained and anger-twisted face.

"You're pregnant! What the fuck?"

The silence of the lambs filled the room with embarrassed muteness, everyone including Billy fearing that his outburst would result in a full-out brawl. Billy fought back his anger. He didn't come here to start something. He shut up and managed to contain himself. He just sat staring at his clenched fists before him on the table. Natalie ignored him and sat down, showing both a degree of agitation and impatience, and a resolve to put things back on track.

"I apologize for the gorilla in the room. Let's get this over with."

It took about twenty-five minutes. A check was pushed across the table. Natalie tucked it in her briefcase and made a beeline for the door.

Billy got up in hot pursuit. Everyone else was relieved that the two of them were out of the room. Hopefully they wouldn't be witness to a homicide. Much too early in the day for that.

Billy caught up with her in the hall before she got out of the building. She whipped around.

"Leave me alone, Billy!"

"What's going on? Whose baby is this?"

"Why it's mine. And Pam's."

"You know what I mean. Who's the father?"

"That's none of your business."

"I assume Pam didn't grow a dick. Is it mine?"

She squared off and looked at him with disgust.

"Come on, Billy. Count. If it was yours I'd be in a maternity ward."

"Then how? A happy hour hump? Did you fuck your boss?"

"Has anyone told you that you're pathetic?"

"A lot of people. So what?"

"A little bit of self-respect would go a long way. This is none of your affair. We're divorced, in case you forgot."

He had no comeback. He ran out of words. He knew what he had to say was bogus.

"Okay okay. I'm sorry … it was just … just such a shock."

"Apology accepted. I still don't want to talk to you. I've got work to do. I'll deposit this check and transfer half into your account." She turned to leave.

"Just tell me, Natalie. Was this the plan all along? Were you going to—"

"Get real, Billy. You know I wanted a baby. For whatever reason, you and I couldn't get it together. It was probably for the best. I gotta go."

He grabbed her shoulder. She looked at his hand like a pile of bird turd had just landed. He didn't care and just tightened his grip.

"I get it now. You were just using me as a stud horse."

Natalie just looked at him and smiled. Her eyes blazed with a cold malevolence he had never seen or could have imagined in her before. It was hard to tell whether she was possessed by hatred, pity, or vindictiveness. Maybe it was all three.

"Pam and I have also applied for adoption. There is a sweet 4-year-old boy living with us. He's originally from Costa Rica. It's a very nice family we're building. I didn't know when I married you, but I can see now that nothing like this would have been possible with such a selfish, immature, self-absorbed jerk as you. You wouldn't have the energy, especially after feeling sorry for yourself every day from morning to night. Let go of me right now, Billy!"

She savagely swung her arm against his and broke his grip.

"Don't ever touch me. Don't ever come near me. Don't even look at me. Never again! Never! You are out of my life. Thank god!"

For a pregnant women with a belly that looked like it could be twins, she moved like a decathlon runner. Before Billy could even think of what next to say to her, she was halfway across the parking lot and getting into her car.

Natalie and Pam. A 4-year-old boy. A new baby.

The entire scene — the parking lot, the cars, the escrow office building — spun around him. It was like his entire life was a carnival Tilt-A-Wheel and he was strapped in with thick unbreakable chains pulled so tight across his limbs and torso he couldn't breathe.

Natalie and Pam. A happy little family.

He couldn't remember why he had come to Newburgh. It certainly wasn't for this.

He heard voices. It was the people who had just bought his house and the real estate agent, on their way out of the building. They cut a wide path around him, now only whispering, stealing quick, furtive side-glances at the ridiculous and rude lunatic they had just spent twenty-five minutes in the same room with. Quick. Just get to the car and get away from here and the crazy man.

And he's so young. How sad.

Billy suddenly realized what a spectacle he was making of himself. He had slumped down on the fake marble steps and was crying like a baby. Loud and red-faced and pathetic. A big, spoiled, obnoxious 'can't get his way so he'll throw a tantrum' baby, but with the bulk and lung power of a full-grown man.

Was this why he came here? To fall apart? Make a total fool of himself?

It took a while, but he pulled himself together and went back inside.

The receptionist called a taxi for him and he waited in the lobby until it arrived fifteen minutes later.

Billy recognized the driver. It was the same guy who had given him a ride to the train station last year when he made his big break from Newburgh.

How weird was that.

Billy wondered if the old man recognized him.

As they crossed the Beacon Bridge to get to the train station on the other side of the Hudson River, Billy looked the length of the riverbanks. Many trees on both sides were still in bloom and there were swaths of color accented by the rich green of new deciduous growth and fresh carpets of grass. He never realized before how much he hated flowers.

"Do you like Bob Dylan, sir?"

"I'm sorry. What was that?"

"Bob Dylan." Sure enough, Dylan's "Blowin' In The Wind" was playing on the radio. "It's the local PBS station. They play Bob Dylan every week at this hour."

"Yes. It's a little before my time but I like his stuff."

"It's timeless."

How many times must a grown man cry?
How many times do you need to say good-bye?
Why do the ones you love always have to lie?
Why does the savagery never seem to soften?

> Why does cruelty descend on us so often?
> How many nails can you drive into a coffin?

Those obviously weren't the lyrics. Billy was putting his own spin on it.
Aural hallucinations.
What a freak.

> The answer my friend is blowin' in the wind.
> The answer is blowin' in the wind.

The driver pulled up in front of the station.
"Good-bye, sir. Nice seeing you again."
The taxi driver did remember him.
Billy handed him a twenty.
He felt very special.
Maybe he was.
Special.
Like the village idiot.

Reverend Welby's Love-Of-Jesus Traveling Tent Show

Billy's head felt like someone had pumped it full of maple syrup and was now trying to reclaim the sticky gunk by punching a hole in back of his skull.

He sat up, opened his bloodshot eyes and groped wildly in front of him like a blind man. When he slowly regained his visual functions, the image of Candy sitting across from him in a wicker chair materialized into focus. She was sipping on herb tea and looking pensively out the window. She spoke to him without turning around.

"You're such a lightweight. I know schoolchildren who can hold their liquor better than you."

"Thanks for the vote of confidence. What you don't know is that I'm entering the Strongman Competition this year. It's in Texas, if I'm not mistaken."

"Spot on, Hulk. Dallas, Texas. Larry Hagman is the Master of Ceremonies. He's reprising his role of JR from the TV show. But I think this year they eliminated the special weight class for shell-shocked veterans and town drunks."

"What happened last night?"

"You can read about it on the internet later. Just Google 'Michigan rube daisy chain huff gas' and you'll get the entire story. For now, we need to get our asses down to Battery Park."

"Battery Park. Battery Park. Why does that ring a bell?"

"Generally, it's acknowledged as the southern tip of Manhattan where you can ferry out to the Statue of Liberty. For us, it's where we're meeting Amethyst for her 'surprise'. She said she has a special day planned for us."

Billy started to get up and winced. He looked down at his briefs, then in them.

41

"Christ! I'm so sore. Did we do something last night? Some weird sex thing maybe?"

"Not a chance, Billy. For me it would have been necrophilia. That probably happened when you spilled the boiling water in your lap."

"Boiling water?"

"You thought it was a cup of tea. But it was a huge pot of boiling hot dogs. A street vendor in front of Trump Tower on 56th. I thought the guy was going to club you to death with a baseball-bat-sized chunk of frozen sauerbraten."

"Are you making this up? Was I drunk?"

"I couldn't make up what happened last night. Drunk. Hmm. It doesn't quite sum it up. Maybe there's no term that's entirely adequate. Let's see. You popped Ecstasy twice in the first hour, claiming the first hit was having no effect. I lost track after your fifth joint, which you horded like it was the last one on the planet. Then you dug in and did some 2C, enhanced with several lines of coke. For an aperitif you sucked down a half a fifth of tequila. Yeah. I think that was it. Thank goodness you showed some restraint."

Billy struggled to his feet and hobbled toward the bathroom.

"I'll be ready by Tuesday."

"You have fifteen minutes or I'll witness for the prosecution on the unseemly events which I personally observed last night. The paperwork is already on the Attorney General's desk."

He was back in ten.

They caught a downtown local and popped out of the Bowling Green subway exit.

Billy was still not happy about being vertical, much less having to actually move.

They headed toward the park and passed some city workers jack hammering a hole in the sidewalk. It was deafeningly loud. Billy thought for sure his head was going explode.

As they walked, he kept his unfocused eyes on the ground a few feet ahead of him to reduce the amount of sensory data going into his compromised nervous system. Candy was graciously acting as his seeing-eye dog as they made their way across the street into the park.

She suddenly started laughing.

"Holy donuts! Is this what I think it is?"

As they approached a gigantic revival tent set up in the center of Battery Park, they could hear the distorted sound of gospel music being pumped through a P.A. system that was obviously not up to the task. The organ wailed, tambourines jangled, as the band rocked out a supercharged roll-'em-in-the-aisles anthem, with the voices of more than 40 singers belting the nasty rhythm-and-blues melodies of the deep South.

Jesus!
The Lord Jesus!
He's the Man with a plan
The Lord and Savior of us all

Candy spotted Amethyst at the same time she spotted them.

"Alright! There she is."

She was standing in front of the huge open flap of the main entrance to the tent. High above her was stretched a full-length oil-on-canvas portrait of Jesus Christ with His beckoning hand outstretched. On his chest was a huge crimson lover's heart encircled with a glowing halo. There was also a giant halo above His head, more of a rings-of-Saturn affair than the traditional cranial nimbus. Jesus was smiling the smile of a game show host, a toothy self-mocking grin that begged for someone to throw a pie in his face.

Amethyst was laughing, waving and jumping up and down, all at the same time. Obviously, she was pleased with herself.

Once they got within striking range, she ran up to them and excitedly hugged them both, then continued to gesticulate with the arms of someone hooked up to an electrical grid.

"Isn't this great! Thanks so much, you guys. I was afraid you wouldn't come."

Billy looked at her incredulously.

"Why are we here?"

Amethyst stepped directly in front of Billy and stared intently into his bloodshot eyes.

"Because you are a truth-seeker."

"I am?"

"At NYU. When we posed for the art class. You were naked. We were naked. You turned dramatically to the class and made a profound declaration of your love of truth. It was an awesome moment, Billy."

"What the hell are you talking about?"

"Yes. I remember it like it was yesterday. You reached up to embrace the entire sky and yelled at the top of your lungs, 'Knowledge is power!' Right, Candy?"

"Hmm. Actually what I remember is that Billy got a huge boner and all the girls in the class were giggling."

"Come on! None of it happened! You're both insane."

"Now Billy, we wouldn't make this up."

"*Totally* insane!"

Candy and Amethyst seemed to find this very funny. It just made Billy's head throb even more. He looked around for a place to sit. There was none in sight.

Candy had inherent trust in her friend but still needed clarification.

"This looks like great fun, Am. But why are we here? Besides the great fun, of course."

"That's it! Why not? But that's not all. It's like they always say at the East Side Anarchist Party meetings. Know the enemy!"

"I have to say, 'Anarchist Party' sounds like an oxymoron to me. But whatever. This is one of those fundamentalist shindigs, right? When do they start boiling the Jewish babies?"

"It's all in the mix. We'll get speaking-in-tongues, paralytics jumping up and doing the jig, voices of the dead over the P. A., blood squirting out of hands, a Holy Ghost cameo, baptism dunkings, conniptions, convulsions, Elvis impersonators, you name it."

Amethyst saved the best for last.

"And are you ready for this? We have our own personal private meeting with the Reverend Shelby himself, right after."

"Blessed are the meek, as they shall inherit the keys to the Canvas Tent."

Though he looked like he wanted to say something, Billy was still climbing the steep walls of his stupor. It was too much for him to comprehend.

"This is way too weird."

"The kettle calling the frying pan black."

Amethyst leaned into them conspiratorially.

"Guys, check this out. He thinks I'm a journalist. Free lance. I'm supposedly doing a feature article for Canadian Sunset Magazine. Eh, hoser? Gullibility is obviously not in short supply around here."

Candy burst out laughing too loudly, drawing both the curious and disapproving looks of those passing nearby, on their way into the tent. She was wholly oblivious of the spectacle she was creating. As Billy looked on in total amazement, she grabbed Amethyst and started an impromptu dance that looked like ring around the rosy.

"Amethyst Reigns! You are truly phantasmagoric!"

They eventually finished their fit of craziness, skipping the all-fall-down finale, then Amethyst led the way.

"Well, let's see what the good Reverend Shelby's got going here."

Amethyst had not exaggerated one bit. They got to see it all. The pitched orations of the Reverend, the miracles, the frenzy, the fainting, the screaming, the crying, the rapturous acceptance of Jesus as a personal savior.

Not that they were indifferent spectators. Not at all. In over two hours of sweat-drenched praying, singing, dancing, pleading, praising, clapping, hooting, hollering, and generally surrendering to the madness of the moment, Amethyst, Candy and Billy proved that atheists can party with Jesus Christ Lord and Savior with as much enthusiasm and abandon — if not sincerity — as the most dumbed-down, brainwashed, fundamentalist Christians around.

Afterwards, as Amethyst had promised, they were brought to the private reception area, a separate office-size tent behind the main big top. A coterie of assistants and brown-nosers surrounded the Reverend as he slouched on an overstuffed couch, sipping on a mug of coffee. He had a towel around his sweaty neck and his perspiration-soaked dress shirt was open down to his stomach, exposing the wild salt-and-pepper gorilla ground-cover of his chest. He looked older up close, but his eyes still blazed with the megalomaniac fire of his just completed performance.

One of his bubbly assistants graciously walked them over to him. The others who had been sitting around him dispersed, freeing the seats for Amethyst, Candy and Billy.

"This is Mary Jane Cannibis, the reporter. She's doing an article for Canadian uh …"

"Canadian Sunset. And these are my close associates, Billy Idol and Candy Bunk."

Without standing, the Reverend extended his hand for a round of handshakes.

"Bless you, Mr. Idol. Pleased to meet you. And you …" He gave Candy a quick physical assessment and seemed rather pleased with the initial findings. "… *Miss* Bunk? Nice to meet you and God bless."

Candy winked flirtatiously. "My friends call me Candy."

"And Miss Cannabis …"

"Can-*ni*-bis. It's an 'i'. And the accent is on the second syllable. Not to be confused with the drug which has become the horrible scourge of my generation. I've gotten an awful lot of teasing about my name over the years. And Reverend, just call me Mary, please."

"Yes. I'm sure you have, Mary."

"Do you mind if I smoke, Reverend?"

"Not at all. I think I'll join you." He reached behind him and retrieved a pack of Marlboro Lite Menthols, then turned and offered her one. "Here you go, my dear."

"Thanks. I have my own."

As the Reverend lit up, Amethyst pulled out a perfectly-rolled joint, one which a passing glance would judge to be a commercially produced cigarette. When Billy and Candy spotted it, it was all they could do to keep from totally losing it. The Reverend gallantly leaned over and offered the flame of his lighter to Amethyst.

"Thanks."

She smiled and pulled the marijuana smoke deeply into her lungs.

The Reverend also took a long drag on his cigarette, then looked at his watch, impatient to get things moving. He started the ball rolling.

"Anyway, you probably have a lot of questions. But I prefer to just get to the heart of the matter. The message that drives my ministry. The simple but profound idea which I hope each person who attends my services carries away and lives by. You see, the words of Jesus Christ have been misconstrued and manipulated for various reasons over the centuries. Now we have available many easy paths to redemption which are false, paths which frankly condemn the faithful to eternal damnation. One of the myths is that by just 'being a good person', you can achieve salvation and the reward of a place in Heaven. But in Ephesians, the Lord Our Savior is very clear on this subject. Sin cannot be expunged by good works of atonement alone. It is only by accepting Jesus Christ in your heart as your personal savior, accepting His suffering and sacrifice on the cross as His personal intervention with God the Father on our behalf, it is only embracing Him thusly, that opens the doors of Heaven to us. Let me offer an example."

The Reverend took another long drag on his cigarette, momentarily closed his eyes as if in prayer. He slowly released the smoke and it recycled back up into his nostrils, then put the cigarette down in an ashtray and looked intently at Amethyst.

"How many times do you think you have lied, Miss Cannabis? Roughly. In your lifetime."

"Reverend, you really should just call me Mary Jane. I would feel more comfortable."

She perfectly imitated the Reverend, taking a long hit off the perfectly rolled joint, closed her eyes, recycled the hemp smoke through her nostrils for maximum effect, then looked intently at the Reverend.

"Let's see. Lies. White lies and grey lies and dirty rotten lies. That's impossible to say. Likely it's in the thousands."

"How do you think the Lord feels about that?"

"I have no way of knowing. But probably not too happy. Not happy at all."

"Do you think you've been forgiven?"

"Reverend. I'm a good person. Lying is not all I do. In fact, it's pretty rare that I lie. And in the meantime, between the occasional fib here and fib there, I think I do a lot of good in the world."

"So you feel that because you do good things, you will be forgiven for your transgressions and ultimately will be rewarded with a place in Heaven."

"That's not for me to say. But yes. I sure hope so. It's not like I've spent my life hacking up babies and feeding them to my friends. Or making porn films."

"I am — and I base this on the gift given me by the Lord Savior of being able to sense the essential worth of a person — I am sure you are a good person. But be careful. The Bible is very clear on this. It is not by good works alone that we can atone for our failures here on Earth. The only way to get to Heaven is accepting Jesus Christ into our hearts."

Reverend Welby then turned to Candy and despite his best efforts could not help but do a another quick survey of the highlights of her erotic assets. He took in the length of her body, pausing in a flickering glint to savor her breasts. By intentionally slouching down in her seat and spreading her legs provocatively, she made it virtually impossible for him to keep his gaze focused on her face. He was obviously drawn in by the sweet magnetism emanating from between those long lovely legs.

"Let me ask *you* now, Miss Bunk. I'm sorry ... Candy. How is your relationship with God?"

"Great. How's yours?"

"Fantastic. Excellent. Praise the Lord! So for you, can you give me a little heads-up on what that relationship is?"

"That's kind of personal. It's a personal relationship, you see. But I can tell you some of the things I've learned. Just this morning, God was telling me I should beware of false prophets. Men who claim to speak in His name."

"False prophets? Yes, we all must be careful. The Devil wears many different wardrobes."

"God is particularly pissed off about the way His word is being twisted. Cheapened. He says that there are too many people running around these days saying they speak for Him. Putting words in His mouth that aren't His. Making

Him sound like a third-rate snake-oil salesman with a two-bit education from some half-assed seminary in the Midwest. God specifically told me that His thoughts are not just bumper stickers for monster trucks and NASCAR equipment trailers. He especially resents those who run around aggrandizing themselves in His name. You know the types. Like those televangelists who are always asking you to put your hands on your television screens to be healed. Then they suck all the money out of your wallet so that they can buy a new fleet of Cadillacs. Those guys are going to burn long and hard. At least that's what He said. I'll tell you something, Reverend. The Guy sure talks up a storm. Whatever."

She shrugged and her skirt hiked up a couple more revealing inches.

The Reverend's capped and professionally-bleached smile was starting look a little forced. It was clearly not in his game plan to ever lose control of a conversation. This was a new experience. He dug in his heels to regain the initiative.

"Very interesting. Yes. So Candy. How many times in your lifetime have you lied? Just a rough estimate."

"Let's see. Hmm. Rounding it off. Well ... actually I have never lied. No. Not once."

"You're saying you've never lied. Not even a tiny white lie?"

"No. I haven't. Why would I lie? It's wrong to lie. You should know that."

"Right. Yes, it is. It *is* wrong to lie. Then let me ask you this. Have you ever disobeyed your parents?"

"No. I haven't. That would be disrespectful. A bad thing. 'Honor thy father and thy mother.' That's one of the Ten Commandments."

"You've never disobeyed your parents. Not once. That's very commendable. Let me see." Quick glance at Candy's crotch. "Have you ever had sex outside of marriage? You're not married, right? So have you?"

"Have I had sex? Never. Not even a hand job. Or a blow job. What kind of girl do you think I am, Reverend?"

"I ... I—"

"I look at it this way. There you are. And here I am. I'm not the one looking at your chest wanting to lick my way down your body. I'm not the one looking at your crotch thinking how good it would be to sample a little of this and a little of that. The wife wouldn't know and the Lord has died on the cross so that all of us, if we just follow Him around like a bunch of lost puppies, can get into Heaven anyway. So it all works out pretty good in the end no matter how much tail you chase on the side, right Reverend? Am I getting your message straight here?"

"If you're implying—"

"Here's the way I see it. God agrees with you on one count. At least that's what He's been telling me for some time now. As I said, I was just talking to Him this morning—"

"Hold on! That's blasphemy. You're telling me you talk to God? Directly to God?"

"What? Of course, I talk to God. All the time. Don't you?"

"Well … yes. Yes, I do. Of course."

"And does He tell you that you're full of shit? Because that's what He's telling me."

"Listen, young lady. I will not tolerate any more of your insults. And you are not to use that kind of language."

Reaching up and taking in the stained walls of the tent with his hands.

"After all, this is the house of the Lord."

"Looks like a circus tent to me. But whatever you say. All I'm saying, Mr. Reverend, is the Big Guy is pretty upset with you little guys. Going around acting like you have some pipeline to Him, some privileged access to what He's thinking and what he really means. Turning his message into a variety show. Or in your case a circus. Raking in the dough. Selling salvation like it's saddle oil or kettle corn."

"But He says right in Ephesians—"

"Quoting the Bible! That's another one that makes God go ballistic. In the first place, God will be the first to tell you, the Bible is a manmade document. Campfire stuff. All those nomadic Jews and homeless apostles sitting around in the desert at night with nothing better to do. Plus He thinks the writing sucks. He's always telling me, 'No one talks like that. Especially me.' And in the second place, there's more versions of the Bible than there are New York telephone directories. They've been hacking it up and rewriting it for so long, no one knows what it says anymore. Did you know, Reverend Welby that God has a huge library in Heaven that makes the Library of Congress look like a corner news stand. And you know where they keep the Bible? I love this! It's filed under Children's Fiction."

"Just hold on here. How can you claim to know this? How do I know you speak for God?"

"You can't. And how do I know you speak for God?"

"I'm an ordained man of the cloth. I have been given the power to heal in His name."

"I see. Let's get back to that Bible you love so much, Reverend. Are you familiar with the passage where Jesus says, it is easier for a camel to pass through the eye of a needle, than for a man of wealth to enter the kingdom of Heaven?"

"Yes. Of course. What's that got to do with—"

"Tell me, dear Reverend. What kind of house do you live in? How many cars do you own?"

Candy pointed at his wrist.

"How much did that Rolex set you back?"

A flash of anger and desperation crossed the pastor's face, leaving his brow hunkered down in a deep furrow. He waved at his assistant to come right over.

"Or let's get to some of your questions. How many lies have you told? How about today? Any lies up there during today's performance? How about sex outside your marriage bed?"

With the subtlety of a third-base coach, the Reverend with a slashing motion across his throat signaled to his assistant — who on approaching had already registered his distress — that the interview was over. She went directly to Amethyst, who sat with an amused expression on her face. The assistant grabbed her hand and pulled her to her feet.

Amethyst held out the joint to her.

"You seem a little tense. You want some of this?"

The assistant obviously had no idea what she was looking at. After momentarily looking confused, she quickly again donned her damage-control smile.

"Thank you so much for coming today. The Reverend has a busy schedule, as I am sure you know. We, of course, require advance approval of your interview before it can be published. Just send the transcript to me. Here's my card."

As she spoke, Reverend Shelby beat a quick retreat through a rear flap of the tent, scrambled into his 85-foot motor home, slamming the door behind him.

The outside of the monstrous gas-guzzling condo on wheels was painted with angels and clouds, a portrait of the jester Jesus like the one suspended above entrance to the revival tent. There was a flashy close-up of the Reverend himself below a banner which read ...

REVEREND WELBY'S LOVE-OF-JESUS
TRAVELING TENT SHOW AND PORTABLE MINISTRY
"Bringing the Divine Message of Jesus Christ to your Community."

The three of them were briskly escorted out by the assistant. A couple of body guards in three-piece suits appeared at the front of the tent to guarantee an expeditious exit, should any encouragement be necessary. Billy gave them the peace sign. Candy and Amethyst were talking and giggling as they made their way to the cordoned perimeter of the revival grounds.

"I'm sorry if I ruined your interview, Mary Jane."

"That's why I invited you. You were terrific! You kicked his holy ass."

They celebrated their salvation and redemption by sitting on a bench looking at the Statue of Liberty off in the distance of the harbor, while they ate hot dogs with mustard and sauerkraut. For Billy, it was too much a gastronomical reprise of the previous night and he tossed his up into a waste container which said on the side, *Please Recycle*.

They spent the rest of the day at Amethyst's place watching *I Love Lucy* reruns on DVD. Whenever Ricky's band played, the two girls did their own version of salsa dancing.

Billy just sulked and drank mineral water. Occasionally the girls would come over and try to get him to stand up and dance. He passed. Went back to sulking.

He silently repeated a mantra that he would never drink again.

The same one he would repeat after the next time.

And then the time after that.

And then the ...

The Lottery

Occasionally — just occasionally — Billy would wonder if he was slowly becoming a carbon copy of his father. After all, for nearly a year, Billy had become the Big Apple version of a couch potato. He was worthless to everyone, including himself. It felt like he had forgotten how to smile. He was miserable. And he was drinking like the Nicolas Cage character in *Leaving Las Vegas*.

There was one major difference with his dad. That was the complete lack of pattern or predictability in Billy's current lifestyle.

His father on the other hand, from what Billy could tell, embraced a daily existence where all six sides of the dice had the same number.

Despite in his leisure time becoming an over-the-hill Hell's Angels wannabe, Harold wrote the book on predictability and routine. He went to bed and got up the same time every day. He went to bed angry and he got up angry. Except perhaps when he was riding his hog in the thundering herd of his motorcycle buddies, the guy constantly seethed. Life was hugely unfair to him. He let the world know.

The robotic regularity of Harold's personal life mimicked the mechanistic repetition of his daily work — thirty-three years working on the assembly lines at various divisions of both the Chrysler and General Motors auto factories in and around Detroit. Last Billy had heard, his dad was back at the Buick and Cadillac final assembly plant, just a stone's throw from their new home in Hamtramck.

As if he cared. Billy did his best to not think about his father and listened with quiet courtesy or sometimes innocuous jokes, whenever his mother reported goings on related to the man. He respected his mother's loyalty, even if he couldn't comprehend it.

It was just before noon. Candy had just left and Billy was trying to make some breakfast. He had dropped an egg and was crouched over contemplating with almost childlike wonder, the yellow slime spreading on the linoleum of his kitchen floor, when his phone rang. Billy hated phones. More than broken eggs.

At Candy's suggestion, he had a caller ID phone now. It displayed a Detroit number.

His mom. Okay. Phones were a good thing on rare occasions.

"Billy! I have some great news. It's about your father."

"They found a brain donor?"

"You are such a silly boy. No, we're rich! Your father won the lottery!"

"You're serious?"

"Serious as a heart attack. Two-and-a-half million dollars!!"

"Mom! That's outstanding! Wow! That's incredible! So what now?"

"Your dad quit his job. We're going to travel."

"Travel? He's afraid to leave Detroit."

"Hey, come on now. He went to Mackinac Island once. He seems to really like Las Vegas. Anyway, I am so happy! Finally, I get to go somewhere."

Go somewhere they would. After a few feverish shopping sprees, Harold and Irene sat down with a local travel agent and planned their first vacation in over thirty years of marriage.

Kenya, Africa.

Harold had grown up on Johnny Weissmuller's Jungle Jim movies and weekly TV shows. He apparently still harbored fantasies from early youth about African game-hunting. With some money in the bank — a lot of money — he licked the lips of his hibernating imagination and could vividly picture himself in a pith helmet, toting an elephant gun, and bringing down the big African beasts of his carnage-filled boyhood daydreams.

For Irene, Kenya was as good as anywhere. As long as it wasn't Detroit, she was fine with it. The pictures and travel pamphlets provided by the travel agent helping them plan their trip, looked fascinating. The tall elegant Maasai tribesman, the beautiful stretches of grassland, the animals — wildebeest, lions, antelopes, giraffes, buffaloes, cheetahs, jackals, hyenas, zebra — it all looked so exotic and wild and exciting.

As they were sitting at their kitchen table strewn with brochures, she looked at the weathered face of her husband and risked some romantic sentimentality.

"It's never too late for a real honeymoon."

Harold only half-heard her and smiled back, as he pictured the huge heads of several beasts of the African wild mounted above a yet-to-be-acquired fireplace, glass eyes staring back in death, the decapitated animal mugs mounted beside the highly-polished long-barreled weapons of slaughter, which he had used to pump bullets into them.

Big bad Harold Green, retired automobile maker, big-game hunter.

He wasn't a changed man. But he was a changing man.

He was also a worried man. Irene had been losing weight. Something was wrong.

At least they had money now. Money can fix almost anything.

Irene had an appointment with her doctor next week. No sense thinking about it now.

Certainly there was no reason for her to bring it up to Billy. It was probably nothing.

"I'll bring back a souvenir for you. What do you want from the deepest depths of Africa?"

"How about a machete? It's getting crowded here."

"I'll bring back one of those masks the medicine men wear. That should clear a path for you."

"When are you leaving?"

"End of next week. We have a few stops to make along the way back. London. Paris. Madrid. Rome. Oh Billy! I am so excited! I could never have imagined this in a million years."

"You deserve it, mom. Too bad you don't have better company."

"Now Billy. Your dad is slowly coming around. I know you won't believe this. I can hardly believe it myself. But he treats me pretty good these days."

"You're right. I don't believe it."

"Hey, Billy Boy. Do you need some money? I know it's been difficult for you. We've got tons. It would be no problem."

"I'm fine. We sold the house in Newburgh. With that, I'm the Warren Buffet of Avenue C. The bums form a reception line and bow down to kiss my wingtips when I come home."

"You are the funniest boy a mother could have. I promise I'll write. I'll send some pictures. Next trip you have to promise to join us. Maybe we'll stop in New York on the way back. Alright. Bye-bye for now. I love you, my favorite son."

"Bye mom. Be a good girl."

Militant Meditation and Dumpster Deaths

By late spring of that year, with aggressive recruiting, Apocalypso had established a sizable grass roots following, promoting a message and persona which reached deep into a growing disaffection and sense of isolation in New York. The most loyal of these constituted the initial solid core of his movement. These were individuals predisposed from prior quests for spiritual revelation and personal tuning, to be receptive to his teachings — New Agers, secular humanists, Buddhists, devotees of Osho, 60s and 70s survivors of Maharishi Yogi's Transcendental Meditation, and scattered others who had with the onset of the new Millennium, replaced their gym workouts and penny stock trading with a workout for their soul, an investment in their karmic balance sheet.

Then his appearances even began to attract others. There was something so fundamental, simple, honest and appealing about his approach to self-healing and personal empowerment, it often reached far beyond the touchy-feely crowd, even resonating with housewives and ordinary blokes, for whom the Pablum of television and the occasional Sunday service or self-help prescriptives, no longer did the job of refurbishing and reinvigorating their meaningless, humdrum lives.

However, since he had from the beginning strategically tailored his message for maximum effect on those who he knew he could initially reach — the touchy feelies — the core of his teachings had changed little over the past few years.

Apocalypso now became increasingly convinced that this message soon had to start evolving, or risk becoming just more of the same old blah-blah blather. The American public was restless and fickle, with a pathological addiction for new, whiter, brighter, shinier. This is how things had been, and probably always would be. Pandemic ADHD drove change and innovation.

Once Apocalypso started thinking along these lines, he found himself questioning, and reformulating from top to bottom, the entirety of his enterprise. He realized how limited his approach had been until now. How quaint and provincial his little ashram in the East Village was.

Sure. He was helping people. But he had gotten into the whole guru business to try to make some big changes. Some *serious* changes. And there was no way he was going to seriously change the world by going at it one person at a time, not in this lifetime anyway. He had to start thinking big. The slow patient plodding of evolution was not cutting it. What the world needed now was revolution. Both a revolution of the spirit and a revolution of the system.

He formulated his new strategy. And came up with his own personal five-year plan.

But he would have to move judiciously.

First, he needed to make sure he didn't alienate and lose any of those already loyal to him. To keep those already captive in the fold, he would very gradually move the path of enlightenment to its new terrain. He would bit-by-bit build on the metaphysics he had in place, slowly and subtly transforming it into a theology of personal activism.

While thus extending the scope of his message, he would start reaching out to a wider audience, and substantially enlarge the pool of potential donors and recruits for his moral-political agenda. The bigger and more embracing his message, the bigger his people's army.

No child of enlightenment left behind.

No potential child of insurgency left outside.

There was more.

Just as important as numbers, if his organization was to become an effective agent for change, he needed to get all of the gentle, docile, peace-loving — not to say comatose — current members of his sleepy ashram off their stationary butts and doing something. As Candy had so eloquently put it, he needed to "get the lard-asses moving."

On a purely practical level, all of this added up to the same thing. There would be less praying and more yelling. The quiet hum of the mantra would gradually be replaced with the loud roar of a call to action.

In his public appearances now, Apocalypso started to make the case for an energetic activism. Scare tactics seemed to be the most effective way to get everyone's attention. A spoonful of paranoia goes a long way.

> *"Already we see the harbingers of persecution. Who are we hurting? No one. Who do we threaten by our meditation? No one. Who do we harm with our universal love? No one. Nevertheless, they're coming after us. They're coming after us with bad intentions. I see it. You see it. So we, who embrace peace, non-violence, and perfect harmony for all living creatures, are now forced to accept a new reality: Enlightenment within is not enough, if we are destroyed from without by the forces of darkness and ignorance."*

Actually, this wasn't histrionic crusading. It was true. Beyond the usual harangues about pagans and heretics by the fanatical preachers of the Christian right, Apocalypso and the Ashram of the Urban Night had recently attracted enough attention to be specifically singled-out by several of high-profile preachers and priests, in a number of well-publicized sermons. It was the price of popularity and success.

It wasn't that Apocalypso was pulling from the rank and file of the established Christian and Catholic churches. Most of these folks were locked in for the long haul by their narrow beliefs and unquestioning allegiance.

It was just the *idea* of it.

That this upstart, illegal alien Cuban refugee — an accusation that was completely false, since he was born in Miami to Cuban parents, both of whom were U.S. citizens — that this hyper-virile, hippie long-hair, bare-chested Desi Arnaz-Ricky Martin clone, could attract a huge following with his un-Christian, blasphemous babbling about spiritual healing and moral renewal, was an affront. It was offensive. It was un-American. It was atheistic. It was dangerous.

Apocalypso welcomed the publicity. As far as he was concerned, any press was good press. It got him in the public eye and made it easier for him to get people's attention, the first step in recruiting them.

At the same time, he couldn't just stand by and let the establishment clergy rip him a new asshole.

It was time to get tough. It was time to flex some muscles.

Apocalypso created a new motto, which he had emblazoned in big graffiti-style spray paint letters on the inside wall of his Ashram on 1st Avenue.

Militant Meditation:
Love the Oneness of All.
Defend it from division.

This became the spiritual call to arms from which the new Apocalypso would emerge. Louder, bolder, more assertive, more zealous, more streetwise, as much tuned in to the world around him as the world within. In a word … political.

The new Apocalypso increasingly sprinkled his teachings and public statements with phrases that were provocative, controversial, confrontational, even incendiary. Any undergraduate student of political science would recognize chunks of language borrowed from Marx and Engels, Eugene Debs and Upton Sinclair, from icons of revolution like Lenin, Trotsky, Mao, Che Guevara, Fidel Castro.

Meditation and prayer, rather than being the means to withdraw to the quiet sanctums of inner peace and repose, now became the technique for centering and focusing one's energy, in preparation for the battles that needed to be fought outside of oneself.

It was a slow, subtle and well-crafted transformation, but viewed over time, had to be judged as a major paradigm shift for Apocalypso's metaphysical beliefs and real world game plan.

It was puzzling to anyone who wasn't familiar with Apocalypso and his enormous oratorical gifts, that this new edginess and migration toward the rough and tumble of real politik didn't alienate the incense-burning, Om-chanting core of his following. It seemed reasonable to expect that these recluses, escapists, self-styled ascetics and monk-wannabees, would have rebelled against leaving the protective cocoon that meditation and turning within provided. But right in line with his carefully wrought strategy, Apocalypso kept the metaphysical components of his teaching intact, even if they became increasingly diluted over time by his campaigning for political awareness and in-the-street activism.

In essence, it was all about tuning the message and massaging the temporal lobes, while giving everyone a good swift kick in the ass and yelling at them to storm the fortress walls.

Billy was walking up 1st Avenue on his way to meet Candy. They had a movie date to see a just released movie at the Regal Union Square multiplex on Broadway. It was some weird thing called *XXY* about a girl born with male genitalia. He could always count on Candy to find the most off-the-wall thing out there, and insist it was a "must see" for them.

A young boy maybe 17 with his head shaved, wearing an off-white Tibetan prayer shawl over shoulder-to-toe military camouflage, approached him.

Oops! Correct that.

It was a young *girl* with her head shaved.

She gave Billy a slight bow with her eyes closed and her hands in prayer position before her.

"Have you heard of Apocalypso?"

"If I'm correct, I'm hearing him right now."

He was. They were right in front of the Ashram of the Urban Night. It was basically an empty box storefront, which became available three years ago when a convenience store had been held up so often, the owner just packed up everything in a rental truck and drove away in disgust. The sign out front still read *Falco's Easy Stop - Hot Coffee To Go.*

Billy rarely walked this stretch of 1st Avenue, never walked on this side of the street, mainly to avoid the very situation he was in right now. He still had a strong aversion to Apocalypso and his organization. Billy's initial impression that the guy was a full-tilt kook and fraudulent opportunist was still pretty intact.

Blasting out into the street was a harangue by the holy man himself. Billy, or anyone passing by for that matter, could look through the front window and see who was doing the talking. Apocalypso in the flesh. The man. The legend. The myth.

> *"Let us reach inside to that calm pool of certainty that is the Universe's gift of enlightenment. Then let us take that gift out into this divided and divisive world, into the streets, into the homes, into the hearts of Americans, so that we may again become a family. Recognize and again be One with the ..."*

Billy had to admit. He was good. The guy had it together.

But ... he didn't have the time or the patience for this right now.

"Thanks, sweetheart. But I've got plans tonight."

"You are always welcome here, sir. Please come back."

"Awesome. Maybe some other time."

Off he went to spend two hours sitting in high-tech, air-conditioned comfort, to see a cinematic tearjerker that held no interest for him and bore no discernable relevance to his tearful, irrelevant life.

That evening Billy finally found out what Candy did to make money.

She was a tattoo artist.

Not a tattooist, which is the person who puts the ink to the skin. But the person who designs the tattoos.

It made sense. She was covered with some of the most unique and visually mesmerizing tattoos he had ever seen. Now he realized they must be a portfolio of her own designs.

The onset of Billy's revelation occurred as they were coming out of the movie and some guy recognized her. He stopped them in their tracks. He took off his jacket and rolled up his shirtsleeve to show her how great his tattoo looked, then went on to rave about the design, and claimed that he had to keep it covered because strangers would constantly stop him to have a closer look, even people who didn't have any tattoos themselves.

"Susan! You're the best."

When Billy finally coaxed it out of her on the way to Miss Piggy's Sweets & Succulent Morsels, he was then able to piece together the whole thing. Whether she was being humble or evasive, he couldn't tell. But under her real name, Susan Kalkin, she was widely considered in body art circles to be one of the top three designers in New York City, her work heralded across the board. While she was widely plagiarized, she still managed to be one of the most highly-compensated people in the field. She only took on a few clients at a time but made between $1500 and $5000 for each design.

This success had all happened in the past year. She was certainly extremely happy about it, but still rather dumbstruck by the whole thing.

From Billy's perspective, this explained a lot. Though she hardly lived extravagantly, she never seemed to worry about money. She always wore great clothes. Billy couldn't ever remember seeing her in the same outfit twice. She frequently had to be places, but there was never any pattern to it, at least that he could see. It was obvious from the beginning that she didn't have a straight job.

They reached Miss Piggy's, miraculously got a table — it was very popular and always packed — and were now sitting with a gigantic mound of Mud Pie between them, spoons poised for their assault on the confectionary bomb, one which would send their blood sugar levels into the stratosphere.

"Why didn't you ever bother to tell me?"

"It never came up."

"It's certainly something I'd want to know about."

"Last time I looked you had as many tattoos as John Kerry. Now you know the awful truth. Does it change anything?"

"I guess not."

"Why does everybody think that what you do is who you are?"

"For most people it is."

"So that means you're a nothing?"

"I guess it does. A big fat zero."

"You said it, not me."

Billy suddenly looked angry.

"Well, you said it first."

Candy tried to make light of it.

"I was being ironic. But I guess you're right."

Billy played with his spoon. He looked at Candy. It was obvious he was pissed.

"So. I'm a big nothing?"

"It seems that way."

"You could help me out here. Where is the witty comeback? The snappy rejoinder?"

She put her spoon down and rolled her eyes.

"Why would I do that?"

"Because I'm such a great guy?"

Candy stood up, grabbed her untouched latte, took a quick swallow and poured the rest onto the Mud Pie. She looked more hurt than angry.

"You may be. But right now you're hopeless."

"Hopeless?"

"Hopeless and pathetic."

"Fuck off."

She grabbed her handbag, then paused before leaving.

"I really don't understand. You have so much going for you. What a waste of protoplasm."

"Fuck off. Fuck off! FUCK OFF!!"

"I heard you the first time."

Then she was gone.

Billy sat there and watched the Mud Pie melt. In twenty minutes, it started to drip over the edges of the plate. At least one waiter and a number of customers were glaring at him, pressuring him to free up his table so that they could sit down.

Finally he paid, got up to leave, and wandered out. He was still angry and mindlessly walked in whatever direction he was going. It took a while but he finally cooled down a bit.

It was shortly after 10 pm when Billy started to make his way back to his apartment. He was heading east on 8th Street but as he crossed 1st Avenue, he noticed a huge commotion a couple blocks down. The street was barricaded, there was a sizable crowd, numerous flashing lights, and men in uniforms scrambling around.

Billy suddenly realized all of this was taking place right where he had briefly stopped earlier this evening, at the Ashram of the Urban Night. He went to see what was going on.

From the number of police cars, assault and support vehicles, mobile news vans, ambulances and fire trucks, it looked like they had Osama bin Laden and the entire Nation of Islam trapped in the building. The police led about twenty apprentice monks, lay staff, and a handful of innocent visitors who happened to be there at the time of the raid, onto the street, where they were handcuffed and made to sit in a row on the curb. Several cops in riot gear stood over them with weapons drawn, while the building was searched.

This would be the first of several such raids on the ashram over the next few weeks. The police went in allegedly with certain knowledge that there were illicit drugs and illegal weapons on the premises.

Of course, they found nothing. Apocalypso's official program of spiritual purification strictly forbade the use of drugs, even discouraged drinking alcoholic beverages.

As for guns or weapons of mass destruction, the only thing they found was a slingshot fashioned from some rubber bands and two Bic pens that had been taped together to form a V. Well-aimed it might be able to take out beefy housefly.

Figuring that Apocalypso's guard might be down after the first couple raids and the sought-after contraband would reappear, they returned almost weekly. Each subsequent assault on the unimposing storefront ashram became more dramatic as their frustration snowballed. After the fourth raid, the staff bought their own plastic handcuffs at a toy store, and the next time they saw the small army of police assemble on the street, they came out already cuffed, then lined up on the sidewalk laughing. Each held a hand-written confession in his hands.

I confess to making fun of the NYPD.

It became such a joke that for the final raid, Apocalypso had a huge pot of coffee and trays of donuts waiting for the cops as they stormed into the premises. What the press didn't catch on camera, the ashram's staff did, using both still and video cameras. The photos and footage made the NYPD look like the Keystone Cops' rightful heirs to buffoonery on the beat.

Apocalypso then wrote and hand-delivered a letter to the NYPD Police Commissioner.

```
June 18, 2008

Dear Commissioner Kelly,

There seems to be a great deal of interest within
your department in our humble organization.
Several times in the recent past, you have
visited us and searched our premises from top
to bottom. Your search warrants list items which
would never be found here but that has not
discouraged you from sending dozens of your best
men, armed to the teeth and ready to do battle.

While we are puzzled at this gross waste of
resources on our peaceful and loving ashram, we
understand you have a job to do and thus will
never stand in the way of what you perceive as
your public duty, regardless of how foolish and
misguided it is.

In fact, to facilitate your efforts, I am
enclosing with this letter, a full set of keys
to our facility. You are welcome to come here
anytime to do whatever you think you need to do
to protect the public from our message of
universal love and peace.
```

It would be better for everyone if you came at
night, so as to not interfere with our teaching
and exercise of quiet meditation.

Please turn off the lights when you leave.

Thanks.

> Yours in the guiding
> spirit of universal
> brotherhood and love,
>
> *Apocalypso*
>
> Apocalypso, Mentor
> Lama Bodhisattva

He then published it in several newspapers, including the Daily News and the Village Voice. Accompanying the letter were photographs which made it look like half of the law enforcement personnel of New York City were on the scene. These full-page spreads were headed with the question:

Haven't the police got better things to do
than waste taxpayer money?

The ads landed like a cluster bomb on City Hall. Reporters and pundits at every end of the political spectrum jumped on the bandwagon and ran with the story.

Most people couldn't have cared less about Apocalypso — in fact, until this incident 99% of them had never heard of him — but they did care about the way their money was being spent. For three days the public outrage, cries for heads to roll, and reviling of official waste and police incompetence, filled the airwaves and grabbed page one and page two of many editions of the daily press. Mayor Bloomberg and Police Commissioner Kelly mounted a feeble defense but were resoundingly mocked and denounced.

As with all news stories, it eventually faded, as the public's attention moved on to the latest sensationalized disasters, public scandals, and celebrity gossip.

But while the story ran, the voices of the judges were loud and unequivocal.

Apocalypso had definitely won Round One.

Something else happened that evening of the first police raid of the ashram, a tragic and horrifying incident, setting up the next mauling of the NYPD at the hands of the Apocalypso public relations machine.

After their brief but emotionally charged clash — the first thing resembling a fight they had ever had — Billy had stormed out of Miss Piggy's, angry at Candy, angry at himself. Just plain angry.

But by the time he got to the East Village, he had pretty much calmed down. Observing the raid on Apocalypso's ashram for thirty minutes or so further distracted him. When he got to his flat and sat down, whatever injury he had felt from Candy's barbs about him being worthless had been replaced with remorse. He knew her well enough to know that most everything she said, regardless of how harsh her remarks might seem on the surface, were to a large extent innocent, and purely a product of her twisted sense of humor and penchant for sarcasm. Frankly, she was one of the funniest people he had ever met.

Tonight had maybe been different. She genuinely seemed upset with him. Really fed up. The problem was, joking or serious, she was right. Maybe that's what really bothered him. It's no fun being nailed to a cross, even if you know in your heart you deserve it. *Especially* if you know you deserve it. No way to play the sympathy or self-pity card.

He pulled a wine cooler out of the refrigerator. He passed on smoking a joint. He wanted to be somewhat coherent when he spoke to her.

Billy waited another half hour. Candy should have had plenty of time to get home.

But when he called her, her phone rang three times, then went to voice mail. He tried again. Same thing happened. So it went for the rest of the evening. He tried to space the calls out fifteen minutes apart. Sometimes he got so impatient it was much less. She never answered.

Billy came to the conclusion she was avoiding him.

Two could play that game.

Now a joint seemed like a damn good idea.

He toked away, popped a couple Xanax, then lit a candle and turned off the lights.

After Candy left Miss Piggy's, she went straight home.

When she entered her building, the smell was overpowering. Someone right there on the first floor had left a bag of garbage sitting in the hall, probably with the intention of taking it out, but then forgot. Candy picked it up and took it around the side of the apartment complex.

That was when she saw her. Veronique Desqué. The French girl. Her next door neighbor. Just lying there hacked to pieces.

Veronique was the first in a series of brutal homicides which were dubbed by the press as the dumpster murders.

Candy was shaking when she dialed 911. The police arrived and were there for several hours. After asking her hundreds of questions, taking her statement, bringing in a crime scene psychologist to offer Candy some company and professional support through the ordeal, she was finally barricaded in her place alone, four deadbolts in place, three detective business cards on the table in front of her, in case she saw or heard anything suspicious. A glass of orange juice poured but untouched sat on the kitchen counter.

As irrational as it was, she was scared to death. Killers don't return to the scene of the crime the same night. Despite that, she felt horribly vulnerable, powerless, desperate.

She called Billy a little after 3 am. He sounded groggy. She obviously had awoken him. But she immediately recognized his slurred, sluggish speech was not just the product of deep sleep. She had so much experience with this, she probably could have accurately listed all of the intoxicants he had ingested to get to where he was now.

"Billy. I know you're fucked up. But I really need your help. Something's happened here. Can I come over right now?"

There was a long pause. She wondered if he had passed out. He dropped the phone. Picked it up. Finally, she heard his garbled voice.

"Tomorrow ... see you tomorrow."

"Please, Billy. It's important."

"I'm worthless. A waste of good protoplasm. Find someone else."

Click.

Candy made it through the night, sleeping very little, jumping at every little sound.

Billy never knew why she called that night. Nor did he know that Candy had been the one to find the blood-splattered, naked body of the first victim of the latest vicious serial killer to spread terror throughout the city.

Over the course of the next six months, the bodies of 46 attractive young women, raped, murdered and often mutilated, were found in dumpsters all throughout lower Manhattan.

As more victims were found, the hunt for the killer became the centerpiece of television news programs and increasingly sensational headlines for the daily newspapers.

This played right into the hands of Apocalypso, providing him with the ammunition he needed to segue from his first round of ads and posters lambasting the NYPD.

A whole series of new ones started to appear, again in newspapers and on the hundreds of plywood construction site walls throughout the city. They showed photos of young female bodies being hoisted out of dumpsters with an appropriate caption.

Where is the NYPD when you need them?

There was one showing a grumpy meter maid arguing with a man as she wrote him up.

Plenty of time for parking tickets ...
but what about the killer?

On some posters, juxtaposed against the grim photo of the latest victim, was a picture of either the Ashram of the Urban Night or sweet and innocent members of Apocalypso's staff. Sometimes a photo of Apocalypso himself showed him giving food or clothing to the needy, leading prayers, or dancing with children onstage at one of his rallies. Then the challenge.

Which is the real threat to making New York
a good and decent place to live?

After victims 32 and 33 were found, Apocalypso went all the way back to the very first girl slain, the one Candy had discovered outside her apartment. A member of Apocalypso's staff bribed a photo journalist who had been at the crime scene and obtained a picture of the girl's bloody corpse splayed across the garbage in the dumpster. Her eyes were open and her face was frozen in a ghastly expression of complete terror. It was a horrifying sight.

The grisly photo was printed on a poster with her name and *Victim #1* at the top. Underneath was a photo of the police raid on Apocalypso's ashram, one which caught two police officers in the foreground laughing about something, as Apocalypso's staff sat on the curb in handcuffs, looking about as threatening as 4th grade school children on a field trip to the library. The caption was a damning indictment of the quality of police work in the city.

This is what the police were doing when
Veronique Desqué needed their help.

This poster became a rallying and talking point for weeks to come. Apocalypso just kept them coming.

For more than six months, the cries of the public became more and more shrill as the police became more and more frustrated. The bodies were piling up at a rate of nearly two a week.

Young women went about the city in fear of their lives, and both the citizenry and their various media spokespersons became more and more outraged at the ineptness of the NYPD, the misallocation of its resources, and the gross misalignment of its priorities.

The police were probably doing everything they could, despite the common perception.

But by the time the serial killer was apprehended — he turned out to be a well-groomed, smartly dressed 35-year-old derivatives trader living in Brooklyn — Apocalypso had turned the gruesome murders into a huge public relations victory.

He had unequivocally won the second round of what would turn out to be many clashes over the next two years — a battle for the hearts and minds, sympathy and respect of the citizens of New York.

Chapter Three

CARBON-BASED LIFE FORMS
Autumn 2008 – Winter 2009

Carbon and Pain

Billy was sitting on the floor of his flat staring at his shoelaces, trying to decide if he should buy some new ones — ones which made more of a statement. He had been at Washington Square yesterday, watching a team of five early-teen hip hop dancers doing their thing, mega boom box pumping out some gangsta rap, as they tried to pry some money out of curious spectators. More than the dancing, which was extraordinary in its own right, Billy was blown away by their brightly-colored, extremely flashy shoelaces.

There was a knock at the door but before he could get up to answer it, it swung open and Candy came flying into the room.

"You really should think about keeping your door locked. Anybody could barge in here."

"That's for sure."

"I need to reduce my carbon footprint."

"What?"

"I've been thinking. I mean, we really all need to. But I can't be responsible for everyone else's irresponsibility. It starts right here with me."

"What are you talking about?"

"My carbon footprint. Aren't you listening?"

She looked at the pile of pizza boxes and crumpled sandwich wrappings overflowing the waste basket in the kitchen. Billy continued to ponder his shoelaces.

"You should try leaving this dump occasionally. There's a whole world going on out there."

"I went to Washington Square yesterday."

"Well, maybe you noticed then. We're destroying the planet."

"There were some kids dancing hip hop. Drug dealers. A ranter spouting from the Bible. The usual crowd."

"Billy. Wake up. Look around you. This city. The cars and buses. It's a cement jungle. Nothing is natural. Rampant destruction of the native habitat."

"So? When it's destroyed, we'll all be history. There'll be no one around to worry about it."

"Brilliant. You are such a knee-jerk nihilist. Default mode zero."

"Alright. Let's just say for argument's sake that the world is worth saving. I still don't know what you're talking about."

"A person's carbon footprint is how much a person contributes to the degradation of the environment. Especially to global warming. The Earth is becoming a pressure cooker. We're the stew."

"I can't get my head around that. Of course, I understand it. It's a problem. A big problem. But I'd rather put my energy into reducing my pain footprint."

"Sounds very Oprah."

"Thank you."

"It wasn't meant to be a compliment."

"I was being sarcastic."

"Okay. Since you aren't moved by one of the most monumental challenges in the history of mankind, we'll go with yours. Let's say that there is such a thing as a pain footprint. How do you propose reducing it? Wait! Let's back up. What the hell is a pain footprint?"

"The sum total a person dumps on people around him. Inflicts pain on others."

"Oh! I get it. Like the amount others have dumped on you. That's really where you're going with this. You take self-pity to the level of Nietzschean metaphysics."

"Fuck off, Candy. You are way too brutal. I didn't say anything about me. Okay. I will admit, that's where the awareness started. Look at my dad. What a bitter fucking asshole. He thinks the world ganged up on him at some point. So he passes it along. Makes everyone around him miserable. His pain footprint must be the size of Montana. Or New Zealand."

"Montana is bigger than New Zealand."

"Whatever. I want to break the chain. Stop passing it along. It doesn't accomplish a thing."

"You haven't figured anything out, I swear. You sit around this rat-infested bomb shelter brooding all the time. Pondering, analyzing, mulling, ruminating, contemplating, meditating. And then you talk this nonsense."

"I don't have rats."

"What's that then?"

She pointed at a rodent which was crawling from behind the refrigerator and making its way up onto the kitchen table over to a half-eaten bologna sandwich.

"A gerbil?"

"Billy. You're carrying a load of laundry down the stairs. You fall. You tumble to the bottom. It causes pain. What are you going to do? Blame the manufacturer of the laundry basket for not mounting side-view mirrors on the basket? Blame the carpet manufacturer for not putting a high-traction coating on the carpet? Sue the shoelace manufacturer for making shoelaces that come untied?"

"What a coincidence! I was just thinking about buying new shoelaces. "

"Pain happens. It's life. Once it's there, all you can do is make it go away. Or at least hurt less. And if you're hurting, it's your problem. No one else's. You know why? You're the only one that can do anything about it. So deal with it. But that's the difference between all this touchy-feely stuff and what I'm talking about."

"What *are* you talking about?"

"What was I talking about? Hmm?" Candy went over to him, got down on her knees and putting one hand on each of his shoulders, started to shake him.

"Earth to Billy. It wasn't that long ago. Carbon footprint. Carbon footprint, Billy. Something which impacts each and every one of us, and something each and every one of us can do something about."

"I never thought it was important to be liked. I never cared about being popular. Noticed? Yes. But not about being popular. Now I feel so isolated. I know I've hurt people. I've hurt you, Candy. How can I live with that? How can I go on hurting other people? I don't want to hurt anyone any more."

"Jesus! See how you are. You always turn some worthwhile, completely socially relevant discussion into pining about your own pre-adolescent growing pains. I can't listen to this. You make Britney Spears sound philosophical."

Billy leaped to his feet. He reached for a shirt and started getting dressed.

"Okay okay! You're absolutely right. I get it! Are you coming? I'm heading out now to gather some firewood. We can ride a couple mules down to Battery Park later and collect some berries for dinner. You can knit a hemp blanket while I share the oral history of the Algonquin Indians with the hunter-gatherers coming ashore from New Jersey."

"Did I say nihilistic? I hope it's not too late to add cynical to that."

"It's never too late. I know! Let's propagate the species."

"Granted, it won't contribute to global warming."

"Or expand the hole in the Ozone Layer."

"It's a small start but a good one."

"I have a redeeming side."

"Let's not push it."

While what followed did nothing to solve the enormous problems facing mankind at this critical juncture in human history, the total amount of good feeling and love within the small confines of Billy Green's rent-controlled dump on Avenue C was enormously increased over the next three minutes. They fell asleep shortly after, over a bottle of plain label white wine.

The next morning Candy would get a fresh start on reducing her carbon footprint.

The next day for Billy would end with an earthshaking thud.

Sometimes fate wears a mighty big boot.

Just like Candy had said.

Pain happens.

A Call from an Anonymous Sleazebag

It was evening. Around 9:30. Earlier Billy had gone shopping. It was way too exhausting. He had nodded off trying to decide which pair of shoelaces he should try first. The metallic blue pair was in his left hand. The braided yellow and purple in his right. He was sitting half-upright and could be heard faintly snoring.

The phone woke him.

"Billy Green? Is this Mr. Billy Green?"

"Uh … it is. Who wants to know?"

"Marty Dykstra here. Close personal friend of your family."

"Marty who?"

"Dykstra. Marty Dykstra. I'm an attorney."

"Never heard of you. You're saying you're their attorney? They never mentioned having an attorney."

"I'm a good friend. Have been for many years. And yes, I've helped them out with legal stuff. When they bought their house. Their wills. You know, boilerplate stuff."

"If you say so."

"Billy. I have some terrible news."

"What are their names?"

"What a stupid fucking question! You don't know your folks' names? You lived with them for eighteen years, Billy."

"No. I think this is a crank call. I don't think *you* know their names. What are you selling?"

"For fuck's sake listen to me! This is not some goddamn game. Harold Green, formerly called Duke, and Irene, maiden name Jovovich, have been killed in Kenya. A horrible accident when their jeep turned over. They were on a safari. Billy! Both of your parents are dead."

It took a full five seconds for those words to coalesce into something he could comprehend.

Both … of … your … parents … are … dead.

Then instantaneously, Billy felt himself accelerating feet first into a void of blackness, a vast dark force sucking him into a bottomless abyss. His stomach juices rushed up into his throat with a sour bewilderment, emptiness, fear. His throat tightened and it was impossible to breathe. A hot white bubble filled his head. His brain was on fire. It felt like a volcanic furnace was pushing his eyes out of their sockets, splattering them and his molten tears into the desolation of his suffocating trappings. He struggled to breathe and when he finally did, fought a rapid series of hiccups. He was just able to get enough breath to remain conscious, as the room tilted and swirled around him. His lips tried to form words but he had no idea what he was trying to say.

"Are you still there?"

He violently shook his head to wake himself from the nightmare. But he found he was still exactly where he feared he was, still hearing what he never imagined he would ever have to hear.

Both … of … your … parents … are … dead.

"Yes. I'm still here. I … I … don't know what to say."

"I understand. I completely understand. I didn't either. I dreaded making this call. But you had to know. And well … whatever. I'm very sorry, Billy. You don't know me. But I mean it. I'm very sorry."

Billy hurt so bad he was beyond crying. His voice came out in tight rasping bursts.

"What do I do? I … I don't know what to do."

"It will be a few days before the bodies are returned to the States. I'll take care of what I can here in Detroit. I'll call you."

"Should I come back now?"

"No, not yet. There's nothing to do. Wait till I call. Then we can talk about arrangements. And Billy?"

"Yes?"

"I know you're a smart kid. Strong. Solid. Capable. Your parents were very proud of you. Your father bragged about you all the time. This is a horrible tragedy. But hang in there."

His father bragged about him all the time?

"Thanks. I'll try."

Pain Happens

Funerals are strange.

Thank God they only happen once in a lifetime. For the dead person anyway.

What a bizarre rite of passage they had become in these modern times. Black stretch limos. Police escorts. The funeral homes decked out like a Playboy Mansion for the Adams Family. Graveside eulogies by hired-gun ministers or smooth-talking priests who might not even know the deceased.

Funerals are big business.

They get you coming and going. Right when you're paralyzed by grief, they come after your wallet, making you feel that if you don't buy the most expensive casket and memorial package, you must be some ungrateful, insensitive dick who really could care less about the poor unfortunate corpse. Billy recalled a very outlandish movie from the 60s called *The Loved Ones* about the funeral business. The ultimate memorial tribute to the deceased was the astronomically pricey option of shooting the casket into space in 'an orbit of eternal grace'. Right. Maybe he should contact NASA and put his dead folks on the next shuttle mission.

Funerals are really for the living.

But let's face it. Without at least one dead body laying around, you don't have much of a funeral.

Billy had two. Double bang for the buck.

Funerals kind of make sense.

Then again, they don't.

Parting is such sweet sorrow, you know.

But the man or woman of the hour get none of the sweetness or the sorrow. They're dead. They can't see or hear a damn thing. Don't smell the flowers. Don't get to hear all the lovely things being said about them. Don't get to find out just how much they were appreciated. Don't get to hear everyone carry on about how much they're going to be missed.

Don't get to enjoy and revel in perhaps their last and only shot at 15 minutes of fame, since their lives were so ordinary, unnotable and unpressworthy.

Don't get to eat the finger food, drink the beer, sip the tiny cups of cola, cider, cheap watery coffee and tasteless tea.

Don't get to laugh it up among their friends and relatives, most of whom were too busy until now to get together and spend a day with them.

How fair is that?

A funeral would really make sense if the dead person were still alive. Say you're getting on in years. You stop to think, 'Hey, I've probably only got so long on this planet. Time for my funeral.' Sort of like a living will.

Yes! A living funeral.

Cool.

Everybody gets together as if you've died. After all, you will. It's as inevitable as a flat tire, or Botox for over-the-hill movie stars.

You arrive a little early and get gussied up to look like a drag queen.

You lay in the casket maybe in 60-minute stretches. People come up, cry, say wonderful or sorrowful things. You get to answer them. 'Thanks, Martha. You know, I always loved your cooking.' 'Hey Bill. We had some good times, eh?' 'Marianne. I always wanted to fuck you.' 'Jim. Did you ever pay me that 20 bucks for the Colts-Broncos game back in '96?'

This could work!

Maybe in addition to a mandatory retirement age, the government could have a mandatory funeral age — say 50. You hit fifty and you get time off work to attend your own funeral.

It actually makes sense.

A lot of sense and no sense.

Because no matter how you frame it, massage it, or spin it, people just can't deal with death.

Which is why funerals are — in every way, shape and form — other-worldly. Even the living attending a funeral seem to operate in a parallel universe, having to confront the reality and inevitability of death, but having for their own sanity to deny any of this applies to them.

Otherwise how could they attend such a depressing and fatalistic affair? How could they even go on with their lives, if they didn't secretly believe they were immortal?

Indeed.

Billy stood there between the two dead bodies. On the bridge to the other world. Between here and wherever they were now. Whatever it is that lies beyond. Eternal bliss in Heaven? Eternal damnation in Hell? A long cruise on a ship through the Oneness of the Infinite All? An absolute insensate void? Everythingness. Nothingness. Everynothingness.

There was one uncomfortable certainty. Only one.

Despite the advances in the technology of casket-making — high-tech materials and sealing techniques — sometime down the road, they would become fertilizer. A worm feast.

Scientifically speaking.

Science and empirical certainty notwithstanding, it didn't seem possible to Billy that these two dead carcasses were once the living, animated flesh of two people, for better or worse — through best and worst — who gave him life, assured his survival, nurtured and taught him how to function, guided him through the treacherous but amazing journey of the first eighteen years of his life … it just didn't seem possible.

Open casket funerals.

What an insult to the eyes and a mockery of life.

One last look. But not at the end of life ... just the beginning of decay.

His mother looked decent. They found a lovely taffeta dress, very summery and celebratory. Her smile looked real. They didn't have to do anything. Billy always thought of her smiling. Through everything. Even that horrific business with the breast cancer. Now she just looked like she was sleeping.

A long perfect peaceful sleep after a tough life.

Which is why they should have closed the casket. Give her some privacy. Show her some respect. Rather than display her as an inert mannequin, a mâche facsimile of the vibrant, beautiful person she had been throughout her life.

His father looked ridiculous. Where did they find that suit? He couldn't remember ever seeing the old man in a suit. What a sham. They should have laid him out in an old wife-beater with pizza sauce stains down the front. They had his hands folded in prayer. Where was the bottle of beer? His face had so much makeup, he looked like Ronald McDonald. And how ironic. They must have used vice grips and superglue to set those acrimonious lips into that self-mocking forgery of a smile.

Which is why they should have closed the casket. To spare everybody having to look at this pathetic slob. The last chapter in the Book of Duke. A sad commentary on what happens when a man loses all his self-respect, his regard for those around him, his love of life, and his desire to make the smallest contribution to the world.

Then again. Maybe in his case leave the casket open. As a warning.

Be careful. This could be you, motherfucker!

Billy glanced around the room.

Who were all these people? People coming up to him. Commiserating. Offering sympathy. Shaking his hand. Hugging him. Putting their wet cheeks against his dry ones.

If his mom and dad had a social life, they had hidden it well. From him anyway. He didn't recognize anyone. But the funeral parlor was packed. Everyone seemed to know him.

Billy, I'm so sorry.

You're sorry? No ... *I'm* sorry.

Or was he?

After all, they weren't exactly in the bloom of their youth.

His mom looked okay. But the cancer had aged her beyond her years. She was very drawn and her hair certainly never came back the way he remembered it from his childhood.

His dad looked like shit. Surprising they could close the casket over that belly. The man had eaten enough food and drunk enough beer for three lifetimes. He'd gotten his money's worth.

Then again, it's never enough. People cling to life till the last cell shudders and turns into a defunct piece of slime. When you're facing the Grim Reaper, no matter how old you are, you're too young to die.

Billy was sure that's how it felt when you got older.

Of course in this case, they never had time to think about it. They never saw it coming.

Billy tried to picture it. It wasn't easy, on a lot of different levels. He could almost see them in their beige safari shirts and hats, finally freed by winning the lottery to live out some ill-formed fantasies of the good life, riding across the savannah in Kenya, looking through binoculars at the wild beasts of Africa. Then? What? The jeep begins to roll. What were those last few seconds like? Did their lives pass before them like they always say happens? Were they instantly killed? Did they lay there bleeding, groaning, suffering a slow horrible death? Did they get to say good-bye to one another? Did an image of their boy Billy pass before their eyes, however brief, before they were overtaken by unconsciousness and death?

It was masochistically cruel what the living did — what Billy was doing right now — in dissecting the moment of death. But impossible to avoid. Especially standing as he was right now between the two caskets. Tortured by the mental autopsy he couldn't stop performing on that tiny slice of time when death claimed them — when they went from being the living creatures he so casually took for granted, to the lifeless lumps of decaying protoplasm they would now forever be.

Would he miss them? He wasn't sure. Right now he was still in shock. But realistically, going away to college was liberating. A welcome relief after years of longing for an escape. And he couldn't remember one moment while he was at Cornell when he truly missed them. Or anytime since then. Not while he was in Newburgh. Or now living in New York City. How long had it been? Eight years since he had left home. Eight years.

He certainly hadn't missed his dad. While he loved his mom and truly appreciated everything she had ever done, he couldn't say he ever had an overwhelming craving to go back and spend time with her. They had seen one another how many times in eight years? Maybe three or four times? He had avoided returning to Detroit during his breaks at Cornell, always using the excuse he needed to work. When he was with Natalie in Newburgh, and now that he was living in the Big Apple, it never seemed like the right time. Or like he had time. But if he had really wanted to, he could have made the time. Where there's a will there's always a way. That was the reality. A depressing reality as it turned out.

Would he miss them?

Would he miss them?

Everyone else seemed to think he would.

Billy, I'm so sorry.

Yes, you are. I can see that you're sorry. I'm sorry too.

For everything. And for nothing.

The big finale was graveside. Some incoherent priest mumbled incantations from the appropriate section of the Catholic missals — stuff Billy had already heard a few hours before at the mass in their honor — mixed in with random homilies reinforcing his firmly-held belief that Catholicism had no redeeming qualities. Father Arnold Benedict raced through a perfunctory benediction. Billy's parents were then tucked away beneath shovels of dirt tossed by him and a couple others onto the lowered caskets, the few shovels of earth being purely symbolic, since a couple Mexicans stood twenty yards away under a tree waiting to finish the job. Billy glanced over and thought he saw them sharing a joint. After the weepers and other somber spectators left, they would fill in the holes and put the grave markers in place. Billy hoped that they weren't too stoned and were literate enough to put them over the right graves.

Lacking any instructions to the contrary, Billy had come up with the inscriptions for the tomb stones. Marty Dykstra raised holy hell but Billy stood his ground and in the end prevailed. They were probably a little too bona fide.

Irene Jovovich Green *1954 - 2008* *"She was a saint and a* *martyr of marriage."*	**Harold 'Duke' Green** *1951 - 2008* *"Life sucks and* *then you die."*

It was done. It was over.
He would feel lousy for a while.
He would lament their lives cut short.
He would grieve. Yes. He would grieve.
Mourn the senseless loss of their lives.
But he had to be completely honest.
He would not mourn for himself.
And he would not miss them.
It was a painful reality.
Candy was right.
Pain happens.
That's it.

Another Call from the Anonymous Sleazebag

"Billy. Dykstra here. I have to see you before you go back."
"Okay. I'm not leaving till tomorrow night. Taking the redeye."
They set a time to meet next morning. 9:00 am at Dykstra's office in Rochester, up on the north side of Detroit, not far from where Billy grew up.

Billy was a few minutes early. The extremely well-endowed secretary, clearly proud of the chest which had either grown to abnormal size on its own, or been artificially created by implanting two bowling balls, bent over to allow a thorough appraisal by Billy as she put down a tray of coffee, Cremora and sugar, on the reception room table in front of him.

Billy hated large breasts. This pair, crisscrossed with prominent blue veins, really put him in a foul mood. He didn't want to burst this babe's bubble, but all he could think of was a field trip he had taken in elementary school to a dairy farm. Big veiny udders bloated with milk. The legs of the cows caked with cow shit. That place sure smelled bad.

At 9:10 am he was escorted into Marty Dykstra's less than lavish office. It would have easily passed as the office for a paint wholesaler or cigar importer.

"What kind of law do you practice, Mr. Dykstra?"

"Just call me Marty. We're more like family, you know. Never charged them for any of this. Then when they won the lottery, I got a check for $50,000. Your parents were very good people. Let's get down to business. Any questions?"

"Not that I can think of. I'm still pretty shell-shocked, Mr. Dykstra."

"Marty. Just call me Marty. First of all, Billy, let me tell you that as we sit here today, you are a relatively rich man."

"Rich? How rich?"

"After my reasonable few bucks, minimal probate fees to properly record property transfers, and so on and so on, let's see. Try two million, two hundred twenty seven thousand, eight hundred sixty one dollars."

From the look on Billy's face, Dykstra could see it was not computing.

"Here. Let me write it down for you." He handed Billy a Post-It Note.

$$\$2,227,861$$

"Exactly $2,227,861? How can you be so sure?"

"It's been obvious from the start that you think I'm some two-bit hack. But I actually know what I'm doing."

He pulled an envelope out of the briefcase he had beside him on the floor.

"This here is a cashier's check in the said amount, plus a complete accounting for everything. I will be forwarding the title for the house when I get it from the title company, as well as for the car. If I incur any unexpected expenses, I'll bill you. Okay? Like family. That's how I see it. That's how I do business with family. I just need you to assign me limited power of attorney for a couple things. It should all be wrapped up within a month."

Billy took the envelope and gasped as he looked at the check. Then he felt his face flush with embarrassment for how badly he had misjudged this man.

"I'm sorry. I—"

"Don't worry about it. I know I don't cut a very impressive figure. No Perry Mason here."

"Who?"

"Never mind. Listen, Billy. As completely life-altering as the money is, that's not the main reason I wanted to see you in person. I could have just FedExed that stuff to you and been done with it."

"There's something else?"

"Billy. I know how rotten your dad treated you. And I know how much you loved your mother. I knew them both really well even before you were born. I knew the Duke Green you never saw. I also saw how he changed. Just kept sliding. Until … well, you know how he ended up. This accident must really have your head spinning. I'm sure that most of all you feel horrible about your mom going so soon. But … but I don't know quite how to put this. Let's just say her dying now was not … I just … this is really difficult to talk about …"

Dykstra again reached in his briefcase. He pulled out a letter. It was not sealed. Probably the attorney had already read it. The outside just said *Billy*, written in his mom's handwriting.

"Billy. Your mom was dying. The cancer was back. When she found out, she wrote this letter and asked me to give it to you if something … give it to you when it happened. After she died. Here it is."

Like the envelope, the letter was handwritten.

My Boy Billy,

You know by now that the cancer came back. I am glad I didn't tell you. But I feel bad I didn't tell you. Maybe you deserved to know.

I know how tough things have been for you the past couple years, with Natalie leaving, you trying to get set up in New York, and figure things out. I didn't want to burden you with my problems. Knowing or not knowing would make no difference. There was nothing you or anybody could do.

I thought you should have the whole story. So here I am writing it down for you now.

We won the lottery about 2 weeks before I told you. But I had found out three weeks before that about the cancer. I hadn't even told your dad, though he suspected something was wrong. It got into my lymph nodes and spread from there. It's called lymphoma. By the time they saw it, it was too late. It had spread everywhere, my liver, my lungs, all over. They said they could give me radiation and chemo and some other experimental treatments. That would prolong my life but that's all. Maybe give me a few extra months. When I went through the chemo and radiation before, I felt so sick, so weak, so miserable. This time I decided I would rather live a short time and not feel so awful than live a little longer and go through all of that again.

Then we won the lottery and I told your father about

my cancer coming back. Your dad and I took it as a sign. Winning all that money. Maybe now, we could afford some new and normally unavailable cure. We flew to Seattle, then to the Mayo clinic in Minnesota. But the doctors all said the same thing. It couldn't be cured. I had at the most four months to live. Probably less.

Your dear dad went nuts. He couldn't believe this was happening. He reminded me of the man he used to be back when we were young and he would never take no for an answer. Of course, as soon as he won the money, he quit his job. But now he was completely obsessed with making me happy. Next thing I knew, he booked us on a round the world trip. We were going to start in Kenya on a safari, then go to London, Paris, Rome, Greece, China (to see the Great Wall), Bangkok (he said we could watch some sex shows to see what we'd been missing - you know, Billy, sometimes your dad can be so funny). Then Japan and Hawaii and come home.

The kitchen table was covered with travel brochures and airline tickets when I finally called you to tell you about the lottery and our trip. I almost told you then about my illness, but it just didn't feel right, and I decided against it.

So here we are. The cancer finally got me. But I want you to know, Billy, I put up the best fight I could. I really thought I could beat it but I was wrong. I am going to miss you, my beautiful boy.

I know you and your father (yes, he is the man who put food on the table and clothes on your back, so he is your father), I know you two don't get along. I guess I know why and understand how each of you feel. But I want you to know that your father in his own way always loved me. He had a funny way of showing it but he did. Lately, now that we're going on this trip together, he has truly been my Prince Charming again. If anything, the guy won't leave me alone for a second. I guess he just wants

74

to be with me as much as he can before I leave.

Try not to hate him, Billy. He has had a tough life. Beyond what he brought on himself, I hurt him, and you just by being there hurt him. I know that's not fair but that's how it turned out. I have always felt terrible about hurting him the way I did and seeing how he took it out on you. But I'm gone now. His life and your life will go on. Please try to be there for him, no matter how much he pushes you away. Do this for me, Billy.

One last thing. People always have said I smile a lot. Even when I knew about the cancer and that I would die. People would ask, how can you keep smiling, Irene? Let me tell you how, Billy. It was you. Whenever something started to get me down, I thought about my beautiful boy, how proud you have made me, how much you have filled my life with happiness. You have been and are the light of my life. Whether I am now in Heaven or in Hell, I can say that my life on Earth was Heaven because of you. I can still see you at every stage of your life, from the day you came out of me, the day you spoke your first word, the day you took your first steps, all of the times we read together and learned new things. Right now, I can see this beautiful man who came from inside me and made my world. That's why I smile so much.

I can't give you any words of wisdom. You are a smart boy with so much to offer to the world. I know things are a little confusing for you right now. But take it from someone who has seen a lot of ups and downs. Take it from your old mom. This will pass. You have a wonderful future. I just wish I could have lived longer to see what's in store for my Billy. Be a good boy.

Love always,
Mom

It took Billy several minutes to stop crying. He looked up and Dykstra was sitting with his back to him. Looking out the window at nothing but the wall of the adjacent building.

"Billy. Your mom and dad had a difficult … a complex relationship. I do know this. Despite appearances, they really loved one another. Your dad knew what was happening. And he wanted to spend every moment he could with her to the very end. The safari was his idea. And he had big plans after that. All the way around the world. He wanted her last days to be special. To be perfect. He wanted them to be together. So now they're together. In death. Whatever you believe happens after that. They're together."

Billy stood up. Wiped his eyes again. Extended his hand.

Dykstra came around the desk and gave Billy a big fatherly hug.

Billy didn't know what to say.

And neither did Dykstra.

Sometimes it's best.

Merely silence.

He couldn't sleep on the plane. His mind endlessly replayed the events of the past few days.

By the time Billy got back to New York, he knew what he needed to do. He needed to cut all ties with Detroit. A clean break. Maybe he was fooling himself. But somewhere in his mind, this was the only thing that made sense. He looked at it all as a chance for a fresh start. What did he have there anyway, with both his mom and dad gone?

He wrote a letter to Dykstra instructing him to conduct an estate sale for everything in and about the house, and furthermore to sell the house and the car. Dykstra could keep 20% of the proceeds for his part in getting all of it done. By the end of the year, Billy received another cashier's check for $476,214.23 with, of course, a complete detailed accounting. Also included was Marty Dykstra's business card and an invitation to his upcoming wedding. From what Billy surmised, Marty was marrying Miss Balloon Chest, his personal secretary.

Guess some men like 'em big.

Carbon Dating

It was strange not having to worry about money anymore. With the inheritance checks and his share of the sale of his house in Newburgh, he had close to $2.8 million dollars. If he didn't go on any wild spending sprees, and if he budgeted carefully, he might not ever have to work another day for the rest of his life.

In all honesty, he didn't really care. Or more accurately, he didn't think about it.

He didn't think about anything.

He just didn't think.

What he did do for the next several months was attempt to create for anyone who happened to be paying attention, the erroneous impression that he was a functioning human being.

He smiled in the right places, chuckled on cue, danced to the music, skipped to my lou, clicked his heels, jumped for joy, snapped to attention, went from a whisper to a scream, rooted for the home team, pledged his allegiance, shot his wad, held his breath, turned the other cheek, just said no, just did it, rocked his socks off, cleaned house, never looked back, stepped up to the plate, on and on.

From all outward appearances, he was in charge.

But the truth was, no one was.

Billy was robo-man, the perfect human sim prototype, programmed from the highest level down to the most basic synaptic switch, to be Billy Green the tragically innocent human machine, popular with the ladies but an enigma to all who knew him, especially to himself.

Which isn't to say he didn't feel anything. He did feel something. But whatever it was made no sense nor did he bother to try to make sense of it. The feelings he had were like the phantom feelings of a missing limb. Fingers could wiggle though the arm was completely lopped off at the elbow. His watch was so tight it hurt even if there was no watch and no wrist to put it on. He could wrap his hand around his dick though he had no hand and he had no dick.

How could anyone make any sense out of that?

If he had stopped to think about it — if he had been capable of standing back and looking at himself objectively — he would been shocked and humbled by how thoroughly he had been dismembered by the loss of Natalie, then in such quick succession both of his parents. How he had effectively been rendered an immobile, insentient amputee. An inert lump. A freeze frame. Inanimate anti-matter. An illegible carbon copy of someone he once knew.

A few times Candy tried to talk to him.

"How are you doing, Billy? Are you okay?"

He always shrugged and said the same thing.

"Just fucking great. I'm at the top of my game."

She stopped asking.

But how could he have answered?

The ontological equation was wrong. It assumed there was a Billy Green in the room.

Asking this phantom Billy how he was doing, was like asking a mute to sing the praises of muteness. Or an unborn child to describe life. Or a dead man to describe death.

Regardless.

Life goes on with you or without you.

Hair and fingernails grow long after the casket is sealed.

And Billy had built up a lot of momentum over his nearly twenty-six years.

He forged ahead like a big chunk of space debris hurling toward some uncertain rendezvous. Some yet to be identified random collision.

Soon after returning from Detroit, he contacted a very exclusive real estate broker. She was visibly suspicious, since he had not come to her through her network of high society referrals, but agreed maybe on sheer impulse or some preternatural instinct to meet with him.

It was a very tight market. She had only one property immediately available.

They set an appointment and she met Billy and Candy on 92nd Street just four blocks from the Guggenheim Museum.

It was on the 15th floor and had a magnificent view.

"I'll take it."

With a visible show of disdain, the real estate broker once again took in Billy's clothes, unkempt hair and the several days growth of not very chic stubble on his schoolboy face. She then looked impatiently at her watch, obviously anxious to stop wasting time and get on to her next appointment.

"There's a substantial security deposit, you know."

Billy pulled a wad of hundred dollar bills out of his backpack the size of a roll of toilet paper.

"Do you want cash? How much? Ten twenty thousand. I like it. I'll take it. Do I have to sign some papers? What."

It was all Candy could do to keep herself from laughing as she saw the woman's eyes bulge at the money Billy was holding out to her.

"We do a full investigation of your credit history, criminal record, references and so forth and so on. You're not a drug dealer, are you?"

"No. But I'm willing to learn."

Billy moved out of his apartment on Avenue C two weeks later.

The last thing he saw as he walked out with a satchel full of wrinkled clothes in one hand and a thermos bottle in the other, was his longstanding flat mate, the one Billy kindly referred to as a gerbil, but who looked like a mouse to everyone else. The little guy peeked around the foot guard of the stove and Billy thought he detected some melancholy in his gray eyes.

"If you're ever up near 92nd and Park Avenue, stop in for some crackers and caviar."

Of course, he had no furniture. For the next two weeks he slept on the floor. Slowly, with Candy's advice and help, he bought the bare necessities as well as a few unnecessities. Everything was overpriced but elegant. But sparseness was the operating term for the place. Billy preferred uncluttered digs as a permanent shelter for his cluttered mind.

He made it known to Candy that whatever their relationship was — both of them seemed content at this point with keeping it free of categorization or rigid inventory — she was welcome there. He gave her a key, made sure the doormen and other building staff knew she was to have free access. Coming and going as she did, most of them eventually assumed she lived there, even if her name wasn't on the mailbox.

The next few months for Billy were as notable for what he didn't do as for what he did.

What Billy didn't do: He stopped drinking, he stopped smoking marijuana, he stopped popping pills, he never had coffee. He and Candy stopped making love. He no longer ever got an erection or even thought about sex. He found nothing even mildly amusing or funny. He found nothing particularly sad or appalling. He stopped eating anything with sugar in it. He stopped killing spiders. He only drank ionized distilled water. He didn't eat meat or fish. He stopped using toilet paper. He never wore underwear. He used no over-the-counter or prescription drugs. No painkillers. No vitamins or food supplements. He never watched TV. He refused to go to the movies. He stopped jaywalking. He no longer bit his fingernails. He stopped apologizing. He avoided looking at sunsets even if it meant ducking into a building. He never carried an umbrella or wore a raincoat. He refused to shake hands, never permitted any physical contact. He never wore a belt or matching socks. He stopped getting his hair professionally cut, instead just lopped it off himself. He never bought anything wrapped in plastic. He refused to go into a room that had fluorescent lighting. He never carried cash. He didn't sigh. He didn't laugh. He didn't cry.

What Billy did: He started each day by listening to the Nine Inch Nails song "Closer" on headphones at maximum volume. He fell asleep every night listening to "The Man With The Child In His Eyes" by Kate Bush. When he was in his townhouse, he wore no shoes and socks and put wads of sterilized cotton between his toes to keep them from touching. He soaked the tips of his fingers in baking soda for 15 minutes every day. He threw mandarin oranges at the pigeons who tried to nest on the ledge next to his balcony. He walked down Madison Avenue and handed out ping pong balls to anyone who would take them. He kept a daily record of the number of times the word 'necessary' was used on the first three pages of the New York Times. He bought a peach on the first of each month and let it grow mold in a dish on the kitchen counter. He shaved off all of his genital hair. He whitened his teeth with a do-it-yourself smile brightening kit bought online.

There was more.

If someone knew he was rich, Billy would intentionally call the person by the wrong name to see if they would risk offending him by correcting his mistake.

He always wore tight pants and stuffed a handful of Kleenex in the crotch to make it look like he was enormously endowed.

Every Sunday morning, weather permitting, he hula-hooped for the Catholics coming and going from mass at St. Patrick's Cathedral, placing a hat directly in front of him already brimming with $100 bills.

Despite the fact that he was having no sex with anyone, he got himself tested for HIV every two weeks at a nearby family planning and sexual health clinic.

Billy also got his first tattoo. It was centered perfectly on his back.

PEOPLE PASS
I GASP AT THE STENCH
CAN'T THEY BATHE
IN SOME PURIFYING SOLVENT
MADE OF TRUTH AND HOPE?

He also did a few comparatively normal things.

He attended the annual Macy's Thanksgiving Day parade. As soon as he arrived, he spotted a balloon vendor and bought the man's entire stock of helium balloons. Then he went around tying them one-by-one on the wrists of what he judged to be the most deserving children along the parade route, the ones whose parents appeared to be less well off.

For Christmas, he bought a book for Candy, *Rachel's Holiday* by Marian Keyes. She loved it and Billy followed this up by buying everything the Irish novelist had written. Eventually, Candy became such a big fan, she started telling people she was Irish, though she actually was Welsh, German and Ukrainian.

In spite of these occasional sorties into the mainstream, the overwhelming bulk of his day-to-day activities appeared from the outside to be a random hodge-podge of dissociated and idiosyncratic busywork.

From the inside, this was not at all the way it looked to Billy.

At the end of five months, the simple truth was, he had achieved a perfect blissful unity with the absence of everything. He had achieved what Zen Buddhists spent years trying to master. He was one with the nothingness of all. He had no cravings, he had no desires, no anger, no happiness, no sadness, no love, no hate, nothing as substantial as indifference.

Nothing.

Billy had retreated to a single infinitesimal point which had folded so far onto itself, that it had no space even for the nothingness that asserted its absence on the empty void of its own non-existence. He was a disclaimer, a repudiation, a renunciation, an eschewal, a non-denial denial. He was AWOL. Alive Without Living.

It all came to a head on Valentines Day.

A little after 7 pm, Candy walked in the door carrying a heart-shaped key lime cheesecake.

Billy was sitting in the center of a circular white rug, which took up most of the area in front of the marble fireplace. His eyes were red and his face was blotchy from what must have been several hours of continuous crying.

Candy stood over him. He looked up at her over his weary drawn cheeks.

"I miss ... I miss ..."

He left it dangling.

"What do you miss?"

"I miss ... everything."

She put the cheesecake directly in front of him.

"Here. Start with this."

"Does it have sugar in it?"

"Enough to power a space ship."

"Perfect."

He wiped his eyes on the sleeves of his shirt.

Then they split the dessert right down the middle. But since Billy devoured his half before Candy barely made a dent in her piece, he started in on hers as well.

Four hours later, he was slumped over right where he had been all evening, sound asleep.

It was probably a combination of sugar shock and physical exhaustion. That night Billy's sex drive had returned with an awesome vengeance. He lost no time making up for lost time.

After three hours and nine orgasms between them, it was physically impossible for them to make love again.

She made only one comment.

"Is quantity a substitute for quality?"

"I see it as a substitute for celibacy."

Nothing more was said. They lay there for some time. Billy didn't look at her but instead stared at the fireplace grating, eventually nodding off asleep. Candy started to get restless. She had no idea if she was welcome there tonight or not. She preferred to error on the side of caution and left shortly before midnight.

She came back the next day a little before noon. He was in the exact same spot. It was hard to say if he had moved anytime in the past twelve hours or not.

There was no evidence that he had been crying but he looked terrible.

"Are you okay?"

"Never been better. I'm at the top of my game."

Again, she should have know better than to ask.

"I know what this is all about."

"Then you know more than I do."

"Billy. This isn't about your parents."

"Here we go again. Blind man's bluff."

"How come you never talk about your wife, Billy?"

"What's there to talk about?"

"She was everything to you."

"How do you know about my wife?"

"You told me. You were probably too drunk to remember. You cried like a baby, carried on like a condemned man on death row, threw your shoes out the window, had what looked like some sort of epileptic fit. I thought I was going to have to check you into Bellevue."

"I don't believe you."

"Her name was Natalie. You met her in college. Got married a year later. Moved to upstate New York. Lived like Ozzie and Harriet minus David and Ricky. You were blissfully in love with her. Then you came home early one night from work and found out Natalie and her best friend were carpet munchers. It went downhill from there. Now here you are rich and fucked-up. So why don't you ever talk about her?"

"When was this, Candy? I don't remember any of it."

"Am's party after the Kings of Leon concert. They had spiked the Mango Tahitis with LSD. You were already halfway to Cancun on tequila when we got there. You threw up in the taxi and the driver was going to beat the shit out of you, until I sweet talked him and gave him a $50 bill for his trouble."

"Jesus, Candy. Your memory is like a Chase Manhattan security vault."

"And?"

"And what? Are you Carl Jung now?"

"Tell me something about her."

"She never wore pearls."

"And?"

"And I don't want to talk about it. It's over."

"But it's not."

"You're talking nonsense now. Let's get a mocha caramel latte."

"All this time you were dropped off on another planet. And now not a single word about it. You were married, what? Over two years? That doesn't go away. It's over now? Just like that? I don't believe you."

"How about a backrub?"

"I don't want a backrub."

"I didn't mean you. I meant me. If I have to listen to this, the least you can do is give me a freaking backrub."

"You are hopeless. And if you think—"

"I am offering to let you give me a backrub. I'd say I've come a long way. Maybe you should think twice before turning me down. It could set me back. Send me back to the land of the charcoal trees."

"You're at the bottom, Billy. It's only up from here. Take off your shirt and lay down."

The backrub lasted only slightly longer than the sex.

When Candy saw him again that weekend, there were clear signs of the old Billy — the one she knew before he went to Detroit for his parents' funeral — reemerging from the poltergeist of the past several months.

She had called him first, then breezed in on her way to meeting a tattoo client further uptown.

An empty six-pack of vodka fruit coolers sat on the sink. His eyes were a little glazed from drinking but appeared to have some twinkle to them. Billy's face was less of an immobile petroglyph than she had seen in a long time.

At the same time, there lingered a hint of despair in the deep space at the back of his eyes.

She sat down next to him. But not touching. Business before pleasure.

She knew better but asked anyway.

"And?"

"The shit almost destroyed the fan."

"Nice image."

"You never change, do you?"

"Can you suggest any improvements?"

He studied her for the longest time.

"No."

"Let's pretend we're in love."

"You have to pretend?"

"No."

"That's more than I can handle right now."

"I believe you're finally on to something."

"I think I want to be alone."

She handed him a small sack of mandarin oranges from her shoulder bag.

"For the pigeons."

"I think I like them now."

"Then they're for you."

She peeled one and put a slice in his mouth.

"You're way too good to me."

"That's for sure."

She kissed him lightly on the lips, then bounded out the door like a ballerina.

He laughed out loud as she closed the door behind her.

It felt good to laugh. It had been a while.

Candy was such a funny girl.

She always made him feel like smiling, even when he couldn't.

He looked at the bag of mandarin oranges and suddenly became very serious.

How did he really feel?

Did he really like pigeons or was he just having a SPCA moment?

Chapter Four

THE FABULOUS FRINGE OF A
MINISCULE MICROCOSM
Late Winter Spring 2009

Little Tantrums

Candy's patience was beginning to wear thin. At the same time she was really starting to worry. It was a agitating combination of disappointment and concern.

Maybe she had been kidding herself. But the breakthrough on Valentines Day seemed at the time to be some watershed moment. Billy had finally showed signs of coming out of his understandable and debilitating depression, holding out the promise of better days ahead.

But four weeks later he again seemed to be careening off in some incomprehensible direction for more rounds of the crazies.

Though she had a key to his townhouse, Candy actually found herself spending less time there — certainly fewer overnights — and more time at her own apartment trying to figure out what she could or should be doing to help him get back on track.

Billy didn't seem to notice or particularly care one way or another. While on some level he had popped to the surface, and had in terms of day-to-day living rejoined the rest of the human race, on another level he was becoming more and more disconnected.

He was losing weight. The whole business of buying and keeping food in the townhouse for basic nourishment had somehow become too daunting or inconvenient for him. Candy had taken to stopping by every few days, if for no better reason than to drop off some meal-in-a-bag takeout.

Today's care package included Kung Pao chicken, stir-fried rice, a half-gallon of freshly squeezed organic orange juice, plus four cream-filled pastries from a Jewish deli right down the street from Billy's building.

She reached for the door but it swung open before she was able to insert her key.

A girl came out as Candy started to step in.

The girl's lipstick was smeared, she had only buttoned one button on her blouse. She was carrying her shoes, panties, bra, and plastic handbag, in one clump pressed against her chest. One of her patterned stockings was halfway down her leg and bunched at the ankle.

If she wasn't high, then she had lost her glasses and was legally blind, since she appeared to be groping her way out the door and down the hall. She turned to say something to Candy, changed her mind and just stumbled on toward the elevator.

Candy looked at Billy incredulously.

"Who was that scaggy creature? Your tax attorney or your exorcist?"

Billy looked up and gave her a sheepish look.

"I ... uh ... that was no one really."

"Billy, forget about it. I don't care who you fuck. I just assumed you were sticking to your own species."

"I met her at the confectionaries cooler at Mini Mart. She really likes Häagen Dazs bars. Almond and chocolate."

"That's so beautiful. And I say thank God in high Heaven you're opening up to other people. Did you get her name before you splooged her with your semen?"

"Aha! I knew you were jealous."

"Jealousy and astonishment are qualitatively very different."

"Did you want to talk about something?"

"I'm pregnant with Kurt Cobain's baby. I channeled him in a ladies room at the Plaza Hotel. Nothing important. I can see you're busy. Gotta go."

"Don't leave on account of me."

"Okay. Then you leave."

"This is my place."

"That is a technicality that some would argue purely an illusion."

"All the same—"

"I wanted to bring you the pie I baked for you. But I ate it on the bus. Actually, several people helped me eat it. I ended up missing my stop. I finally noticed when I saw moose staring back at me through the side windows. I have to say I'm surprised just how easy it is to cross over into Canada these days."

"Candy—"

"Have you noticed that they are replacing all of the fire hydrants on the northbound side of Broadway? I don't get it. What can go wrong with a fire hydrant? Do they wear out? Seems like a big waste of money to me."

"Candy! What are you really trying to say?"

"You've got issues."

"You're pissed at me."

"Give me more credit than that."

"Prove that your not upset with me."

"Prove that you are not a clone of yourself."

"I know things about myself that my clone wouldn't."

"For example?"

"I wear two pairs of socks when I go bowling."

"A lot of people do that."

"I shave my testicles."

"Everybody knows that."

"I really doubt it."

"Oh yeah? Tomorrow, stop someone randomly, anyone on the street. Go ahead, ask them. 'Do I shave my testicles?' See what they say."

"Candy. You can't fool me. Something's on your mind. And it's not fire hydrants or pies or Kurt Cobain's illegitimate baby. What gives? Did I forget your birthday?"

"Yes. That was months ago."

"What's bothering you?"

"You! You bother me. You're pathetic and hopeless."

"And?"

"And if talking shit was money, you'd be Bill Gates."

"Can you be more specific? What exactly is the problem?"

"What's the problem? I was on my way over here to initiate a one-woman intervention, a noble and heroic attempt to rescue you, until I ran into Frankenhooker there stumbling out your apartment like you had taped electrodes to her temples and date raped her."

"She had a note from her mother *and* even signed one of my consent forms. Wanna see it?"

"You know, Billy, for most people — even the seriously demented — flight from reality is an intermittent excursion. They touch back down occasionally and refuel. But for you—"

"For me it's an end in itself. It's all I know. It's what I do."

"No. It's an excuse for what you don't do."

"Alright. I can go along with that."

"Except you have no excuse."

"That's not what I heard."

"You heard wrong."

"I'll be damned."

"Absolutely."

She pushed the bags of takeout toward him and got up to leave.

Billy took a smirking moment to take stock. He really should get this straightened out. Candy might be the hot sex version of a Rubric's cube but he didn't want to hurt her.

"I think you should stay."

She didn't give him a choice. She was gone.

Too little too late.

Nice work, Billy.

Recently, he had discovered the joys of hash. He crumbled a generous portion of the black gum onto the top of a pipe already brimming with weed, then lit up.

Soon he achieved the perfect state for reflecting on his place in the world.

It really wasn't that difficult to figure out.

Things sucked but sometimes they sucked a little less than others. The problem was there was no predicting any of it.

Billy stepped over to the archway which separated the dining area from the kitchen.

God bless the free-market economy! And the enterprising home delivery services of the lovely Miss Frankenhooker.

Billy had twenty 80 mg Oxycontin tablets lined up in a perfect row on his kitchen counter. They looked like the little green Pez candies he remembered from his childhood.

He covered them with a designer dish towel from Williams Sonoma.

The hash-marijuana combination reignited his dormant appetite. He dug into the takeout like he was coming off of a hunger strike. In a way, he was. He couldn't remember how long had it been since he had eaten.

Three more days disappeared.

Time flies when you're contemplating suicide.

There was a knock at the door.

Just as he got up, the door opened and Candy entered with Billy's favorite pizza — broccoli, onions, sausage, and shitake mushrooms — *and* a 40 oz bottle of Miller Lite. She looked more amazing today than ever. Billy looked her up and down. Candy could raise the dead. Sexy, statuesque, thin, graceful, chesty. Her hair was braided into a rainbow and she had two silver rings in her pierced left eyebrow. Her ears had enough silver and gold to put the least sensitive airport metal detector in a heaving St. Vitus dance.

"I thought you might be hungry … what are you doing?"

"Nothing."

She put the pizza and beer down and knelt next to him. She undid his pants and slid them to the floor. Then she quickly disrobed, pushed him down onto his back and got on top of him.

Their moans intertwined in an enchanting acapella song of love and consummation.

She came. He came.

It timed at 3:28 — the perfect length for pop radio.

Efficiently but with the grace of one of Beyoncé's backup dancers, she got dressed.

Billy just lay there staring at the ceiling.

"What's wrong?"

"Nothing."

"So, are you hungry?"

He looked disoriented and reached for the beer. Took a huge gulp. She opened the pizza box, pulled out a slice and lay it on his bare chest. She hadn't eaten all day and was ravenous. She wolfed down a slice, then another, apparently unconcerned with the tiny drop of sauce that ended up on her chin.

"Seriously, what were you doing? Did I interrupt something?"

"No. Just mulling things over. I guess I need to reconsider."

Still prone on the floor, he pulled up his jeans.

"Reconsider?"

"I think I need a plan."

"I thought you said 'plan' was a four-letter word."

She stood up and as she took another huge bite out of the piece of pizza in her hand, walked over to the kitchen to get something to drink more nourishing than Miller Lite. On the way, she grabbed the dish towel from the counter.

The pills went flying off the counter onto the floor.

"Oops! Sorry."

Billy sprang to his feet.

"Don't! I'll take care of it."

But Candy was already on her knees picking them up.

It took only a moment to register.

"Holy shit!! You were going to kill yourself!"

"It's not what it—"

"What were you thinking?"

"I wouldn't have done anything. Apparently I'm too pathetic to even try."

She gathered all the pills and made straight for the bathroom. Billy heard the toilet flush. Candy came back out and stood over him. She looked both hurt and pissed.

She was crying. Billy had never seen her cry.

"You are a crazy fucker, you know that?"

"Get a clue. Who isn't? Look in the mirror, glam goddess. You look like the poster child for a third-world tattoo parlor. Are you Hindu, Sikh, a comic book, or advertising a Buddhist brothel in Kathmandu?"

That was twisted. But in a twisted sense he was spot on. Her body was a potpourri of mystical gibberish. Metaphysical babble and bumper sticker philosophy. I Ching aphorisms. Yin and Yang. Ren and Stimpy. Legalize cannabis. Steppin' out. Kanji. Give peace a chance. The Zulu word for love. Haiku. The center-ring showstopper was the serpent which started at the top of her right buttocks, wound its way up around the left side of her ribcage, and culminated with the jaws-agape pincer of its venom-dripping fangs holding the pink lozenge nipple of her right breast.

Her montage of dermal art was indeed a thing of tortured beauty.

Agony art? Skin games? Apocalyptic ink fest?

"Fuck this." Billy stood up and jerked his thumb toward the door.

"Let's go."

He bent down to pick up a medium-size cardboard box sitting behind a huge ceramic Beijing vase next to the door. He was already in the hallway heading for the elevator before she could swallow the last bite she took of the pizza. She threw the crust into an empty fish tank and ran after him.

"Where are we going?"

"To the future."

"Crazy man."

Billy's doorman hailed a taxi.

It was a pretty typical late-afternoon winter day. The taxi had dropped them at the center of the Williamsburg Bridge. The air smelled like the iron hull of an abandoned cargo ship. Candy stood behind Billy as he stared blankly at a slow-moving refuse barge. It silently glided under them, making its way downriver. Except for the gunmetal blue of the water, everything was tedious shades of musty gray. The clouds hung low like old mattress stuffing. The not-too-distant riverbanks were all but invisible in the industrial haze.

"What's in the box?"

He came out of his brief trance, no longer tethered to whatever daydream or quandary had gripped him. Without any ceremony or ado, he unfolded the cardboard flaps. He stood on the handrail in order to reach over the protective fencing which ran the length of the bridge's pedestrian walkway, then dumped what appeared to be several hundred new, unopened condoms into the river.

Candy was an expert at the cynical laugh. Her eyes rolled under the glittering black frosting of her mascara and silver-flaked eye shadow.

"I see. A box of wishful thinking. But throwing them away is obviously purely symbolic, since you never use them."

"I'm removing temptation."

"Temptation to use them? Right. It's too late anyway. You are probably already a walking catalog of every strain of HIV around."

"You better go."

"Pay me for the pizza."

"You better go."

"Deadbeat."

Who was she to argue? She couldn't fight this.

She couldn't even comprehend it.

Candy was off in a heartbeat. Braided hair flopping, arms waving in exhortation, the iambic kick drum of her tirade soon out of earshot as she clambered, staggered and half-danced down the metal pedestrian walkway of the bridge. Fifty or so yards away from Billy, who looked forlornly at the sedating whitecaps of the river below, she suddenly whipped around and stuck out her thumb. A metallic blue Chrysler PT Cruiser screeched to a halt and was immediately rear-ended by a laundry van.

She resumed walking. "This isn't my day."

Queen for a Day

It was round two. A reprise of yesterday's bout.

Candy was in rare form today.

And so was he, though his rare form was less than sterling these days.

"I have only one thing to say about this, Billy Boy."

"You never have only one thing to say. You don't even stop to breathe."

"I thought about it last night and figured the whole thing out. The amazing thing is that the entire disaster that you've made of your life, the catastrophic way you now live, it all comes down to one thing. Your entire hangman's collection of lethal rope tricks can be summed up in one single word. Women."

"You've lost it, Candy. You're just pissed because you can't have me. You can still fuck me, by the way."

"I *can* have you. But why would I want to. Listen, Billy, you think you have this love thing going on, this big group hug for the three billion women on Earth. You love them. They love you. You chase them, charm them, woo them, lick them, fuck them. I know exactly what's going on here. You run them through here like the migration of sea otters in spring. You think you really got it going on. But the truth is, you're lost and still losing it. You're on a very slippery slope, one that's lubricated with a lot of vaginal mucous."

"It's and interesting point of view. Hey! What's on the tube tonight?"

"That's pathetic, Billy. You don't even watch TV. What I'm saying is simple. Everything, every stupid thing you've ever done, every bad decision, every misstep and misfortune, comes down to your issues with women."

"Does that include you?"

"To the extent that no matter what I do or say, no matter how good I am to you, no matter how much I do to help you save you from yourself, as you keep right on trucking full-speed-ahead down the road of self-annihilation, yes it does include me. You've made me a part of the problem. I can't claim, despite my best efforts, a lot of love, beer, pizza, and speed sex, to be part of the solution."

"Hold on! You think I don't notice? I appreciate it. All of it. I really do."

"I don't think so. You're way too busy wallowing in self-inflicted misery to notice."

"I almost felt like smiling yesterday. It was just before noon."

Candy bolted to her feet and paced in every direction at once. She shook her hands out in front of her, then started pulling on her hair.

"Fuck! I can't breathe. I've got to get outta here."

"Leave? Leave me hanging? Just abandon me? See? Talk is cheap, Candy. You don't give a flying fuck about me."

"I'm supposed to believe you heard anything I've been saying?"

"Just give me something I can use. Please! *Pretty please!*"

Candy stepped over, bent down and started knocking on his head like it was a door.

"Billy! Are you in there? Are you listening?"

"Ouch! I'm right here. Stop cocking me with that bony hand."

She stopped and brought her face in even closer to his. Their noses were almost touching.

"You need a paradigm shift. Got that? A paradigm shift. Good-bye."

She had a thing for quick exits. Candy never strolled casually. Never shuffled thoughtfully. Never sauntered pensively. She always bolted out the door like someone had yelled 'There's a bomb under the coffee table!'

She had only been there for eleven minutes. Only a few weeks ago, it used to take Billy at least an hour to get her that worked up. Their relationship must be maturing.

Of course, that's how things had been going lately. Anonymous bodies came and went. Nobody stuck around. Billy couldn't blame them. He was in constant turmoil and swept into their lives like a Category 5 hurricane. Sometimes he felt bad. Especially for Candy. She was always such a trouper. And in one respect, she was absolutely right. She had not gotten him any closer to dismantling the black existential cloud of impending doom that hung over him 24/7. She *had* become part of the problem, another source of confusion and angst. Billy made sure of that. He was like Typhoid Mary. Or HIV Dave.

He didn't get this last bit, though.

Candy with her brilliant over-simplification. Every single problem, impasse, dilemma, conundrum, roadblock, setback, disaster, catastrophe, all came down to women? *Women?* How did she come up with *that* rubbish? How weird. He loved women! What was the problem? It was the natural order of things. It was his job here on Earth. It was Billy's raison d'être. It was his karma. His destiny. His dick was performing admirably. He didn't see any problem.

Candy claimed he needed a "paradigm shift". What does *that* mean?

Yes, he loved her. Hmm … loved? But how seriously should he take her?

The girl looked like a deranged groupie in an All-American Rejects music video and talked like she had a PhD in Linguistics. How does she find time, after getting ready every day for her Generation Z strut down the hang-tough runway of life, to read so goddamn much?

He thought about it all afternoon and all evening — the sweeping arc of time, and the miles of pain and heartache littering the deserted highways of his mind, strewn with the crash-and-burn debris of his relationships.

What could he say? Shit happens. Sometimes a lot of shit happens. Too much to begin to sort through. It was incomprehensible. Impossibly daunting.

One thing was obvious. He didn't have any problem with men. There were no men. He had no real male friends. No pals, no brothers, no homeys, no hangbuds. Nope. No problem with men.

And he definitely didn't have a career problems. No glass ceiling. No occupational challenges. No job security issues. He didn't even have a job.

He didn't have a political beef. He had no politics. Billy wasn't even sure he could name the President of the United States. Was it still Bush? He recalled that there was a President Bush back in the late 80s. Maybe the 90s. He was just a boy. Couldn't vote back then. Still didn't vote even now. Didn't pay much attention. He knew things were fucked up. It was an age-old story. It would probably never change.

Money? He had plenty of that, thanks to the Michigan lottery and the insurance company his parents had paid so dutifully over the years. The only issue with money was how to spend it fast enough. But he'd figure it out. That was something he could apply his best talents to.

He couldn't complain about what he did day to day. He never did anything. Well practically. Did he get bored? Never. Not bored. Not exactly.

What did that leave?

What did it leave? It left him with a splitting headache. That's what!

His head felt like the linchpin between two boxcars on a railway shipment of industrial waste. He definitely needed to stop thinking about this bullshit. Stop analyzing it. Before it drove him completely nuts! Or drove him completely sane. He wasn't sure which would be worse.

What time was it? Uh oh. 7:30 and he was supposed to meet Amethyst at 8:00 in Tribeca. He'd just make it. He threw on a yellow polyester parka and was out the door.

She was waiting at the top of the subway exit at Canal Street and Broadway. He came up behind her, since he hadn't taken the train but had opted for a taxi.

"I'm your Great Expectations video date."

"You're late. Why are you dressed like Forrest Gump?"

"Well … I … uh—"

"Let's go. We want to get good seats. It'll be packed."

She led they way. Billy could barely keep up without breaking into a jog. He watched her delicious swaying ass in amazement. How can she power walk in those 7" platform boots?

"Where are you taking me, Am?"

"You'll see. This could be good for you. Have you ever done E?"

"No, but my doctor suggested I try it. He said its good for the complexion. Fish oil is best."

"Ecstasy, you moron. Where have you been all your life? Father Flannigan's Boys Home? Anyway, take these. Better than fish oil."

"I don't know, Amethyst. I'm a little fragile these days. Will I lose control?"

"You could wish. But no. It's caramel syrup for your sundae. You'll feel more love than you ever thought possible. Trust me. It'll be great. See. I'm taking four."

They popped the little orange tablets.

She led them down a dark, rather narrow street. They turned left into a service driveway, then crossed over into an alley cul de sac. Centered under a sheet metal canopy was a door with a tiny barred window in the center. There was no sign, just the door.

A half dozen or so girls, late teens maybe early twenties, stood there gesticulating about some crisis of the moment. They were dressed in techno-glitz glamour and studs-and-leather club lingerie. Amethyst in her latex miniskirt and fur-lined vest looked homespun next to these fetishists. Aah! Forrest Gump? He got it now. He was a little underdressed.

After the extremely upset young girls had been sent away unadmitted, Amethyst pushed her face up to the window and spoke to someone who hovered behind the door in black light. His teeth and eyes were glowing an eerie blue-lavender. His face was a hazy green.

"It's me, Castro. You know I fucking *love you!*"

The door swung open and in they went.

It was a club unlike any he had ever scene. Everything was glowing either in the splash of UV bulbs inset over the entire ceiling, or from brilliantly colored neon sculptures, lamps and various dayglow fluorescent fixtures. Very futuristic but at the same time very sensuous. Kind of reminiscent of the milk bar scene in Clockwork Orange. But much more intense and not at all monochromatic. This was a festival of hot greens, intense blues, strident purples, sharp yellows, and glacial whites. Much of the furniture and the floor itself was covered in lush powdery fur, offering a seductive invitation to the eyes and a soft eroticism to the touch.

They took off their shoes at the arched entrance of a foyer, as requested by a beautiful hostess who greeted them and gave them a claim ticket to recover them later. She appeared to be Latino, was dressed in a formal green taffeta evening gown, and with her bleached blond hair, made Billy think of Christina Aguilera.

The main room was high-ceilinged and cavernous. There were at least a hundred small, elegant tables, with two to four places to sit at each one. The tables were clustered rather close together and the entire array sprawled over the club's spacious floor in front of a modest stage. The tables were low — like you might see in a Turkish coffee house — and covered in white linen, each set in the center with floating scented candles and a vase filled with orchids. The seating consisted of flat furry pillows in bright neon colors. Each had the club's logo in an embroidered swath of shiny satin.

Above the stage was a sign, the background of which twinkled to the firings of thousands of tiny purple and green lights. Written the full length of the sign in thick yellow neon tubing was the name of the club...

STRANGE LOVE

Several of the tables already had customers, but Billy and Amethyst sat down at one close to and slightly left of center of the stage.

"This is perfect. We won't miss a thing. I'm thirsty. Carrying cash, Billy Boy?"

"What's your poison?"

Billy ordered Amethyst's mint julep but when he asked for a Miller Lite for himself, the bartender looked at him like he had just requested Drano and dry ice. Billy pocketed the tip.

Shortly after he returned to their table with their drinks, a very tall, lithe brunette came over and sat right next to him. As she leaned lightly against Billy, she looked at Amethyst and gave her a conspiratorial smile.

"Who's your friend here?"

"Leave him alone. He's fucked up."

She ignored the product warning label and smiled sweetly at Billy.

"I'm Sabrina. I'm fucked up too. Pleased to meet you."

She shook his hand with an almost-too-limp tranquility. It seemed a bit odd. But she was gorgeous.

"I'm Billy. But most people call me 'hey you'. You from around here?"

"I have a flat in Chelsea with two of the other girls. It's been ... almost two years now."

"Other girls?"

"Yeah. Girls. Here tonight. You'll see. I gotta go now. Still getting ready and everything. You'll be here for the whole show? Maybe we can pick up the thread later."

"You never know."

Sabrina sashayed off and went through a door next to the stage. Other girls were coming and going at a frantic pace. Even though they seemed in a hurry, they still took the time to stop one another and carry on about something, give Hollywood hugs and cheek-to-cheek air kisses. Their giddy excitement filled the room.

"She said there was a show? What kind of show? And when does it start?"

"Around ten ... but I wanted to get here early. Great seats, eh?"

"I guess that depends on what we're watching."

"Have a little faith. Have I ever steered you wrong?"

"Do I have to answer that?"

They sat for a while in silence. The club started to fill up fast. Soon he was sandwiched in from all sides by the laughing, the smoking, the drinking, the loud, the amped, the excited. Collective anticipation in the room quickly built to a fever pitch, as the bartenders became a strobe light blur trying to keep up with all of the drink orders, and the club's exhaust fans labored to keep the air breathable.

"Candy says I have a problem with women. Actually she says my problem *is* women."

"Tell me something I don't know. How are you feeling?"

"Actually, pretty good. Real good. I feel very close to you tonight."

Amethyst took a drag on her cigarette and exhaled with a knowing, self-satisfied grin.

"Do you love me, Billy?"

"Hmm ... I hadn't ever really ... but I feel really good about you right now. Wow! Yes, I do. I love you, Amethyst Reigns!"

"I haven't seen you smile like that in a long time."

"It's true love. Don't tell Candy."

She really started laughing. A pleasant, bubbling kind of chuckle. She theatrically emptied her glass and thumped it back down on the table.

"And we're just getting started."

It was contagious. Billy could feel the foamy urge to giggle, effervescing just below the surface of his skin, with even more insistent entreaties for outright rafters-shaking laughter rising like gas bubbles from the buoyant hollows of his stomach.

He suddenly tuned into the music that was playing. It was Donna Summers' "Bad Girls". Whoa! He wasn't even born when it was a hit. What a great song!

He started bouncing his head, then his whole body, to the compelling beat. The next table started doing the same, singing along, clapping their hands to the beat high over their heads.

By the time the song started to fade, Billy was on his feet and so were a number of fellow revelers, united in a manic group ritual disco dance. It was Saturday Night Fever all over again. And tonight was Saturday night! Fate or coincidence? Go figure. Ha ha ha ha ha.

Billy sat down, amused by his own breathtaking gift for humor. Though he didn't feel at all thirsty, he sipped on his beer — it tasted good even warm — and gazed around.

As he casually surveyed the crowd, suddenly out of nowhere it hit him like a bolt of lightning. They were almost all women. Can this be right?

"Am! Do you see what I'm seeing here? It's all women. This place is completely full of chicks. I may be the *only male* in this whole stinkin' night club."

"Billy, I hate to break it to you. But if I'm not mistaken, I may be the *only female* here."

"What are you talking about? Are you messing with me again?"

"You'll figure it out."

"How Deep Is Your Love?" by the Bee Gees started to play but was abruptly cut off as the MC for the show appeared on stage and tested the microphone.

"Testes one two. Testes one two three. Okay. Looks like we're ready to go, ladies. Let me welcome you one and all to the world-renowned, infamous and much-maligned Strange Love night club, for its fifth annual Queen For A Day night. I am Priscilla Queen of the Dessert, and as you can see I have eaten my share of the sweet, sticky stuff. Just can't seem to keep my pie hole closed when a good mouthful comes my way. I think most of you ladies can relate to what I'm sayin'. Anyway, in addition to the prize money, the $500 in small denominations stuffed in my panty hose, which you will have to remove with your teeth, while you're handcuffed to my exercise bike, yes, tonight's first place winner will receive a special gift certificate for a free consultation with our dear patron saint, the fabulous Dr. Malcolm Bender. Take that and stuff it in your training bras, ladies! Without further ado, let me bring out our first performer. Her friends at the 146th Street Lube 'n Tune call her Chuck, but we here know who she really is. Let's bring to the stage our own sly and slippery seductress, the oil slick princess, our own wet-back, wet-front, wet-all-over, Miss Chili Pepper!"

As she performed, all Billy could think was this babe was certainly named correctly. A hot and spicy Latino with all the right ingredients in the right amounts. She club-danced energetically, bouncing and stomping the entire area of the confining stage, then stepped down into the crowd itself. All the while, she was lip syncing to a big 80s hit, the Bananarama song, "Cruel Summer". Billy was mesmerized. Miss Chili Pepper even came over to their table at one point. Sitting where he was, put him at eye-level with her butt and crotch, as she seductively gyrated to the music. Before moving on, she reached down into Billy's shirt and gave his chest a quick caress, sending his libido soaring wildly. He urgently gulped the rest of his beer.

That was the pattern of the rest of the show. Priscilla Queen of the Dessert — the only female in the entire place, particularly on stage, who was enormously overweight — would come out, make jokes about her passion for pastries, then introduce some incredibly luscious babe, who would perform a song typically from the 70s or 80s. The only departure from this choice of music, was one girl who danced and lip synced to Christina Aguilera's "Genie In A Bottle", which was a hit in 1999. Billy immediately recognized her. It was the hostess who had initially greeted them.

Eight performers came and went, each bent on topping the others and claiming the prize and title for tonight's contest. Each had a specific theme to their segment. One was a burlesque dancer who performed to a disco-desecrated rendition of "I Want To Be Evil". Another came out as a Flamenco dancer, whose costume slowly shed piece by piece, revealing an awesome set of legs which seemed go on forever, and a mouth-watering pair of breasts. Her music was a Gipsy Kings song, pumped up to ear-splitting decibels. There was a petite and lovely Asian girl dressed as a geisha, who minced around in tiny restrained steps and did her own twist on the traditional dancing of Okinawa, accompanied by the annoying screeching of an 80s Japanese pop anthem.

To close out the official program of entertainment, there was special final performance which did not figure in the contest itself.

But even before that happened, there was another surprise. Priscilla had just come back stage center.

> *"I don't know about you, but after so many hot performances,*
> *I'm so wet I need a life raft. Or at least something to keep my*
> *you-know-what from drowning."*

Suddenly, out of the wings stepped a tall, modelesque, fair-skinned, African American lady, carrying a towelette dispenser. Priscilla feigned shock.

> *"Oh my! Could it really be?"*

The crown went wild! Everyone stood up, clapping, cheering. They started yelling in unison …

> *RuPaul … Rupaul … Rupaul …*

Billy, of course, swept up in the excitement, stood up as well. Though he wasn't sure why.

He leaned toward Amethyst?

"Who's RuPaul?"

She just rolled her eyes, laughed, and kept on cheering with the crowd.

> *RuPaul … Rupaul … Rupaul …*

Onstage, the exotic RuPaul slithered up next to Priscilla, theatrically pulled a couple fresh towelettes from the dispenser, and proceeded to wipe first Priscilla's brow, then her nipples. Finally she gave brief, gentle attention to her crotch. Priscilla dramatically swooned, fluttered her eyelashes, and smiled.

> *"Oh, yes! I feel much better now. Can't have my dessert turn*
> *into a swamp. And … oh my! Aren't you looking good! I think*
> *I'm starting to get wet again."*

RuPaul tossed the dispenser aside and reached between her beautiful and ample breasts and pulled out a piece of paper. She drew her face seductively close to Priscilla's ear, licked her lips, and tucked the paper between Priscilla's pushed-up-and-in boobs.

> *"Here's my shemail address, honey. Don't be a stranger."*

RuPaul planted a wet sloppy kiss on Priscilla's ear, then sashayed off stage, winking and playing the crowd. Everyone now was really going crazy.

RuPaul, *Supermodel of the World* gone, things eventually calmed to what would pass for normal.

Billy sat down.

He felt good. Really good!

But something nagged him.

Rupaul? Why did that sound familiar?

Priscilla now returned to the official playbill schedule.

> *"Before announcing this year's winner of the Queen For A Day contest, we have a special treat for you. This should make those nipples hard, all you princes and princesses."*

The noise level of the audience again started to build, as hoots and hollers almost drowned out the plump mistress of ceremonies. From the audience's quick initial reaction, apparently this was a hotly anticipated item.

> *"Most of you know her, some better than others. Here is our own three-time Queen For A Day winner, a delicious little treat — and I'd lick her plate clean any day of the week — to shake her banana buttered tail feather for you."*

A curtain behind Priscilla, which had been hiding a rear stage exclusively reserved for this special performance, opened to reveal a stark but spectacular set. This new stage area was surprising large, more than double the size of the main stage in front. At the back was a graffitied brick wall with a ladder. Off to one side was an acetylene tank and welding gear. Two intense blue spotlights were shining down from the high ceiling and converged in the middle, illuminating a single chair. The sharply highlighted silhouette of a girl could be seen straddling the chair backwards. She was enticingly clothed in a loose cut-off t-shirt, a tight halter top, dance trunks and sneakers. Her arms rested loosely on the back of the chair and her head was down between them, paused in a moment of calm contemplation.

It was Sabrina.

She instantaneously came to life as the music of pop diva Irene Cara started to slam from the powerful speakers and pulse through the club. Sabrina thrashed, danced, leaped and spun. Torrents of water poured on her from above. Lights alternately bathed her wet, acrobatic performance from every side and angle.

It was an incredible experience, a perfect re-enactment move-by-move, step-by-step, sexy-pose-by-sexy-pose, of one of the most famous dance segments in modern cinematic history. The song was "What A Feeling" from the movie *Flashdance*. Sabrina was Jennifer Beals as Alex Owens — the welder-by-day dancer-by-night — all over again. Halfway through the song, the whole crowd was on their feet. When it ended, their appreciative ovation went on forever.

Sabrina took numerous bows, dripping wet but still able to soak up the audience's abundant love. Finally the curtain closed, and Priscilla minced back out to center stage, peripherally basking in the adulation, as if she had had something to do with the incredible performance they had just seen.

"Wasn't that great! Just like a nice crème brûlée, I never get tired of her. I'd sure like to lick her spoon. Okay. Now to the moment we've all been waiting for. A winner has been chosen by our fine panel of judges. Please stand up my ladies and lords. Come on, everybody. Let's show them some love."

Priscilla led the audience in applause as the judges stood up to be recognized. Two of the five were pretty boys, obviously gay, clearly loving the attention they were getting for their roles in the night's festivities. They blew kisses to the crowd, then to a lot of hoots and hollers, engaged in some deep throat kissing on their own.

The female judges appeared to be a lot older than the other girls in the club.

Billy looked at them a little closer. He decided that they were probably transvestite "queens". They didn't look like his mothers friends, that was for sure. And it totally made sense … queens judging a Queen For A Day Contest. What a hoot.

Wow! …

He was having a great time. He loved them all. He loved everybody!

He got another round of drinks.

"And remember, regardless of who wins, each and every one of you are part of a royal family, you all sit on your thrones …"

Someone in the audience yelled, "I thought they sat on their asses."
Everyone laughed.

"They'd like to sit on your lap, sweetheart. Just lift that pretty skirt."

"Have you figured out what's going on yet, Billy?"

"I'm not sure what you mean. I've figured out I'm having a great time and these are definitely some of the most beautiful women in New York. Is that what I'm supposed to figure out?"

All of a sudden, a pair of arms came around him from behind, and two hands went from his knees, up his legs, across his crotch, up his stomach to his chest, ever so briefly touched his nipples before ending their brief but supremely arousing journey. Billy thought he would bust through his pants.

She brought one arm up around his shoulder and let it rest there casually, as she sat down.

"Hey you! Enjoying the show?"

It was Sabrina. She playfully touched his ear and temple.

"You were amazing! Why aren't you competing? You'd win for sure."

"Been there done that. Now I like just doing a cameo. I think Charize is going to get the prize tonight. Remember her? Red hair? She did the fire dance, you know, with the torches?"

"So without further ado, may I have the envelope, please?"

One of the pretty boy judges was right there, handed it to her, curtsied and scampered off stage. Then he suddenly reappeared with a huge piece of cake, three-layers of chocolate with white icing, got down on one knee and presented it to her. She threw the envelope on the floor.

> *"I'm sorry but you're all just going to have to wait. I have more important things to do right now."*

Priscilla proceeded to eat the cake, making a big production out of each bite, rolling her eyes, moaning orgasmically, extolling the virtues of sugar and chocolate and icing and everything sweet and wonderful. The crowd loved it and egged her on. When she finished, she let out a long gasping moan like she was climaxing. The pretty boy gave her a cigarette and lit it.

> *"My God, that was so good! I think I'll keep you around."*

As she was saying this, she reached between his legs and gave an affectionate squeeze.

Pretty boy then reached down and retrieved the envelope from the floor and theatrically handed it to her. He waved at his friends in the audience and went back to where the other judges were sitting. Priscilla looked at the envelope.

> *"Oh, I remember now. You're waiting to see who is this year's Queen For A Day."*

She opened it and pulled out an unrolled condom. A name was written on it. Before reading the name, she held it up high to the lights to see if there was anything in it. It was empty.

> *"Looks like somebody forgot to load their gun. Anyway, tonight's winner and Queen For a day is a girl that loves to live on the edge …Thelma Louise."*

The crowd cheered as Thelma came out on stage, pulled the straps aside on her evening gown to expose her large exquisite breasts, then accepted the prize envelope. She was also handed a trophy. It was a small bronze statue which combined the signs for male and female — an arrow and a cross — into one unified symbol.

> *"So that's it for tonight. Remember tomorrow is Namaste Night with DJ Quik-E pumping out the best dance music in the city. And I will see you next Saturday for a very special fashion show. One last thing, you lovers of this paradise we call hell, this hell we call paradise. Tomorrow never comes. So live every moment to its fullest, because every day is always today. Good night!"*

Billy was hearing all of this. But he couldn't claim in point of fact to have been paying much attention. Everything occupying his sensory field competed but tossed about like soap bubbles in a breeze.

Moreover, between the ecstasy and the alcohol, Billy had lost all inhibitions. He and Sabrina were all over one another with their hands. She had a very tight body, strong arms and hands, very firm breasts and legs. Around him he saw a few other couples also in the throes of some serious making out. Most were girls on girls. Frankly, in his present hedonistic euphoria, it was a big turn on.

Sabrina leaned over breathing hot succulent air into his ear, followed with a delicate foray with her tongue. He couldn't hold back any longer, and saw no reason why he should.

Billy drew her into a long, hot, tongue-filled kiss.

Suddenly, Sabrina broke it off.

"Everything's good. In fact, you're great. I'll be right back."

She got up and went off to the ladies room. Billy turned to watch her ass the whole way.

"So, Billy."

"Amethyst. Have you been watching this? This isn't some spectator sport. What? Are you a closet voyeur?"

"It's kind of hard not to watch. I'm a bit jealous. But I don't exactly see anybody here who's my type. Are you having a good time? What do you think of this place?"

"Wild crowd. Weird mix. Straights and gays. Looks like most of the woman are lesbians. I'm all over it."

"You *were* raised in Father Flannigan's Boys Home."

"Whatever. I still love you. Don't take it personally. I love everybody here."

"Yourself?"

"Tonight? Maybe I do. It's the drug, eh? You were right. It's a good thing. A very good thing. Want another drink?"

"I'm fine. Suit yourself. Go easy, though, or you'll miss the best part."

"And what's that?"

"Might be coming right now."

She was looking over Billy's shoulder, so he turned to see. Sabrina was on her way back. She slid down next to him and ran her fingers through his hair.

"What a great looking guy you are! Listen I really like you."

He reached to put one arm around her and the other hand on her thigh. She took both of his hands in hers.

"Here's the plan. As much as I'd like to, this isn't going to happen tonight. So I'm going to leave now." She reached in her purse. She had already written it down. "Here is my phone number. I want you to call me and come and see me. That is, if you really think you can handle this."

"Wait a minute. I don't get it. We're getting along great. I can only see good things ahead. The night is still young."

"And if that is true now, it will be just as true next time we get together."

She leaned over and gave him a tender kiss, sans the explicit foreplay of their earlier mashing.

"Good bye, hey you. Really hope I see you soon."

She got up and started to work her way through the maze of tables.

"But Sabrina ..."

She looked back and winked.

"Call me."

Shattered

Despite his chemical euphoria, Billy couldn't hide his disappointment.

"That was cold."

"I don't think so. It was thoughtful."

"Thoughtful? I am so lost. What are you talking about?"

"A lot of them have issues with men. So they play you. Either to see how long they can fool you or to see the expression on your face when you figure it out. It's kind of a sick game. But I misjudged Sabrina. She's really cool."

"Play me. Sick games. What've you gotten me into here? What would I ..." Billy made big quotation marks with his fingers. "...*find out*? I think with what I've been through lately, I could handle just about anything. What am I missing here?"

"Well, Billy since you can't seem to read the writing on the wall, which happens to be written in mile-high letters, I'll just tell you. All of these girls are boys."

Like he had been pulled into the silent void of outer space, all sights, sounds, smells, flavors and feels disappeared from Billy's consciousness. He was locked in the shut-down of total shock. Billy leaned slightly forward over the table and stared at Amethyst's lips to make sure he was getting this right.

"Would you repeat that?"

"All of these beautiful girls are boys. They're on their way to becoming girls. Most of them are pre-op. Meaning, physiologically they're still male."

"They have penises?"

"You have a penis, don't you? It goes with the territory."

"Sabrina?"

"Definitely pre-op."

"How do you know?"

"I've been around this a lot. I just know."

"I've been making it with a guy?"

"You've been mauling a real beauty. Sabrina is as hot as it gets. I wish I were into women."

"But she's not a woman. Not really. Not where it counts."

"And where's that, Billy? Where does it count?"

"Between the legs."

"You never got that far. From what I could tell, you were really digging it."

"I can't believe this. All evening I've been getting the hots for men. Not women! Guys that look like women. But guys all the same. I let a guy lick my ear. Stick his tongue halfway down my throat. Jesus H. Christ. That sucks. Really sucks!"

"Don't be a homophobe. They are what you see. Not guys, Billy. You're not so different."

"Please, don't go there. I am a guy through and through. I'm 100% heterosexual male."

"Then what were you doing making out with a transsexual, who as you pointed out, probably had a dick and balls just like you. Not the standard definition of heterosexual in my book."

"What is going on? A conspiracy to completely fuck with me?"

"Did you or did you not have a good time tonight?"

"I did until now. Now I didn't."

"It never happened? Is that what you're saying? You were ready to plow into that Sabrina like a horny stud horse, Billy Boy. I know the look."

Amethyst was clearly enjoying herself. But why, Billy wondered? Did he have her all wrong? Was she some sort of sadistic bitch?

"What's in this for you? Are you having fun right now, Am?"

"Not really."

"Then why are you doing this? If you want to freeload drinks off me, fine. I can just give you cash, if this is the only way you can handle hanging out with me. Maybe my company's not good enough for you now. You have to amuse yourself by toying with me."

"That's the point. When I met you, you were good company. I thought you were a little too middle-of-the-road but there was something there. You were at least interesting. Now you're a pathetic mess. A little whiny boy. Candy and I have talked about you a lot. She's at her wits end. I guess I had to find out for myself if you were ready to do something about it."

"So you drugged me and mind-fucked me. It's like date-raping someone's brain. Unreal. Was it good for you? Do you want a cigarette?"

"Let's get back to it. You're just playing hide-and-seek. Those girls are girls if that's how you see them. That's the way it goes. So how does Billy see himself? As some reincarnated Casanova? Because that ain't what I'm seeing."

"If I dare ask, what are you seeing?"

"A little girl."

"You see me as a little girl. That's a good one."

"No. I don't see you as one. But I see a little girl inside you."

"Are you out of your mind? Or are you still messing with mine?"

"For fuck's sake, Billy. Get a clue. It's not a bad thing."

"Not a bad thing."

"It happens to be one of the things that makes you an attractive male. I see it. Candy sees it. Most men are one-dimensional gorillas. Life is their big banana and that's it."

"What's your point? I should start playing with dolls?"

"Okay. Please try to listen. You'll really have to concentrate. Do you think you can handle it?"

"No. But shoot."

"Here is the point. All of this warfare you're conducting on yourself and the rest of the human race is just you trying to keep her inside. You either need to let her come out as the real Billy Green or set her free. Either way—"

"Let's get out of here. I don't feel well. Is it supposed to rain tomorrow?"

"Billy. I've said what I have to say. If you want to change the subject, that's fine with me. But let's not play games, okay? I'm here as a friend. We had fun. I tried to help. The end. Roll credits."

"Got it. I just want to leave."

Billy got up and stormed ahead. Amethyst caught up with him at the shoe check booth. They retrieved their shoes from Christina Aguilera.

As they were going out the door, more people were being admitted. The really late crowd. The *really* strange crowd.

Even in the alley, they could hear the 1978 Rolling Stones song "Shattered", pumping out of the club's behemoth sound system.

Billy looked mortified. Angry. Afraid. He walked ahead.

Amethyst was surprised when he then subtly slowed his pace and let her catch up with him. He gradually inched himself closer to her, finally right against her.

They then walked the streets of Tribeca with their arms around each other. They dropped into the subway station for the C and D trains, which would take them to the Lower East Side. Amethyst now lived not far from Billy's old haunt in alphabet city.

For some reason, Billy couldn't make himself go home. Not yet. He was overwhelmed. The Ecstasy, the drinks, the show, his wild flirtation, had put him on some plane he had never been on before. It wasn't unpleasant. More like an inchoate pre-nirvana. A zone of dispassionate quasi-rapture. This was a shift from the numb void he had experienced for the months after his parents died. Very different. He couldn't really say how. But it was different. Maybe he had just been pulled in so many directions over the past two years, tonight it all finally gave and ripped apart. Then something — he couldn't say what — had arrived to fill the center.

Anxiety and resignation. Ecstasy and despair. Love and loneliness. Fulfillment and death.

Isn't everything supposed to be a zero sum game?

If Billy had to sum it all up and be truly honest about it ...

It felt good being with Amethyst. It felt good being at Strange Love. It felt good having the attention of a beautiful babe like Sabrina — even if *she* turned out to be a *he*. It did feel good. Was it the drug? Or did one of the gates finally open up in the system of locks that controlled the pent-up swirl of his emotions? Is this what it felt like to feel? It had been so long. It wasn't like riding a bicycle. It didn't just come back. Apparently he had to work at it. Maybe even start all over.

Amethyst in her own twisted neo-punk way was an extraordinary girl. He knew she liked him. She knew he wanted her. There had always been this smoldering unstated promise that one of these days ... you know ... maybe.

She seemed to know intuitively that Billy was going to stay the night. Nothing was said. Nothing had to be. They arrived at her grimy studio apartment and got ready to crash.

Probably on any other night, Billy would have gone for it. It was hard to believe that earlier in the evening his libido was cranked up so high he thought he would spontaneously combust. Yet now, sex was the furthest thing from his mind.

He felt needy. Vulnerable. Anxious.

Though it was late winter, it was surprisingly warm outside. In her apartment, which had no ventilation and trapped the excessive heat from the cranked-up radiators, it was a furnace.

Billy sank to the floor.

He just wanted to be held.

Perhaps like … like a little girl would.

The room melted like a dream made of ice cream.

Next morning — or was it afternoon? — Billy opened his eyes and found himself naked, with the long graceful arms of an equally naked rock singer wrapped around him in a natural embrace of convenience and ephemeral trust.

He had just woken from a bizarre and disconcerting dream.

A Midsummer Night's Dream

Maybe it was the heat of the apartment. Or the heat of the moment. He was, after all, laying skin-to-skin with a very very sexually attractive girl.

In any case, in his dream it was the middle of summer.

He was completely lost. It must have been somewhere out West. Maybe Utah, New Mexico, or Arizona. He was walking along a dusty dirt road and came to the top of a small rise. There directly ahead in the midst of the barren high-desert terrain was a brilliant green, lush forest. A tropical oasis.

Small plumes of smoke were rising from three different areas of the woods, from what he could tell, not that far apart from one another. Campers? Indians? Wildlife Department?

He was exhausted and needed a place to regroup, recover his strength, eat, maybe even rest for the remainder of the day and night. He was extremely thirsty and had no water with him.

The cool forest held the promise of relief from the sun.

Then things got strange.

Billy didn't know enough about Shakespeare to fill the back of a business card. But he now surmised he must have picked up some impressions along the way. It was none other than the Bard himself who stepped out from behind a huge rhododendron bush, greeting him at the edge of the forest. At least it looked like William Shakespeare. Not that it was relevant. This William Shakespeare had the same crude, nasty manners, body language, and voice as his father.

"You look like shit. Just go in. There are some honeys in there who'll take care of you. Listen! Don't try to fuck them. You got that?"

Billy stepped wide of the sneering Shakespeare-father hybrid and entered the forest, looking for respite from the hot sun.

As he entered the canopy of shade trees, a woman who looked exactly like his mom, seemed to come from nowhere and was now walking beside him.

"Mom!"

Even in the dream, he knew she was dead.

He started crying. She took him in her arms.

"It's going to be alright, Billy. Your mom is fine. She misses you."

"Mom. I never … I wish I could have—"

"Not me, Billy."

She placed her fingers gently over his lips. He continued to cry silently.

"I want you to meet someone you never met. It's your sister."

"I have a sister?"

Candy came out from a low hut off to one side tucked back in the trees. She had a huge smile on her face and her eyes burned bright blue.

"Candy? You're my sister?"

"I'm not Candy, Billy. Why would you say that?"

William Shakespeare but not William Shakespeare. His mom but not his mom who was dead. Now someone who looked exactly like Candy who was not Candy, but a sister he had never met.

No one was who they appeared to be. So it seemed.

"Come with me, Billy. You need to refresh yourself. You've come a long ways."

Billy's not-mom mom stepped aside and his not-Candy sister reached out and took his hand. It most definitely was not Candy. He knew what she felt like. This was a whole different person.

They walked down a long path leading deeper into the forest. Soon they were ducking low-hanging branches and stepping over fallen trees. They then came to a clearing.

There was a beautiful pond, the water so still it looked like glass.

"Go ahead. It'll feel good."

Billy kneeled at the edge of the pond and cupped his hands in the water.

As soon as the water touched his face, he was overcome by an incandescent infusion of love, a slow-motion explosion from deep inside that was both erotic and romantic. He looked at his sister and wanted to touch her, hold her, kiss her, do some very unsisterly things to her. It was like a thousand adolescent crushes all at once.

He reached toward her, thinking for starters he could innocently brush her hair off her face.

His hands were gone.

In their place was a shimmering membrane of light, with tiny luminescent filaments. Not in the shape of his hands. More like fields of energy, little clouds which pulsed and flickered.

His sister came closer but reached into the water and started splashing him. Like they were kids playing in a lake, she kept sweeping her arms in a wide arc and her cupped hands threw more and more water on him until he was drenched.

Each time a new douse of water hit him, he felt urgent rushes of impossibly intense passion fill his body, his mind, every cubic inch of his being. By the time she was finished, he was breathless and totally spent from the fierce waves of infatuation, the divinely-inspired torrents still gently rippling through him.

He looked down at his legs, his torso. He twisted his neck to look at his shoulders. They had all been replaced by the shimmering membranes of filamented light.

"Am I gone? Am I completely gone now?"

"Not at all."

He leaned over the water, which had calmed somewhat from his sister's frenzy of splashing, to view his own reflection.

He screamed in horror.

His face looked like it had been mutilated by tumorous growths, grotesque running sores, and then repeatedly hacked with an axe or a machete. One eye was three times its normal size and hung like a rotten fig on his cheek. His lips were cracked, bleeding and full of puss. His hair was caked with scabs. Maggots crawled in the festering wounds on his forehead and ears.

He held up his hands.

In the reflecting pool, they looked like they had been put in a meat grinder, twisted and torn, with blood running from dangling veins and arteries.

He pulled back and tried to form the words. Desperate to ask what was going on. Why did he look so hideous, so monstrous? What had happened?

He couldn't get his mouth to move. His jaw, throat and lips were locked in a frozen cry of terror and agony.

Now he could see over his sister's shoulder, that a long line of people were approaching. Emerging from a narrow opening in the foliage at the edge of the clearing.

She moved to the side, so they could now get a good view of him.

It seemed like everyone he had ever known passed by for a glimpse of the spectacle of his hideous ruin. His mom, his dad, his teachers, his nuns, the kids he attended elementary and high school with. His college professors, then Julianne, Natalie, Pam, Annie Roberts, the people he worked with at Habitat, even townspeople he only casually knew in Newburgh. Amethyst, Hypo and the other members of Machines of Melanoma strolled by, even Renoir Albertine Toulouse, then Apocalypso. Finally, the real Candy. Glancing at his sister, then Candy, he could see no physical difference.

Each walked by slowly, staring, studying him. Each had a faint, almost imperceptible smile, the exact same non-committal expression, impossible on the surface to read.

But he knew what they were thinking.

Suddenly he was overcome with self-loathing and shame. His grotesqueness overwhelmed him.

He started to cry. He cried harder than he had ever cried in his entire life. Harder than he thought was humanly possible. His body convulsed and he felt surrounded and crushed by the despair and hopelessness of his condition, of his future, and of the emptiness and lack of possibilities of his life.

All he could think about was dying.

"Please! Please! Kill me! Kill me right now!"

"It's not like that, Billy."

"I know what I saw. I know what I've become."

"You can't trust yourself to see yourself. You can only look through the eyes of those around you, those closest to you, those who know you. They are your mirror to the real you. Here."

She reached for him and he could feel her hands on his face. Suddenly, the entire range of his vision was filled with a glaring white field of light. As if walking out of a cloud, he saw himself gracefully, effortlessly coming toward him.

He was completely naked. And he looked nothing short of a god. His body was toned, his skin glowed with a flawless golden perfection, his face was confident, relaxed, intelligent, caring, captivating. His hair was long, flowing, and had never looked better.

Dreaming Billy heard his sister as if from the bottom of a deep trance.

"This is you, Billy."

The Vision Billy came right up before him. He slowly turned so that Dreaming Billy could view the entire beautiful length of his body. When his back was to Dreaming Billy, he stretched his arms heavenward, and looked up. Then suddenly, as if being lit from some powerful beam directly overhead, Vision Billy was flooded with a blinding surge of energy. It was not just light, but something more powerful and profound.

Vision Billy continued to turn very slowly. Now he was completely transformed. His male genitals were gone. He had full beautiful breasts. His face had softened and become feminine and alluring. He was beautiful beyond description. Dreaming Billy started feeling surges of the waves of infatuation he had felt earlier, tinged with more erotic sensations. These quickly evolved into hot waves of pure lust.

Though his sister's hands were still on his face, dreaming Billy saw the female image of himself kneel directly in front of him, then slowly and gently reach with his hand to the area of the luminescent membrane which would have been his crotch.

He felt a surge in his loins that spread through his lower body. His penis felt rock hard and was throbbing, pulsing, relentlessly pushing from the inside. He felt an overwhelming rush as his body convulsed in an earth-shaking orgasm.

That was when he woke up.

Had he really?

He looked down. Semen covered his stomach and the top of his thighs.

Amethyst was still asleep. He carefully untangled his arms out from under her, then slid as carefully as he could off to the edge of the bed, taking pains not to let the copious product of his wet dream drip off of him.

He scooted into the bathroom and started cleaning himself up with toilet paper. He was half done when Amethyst walked in and sat down on the toilet. As the swish of her morning pee could be heard, she noticed what he was doing.

"Hope it was good for you. I didn't feel a thing."

Billy could feel his face blush.

"It was out of my control."

"Isn't everything?"

He didn't say anything.

What could he say?

She was right.

Surrender

Billy found himself haunted in the days which followed. The dream was fresh upon him every waking hour. It seemed to transcend the immediacy of the moment and be more the stuff of reality than reality itself.

Something else kept coming back to him. Flashes of the evening Amethyst took him to Strange Love. Not just the uncomfortable exchange in her apartment afterwards, the bit about the little girl living inside him, but intense rushes both visual and physical — intense as in hypercharged erotic surges in his groin, which gave him a painfully stiff erection. The image and object of his lust?

Sabrina.

This was both off putting and frightening. Billy suspected that at core he was seriously homophobic. Considering all of the conditioning of growing up with in bulked-up, macho Detroit, plus being raised in a Catholic home painted with the Church's largely medieval world view, it seemed impossible that he had escaped a profound and permanent scarring of his impressionable mind.

Sabrina.

That such a brief and superficial encounter would have such a powerful hold on him made absolutely no sense.

But he still couldn't shake it. The more he fought it, the more control the intrusive moments of his recollecting Sabrina exercised over his body and mind. He became a slave to it. Obsessed.

Finally, he just gave up. It was as if he had no choice in the matter.

Time to surrender.

He retrieved the piece of paper she had handed him before getting up and leaving his table. He watched his finger punch in the number.

"Sabrina. This is Billy. I met you at Strange Love. I was with—"

"I know who you are, Billy Green. It's good to hear your voice. If you're not busy, come over."

"I ... I would like to. Right now?"

"Sounds good to me. I'm just about to take a shower. Maybe 7:30?"

Billy got her address. He knew the area of town where she lived. When he put down the phone, he was an oil-and-water cocktail of emotions. Excited. Embarrassed. Giddy. Afraid. Self-assured. Timid. Aroused. He had trouble with that one. But there was no denying it. He was turned on.

She said she was *"just about to take a shower."* He pictured her phenomenal body naked — frontally from the waste up and its full length only from the back — and had to shake the thought. It was just too intense. And he definitely didn't even want to deal with what might be *down there*, if what Amethyst had told him was true.

Whew! Where was this going?

When he arrived and pressed the intercom buzzer, the door release immediately clicked open. She must have been waiting for him.

He walked up two flights of stairs and there was Sabrina, at the doorway to her apartment. She was much more beautiful and sexy than he remembered.

She led him in, made an dismissive sweep of her hand to take in her compact dwellings.

"This is it. Not much to see. But if you have an extra ten seconds, I can give you a tour."

"It's fine. It's very nice."

Billy, of course, was looking at her delicious butt, tightly contained in a pair of jeans which tastefully pulled up and in between her legs to reveal the curves and nuances he remembered from the night at Strange Love.

They sat down on two large floor pillows situated before a small wicker coffee table. Beneath them was a Persian rug which took up most of the living room floor. On the table, there were two glasses of wine, already poured from a half-empty bottle of Cabernet. Finally Billy noticed that a thick plush duvet in rich warm tones which blended perfectly with the rug, was spread out on the other side of the coffee table.

They looked at each other and smiled, then shared a laugh as they both reached for their glasses of wine at the exact same time.

They sipped and watched one another, eyes playfully meeting and exploring the other's face. He caught her staring at his lips, as she took another few drops of wine, then licked her own.

Billy was surprised at how relaxed and comfortable he was. It really felt right.

Sabrina put her glass down and ran her other hand lightly through her hair. Her lips glistened and her eyes were deep starless pools of allure.

"Billy. I am really attracted to you. I mean *really attracted*. Do you think you're ready?"

Her words were like having her fingertips drag down his chest and stomach toward the playground below. His breathing quickened as the hot syrup of lust filled his entire body.

"Sabrina. I'm pretty sure that's why I'm here."

She leaned over and started to brush her eyelashes against his cheek, letting him feel the warmth of her breath and smell the natural perfume of her skin.

After what seemed like an eternity of anticipation — it was only a couple minutes at best — she kissed him. Very delicately at first, then with increasing urgency, passion and wetness. Billy tumbled into the swirling vortex of her kiss. His hands slid under her blouse and up her back, as hers reached inside his shirt and lightly fondled his nipples.

When neither could hold out any longer, off came their clothes, and they moved the party in a desperate wriggling embrace, over to the outstretched duvet.

Billy was on his back and Sabrina was all over him. He couldn't help but notice the press of her rigidly erect penis against his thigh, sometimes brushing his own erection. But in the greater tsunami of erotic sensations, it was only a minor — if unprecedented — anomaly. There was something almost daringly satisfying about it.

He still couldn't look *down there*.

Sabrina kissed Billy's ear, lightly stroked his penis, then rolled him onto his stomach. Playfully she ran a finger down the crack of his ass, reached between his legs and teasingly caressed his balls.

She very discretely slipped on a condom, generously slathering it with Clean Stream anal sex lubricant.

With the gentleness of a mother pampering her baby, she entered Billy.

He couldn't say it was initially pleasant. In fact it was painful.

But it was over fairly quickly. Maybe less than five minutes.

Over this short time, Billy relaxed. The pain of his deflowering gradually melted away. As Sabrina entered and withdrew in unhurried measured strokes — a lover's slow dance of dreams and abandon — he was able to surrender to a building tidal wave of sensations he had never felt before.

After she came, he felt perfectly united with her in the shared calm of her release. Even her final climactic paroxysm was controlled, almost balletic and graceful. As her hardness dissipated, she remained inside of him for a couple minutes and their bodies felt fused in a mutual bliss.

She pulled out. Then with a gracefulness that would be the envy of a Geisha, she kissed his body starting from the base of his spine, working her way up to his neck, then brushed his ear with her lips and playfully put the tip of her tongue inside.

Billy moaned with exquisite pleasure as she slowly rolled him over onto his back under her own body. Her still-hard nipples caressed the skin of his ribcage, then his chest.

Now she reversed direction and worked her way back down the length of Billy's torso. She stopped to lick each of his nipples, then moved down his stomach and finally put his pulsing begging member in her mouth. No condom. Just the pure heaven of her mouth and tongue.

After two of the most pleasurable minutes of his life, Billy exploded. It felt like he kept coming over and over, it lasted so long. It was a 10-megaton eruption which filled Sabrina's mouth three times over and left Billy experiencing continuous mini-orgasmic aftershocks for a full minute beyond.

"Billy Green. You are something else!"

Billy tried but could not get his mouth to form words to reply. He reached down toward her and she slid up into his arms. They lay there like that in a lover's embrace for nearly an hour.

As they were getting dressed — both smiling in varying degrees, and stealing casual glances at each other — Billy noticed something which took him completely by surprise. He was feeling none of that post-coital awkwardness, shyness and embarrassment, that was typical of such anonymous couplings. After all, they barely knew each other. But Billy felt completely comfortable.

It felt right.

Billy then experienced a second shocking moment of revelation. In watching Sabrina — and what a feast for the eyes it still was even post-orgasm — he finally glanced *down there*. Sabrina's penis was still slightly erect, a little smaller than Billy's, youthful, and like his own, circumcised. What shocked

Billy was that he experienced no squeamishness or aversion or any of the emotions he would have expected. There it was. Just a part of her body. She was a girl, but just a slightly different kind of girl. Billy would later learn that t-girls — or ladyboys as they were often called — described themselves in just these terms. "A girl with a little something extra" was the way they put it. That summed it up pretty well in Billy's mind right now. Sabrina was no less a woman than Candy or Amethyst. Just with a little something extra.

Whew! Double whew!

They sat down again on the stuffed pillows, looking quietly into one another's eyes. Billy reached over and touched her cheek with the back of his fingers. She turned and kissed them. They sat for the longest time in silent appreciation.

Finally, Sabrina took his hand in both of hers and caressed his palm.

"That should answer some of your questions. And even if I barely know you and may never see you again, I love you for who you are."

She leaned over and kissed him long and deep. Not tongue-deep but soul-deep.

It was an affectionate and caring kiss that Billy would never forget.

"You should go now. I'd really like to see you again. But I'll leave that up to you. Bye for now, Billy Green."

Chapter Five

WRESTLING WITH DEMONS
Spring 2008

Confusion is Just a State of Mind

Billy was confused. He was certain that in this, he was not alone. Probably 99.9% of the population was confused. From what he saw of the world around him, he seriously doubted that anyone else had made much progress either, at getting *unconfused*. Right now he couldn't worry about them. He had his own problems.

It all came to an explosive head the two hours he spent alone with Sabrina.

Amethyst had tried to explain. Then he saw with his own eyes what a gender bender was.

It didn't entirely compute.

But he knew what he felt. He knew what he experienced in those myth-shattering two hours with the girl that was a guy. Sabrina was all the woman a man could ever hope for.

She even had a little something extra.

It started possessing him. He just couldn't shake it.

Maybe he didn't want to.

Billy looked at the entire spectrum of what is normally considered masculine and feminine. Everyone seemed to be able to at least point at certain archetypes of masculinity and femininity, and know the men that were real men, and the women that were real women.

George Clooney was all man.

Angelina Jolie was all woman.

Man. Woman. Easy to spot. Simple to identify.

But unfortunately, that wasn't the whole story.

Out on the far edges things got really crazy. Way out there on the hyper-extremes.

Some men went so far in that direction, they flew off the edge into some draconian super-male zone, where they weren't even human anymore. Some of them displayed their masculine heroics in action and war movies, or in the staged combat of the professional wrestling ring. They were grunting animaloids for whom higher cerebral functions seemed to shrink in inverse proportion to their bulk. These metamorphs slid back down the slippery trunk of the evolutionary tree. Billy sensed their numbers were on the increase with all of the steroids and other drugs available on the market for re-engineering the human body, plus all of the entertainment and media that appeared to be specifically designed to make people as dumb as a doorknob.

Similarly, out beyond the fringe on the other extreme, were women who likewise ceased to be human, such übersexual creatures whose fine perfection and hyperbolic delicacy rendered them unapproachable and asexual — angels and androgynous faeries, wonder women and super-vixens. Hollywood was full of them, products of pathological levels of self-indulgence and cosmetic surgery. They were even becoming common on the streets of New York and Paris, Milan and Madrid. Plasticized Barbies who looked like they would pop if you pricked them with a pin.

Nevertheless …

Look from one end of the spectrum to the other, it at least made *some* sense.

Here was the catch: no matter where you placed the outer limits of gender, the real problem remained the same. It was what was in the middle that had become a big soupy mess.

The blurring had all started in the 60s, basically spreading from the west coast across the country in a cultural firestorm that annihilated a whole range of taboos. Boys en masse began wearing long hair and trading in their leather jackets and t-shirts for bellbottoms and hip huggers, loose frilly shirts from Kathmandu and Calcutta. They wore earthy sandals, leather body and hair ties from Marrakech, wreaths of flowers, jewelry and earrings — which happened to be the same clothes and styles the girls were wearing.

The freewheeling discofied 70s, New Wave 80s, even the gothed out Glam Rock 90s, each a decade with its own twist of dissident decadence, saw the perfect collusion of the fashion industry and hyper-consumerism to keep gender stereotypes from ever re-grouping to the straightforward and unaffected images of the 50s — *Father Knows Best. Ozzie and Harriet. The Cleavers. Donna Reid.*

Nothing would ever be so simple again, as basic biology was trumped by pop culture and fashion.

All that historical analysis aside, the entirety of Billy's current conundrum could be reduced to a single question.

How could a girl with a dick be so utterly and perfectly feminine?

Feminine the way that it makes you hurt and weep and crave and lust until you can get some.

Sabrina was more feminine than 99% of the women in his hometown of Detroit. Maybe of the entire state of Michigan. As sexy as any woman he had ever met.

For days and days Billy pondered those two hours with her. Why was it so incredibly good? What on the surface would appear to be a totally kinky sexual experience, turned out in fact to be one of the most amazing human encounters in his life.

Sure. Sex is always good.

But with Sabrina there was something else in play. That's what he needed to figure out.

The girl was a guy. But not a guy. Kind of. But not really. Maybe not at all.

It was just like Amethyst said, when Billy was fighting his knee-jerk revulsion at making it with a another male that night at Strange Love. The entire time that Billy thought Sabrina was actually a girl, he was having the time of his life. She looked like a girl, felt and smelled like a girl, kissed like a girl, embodied all of the feminine beauty and sexual allure of a girl.

It was only when he let her apparent possession of male genitalia start messing with his head that he freaked out.

There was only one conclusion he could draw, regardless of how much it ran contrary to his narrow conditioning and preconceptions of rigid gender roles: A girl is a girl if that's how you see her. If that's how she saw herself. If that's how she presented herself to the world. And if that's how the world accepted her. At least on the surface.

The problem wasn't Sabrina or any of the others in the club that night.

The problem was him.

Amethyst had later that evening raised an even more fundamental question. It was a question which cut to the core of his identity, and painfully hovered over the open sores of his failed marriage and lifelong alienation from the rest of the human race.

What was he? Was Billy Green a man or a woman? Was there actually a feminine side to him trying to break out of the cocoon that he had trapped her in for his twenty-six years? She had called it 'a little girl', a characterization which offended him on so many levels. But he got the point. There was something very strange going on inside Billy Green.

As much as he hated to admit it, maybe Amethyst saw something he couldn't possibly see. Maybe this was the key to all of his confusion.

He suddenly remembered a song by an English band whose heyday was the 60s and 70s. When it came out, apparently it had caused a raging controversy. Whew! Things sure had changed. By today's standards, it was Sesame Street material. It was called "Lola".

> Girls will be boys and boys will be girls
> It's a mixed-up muddled-up shook-up world
> Except for Lola
> Lo-lo-lo-lo Lola

It was a mixed-up muddled-up shook-up world alright.
He could be the patron saint of confusion.
The poster boy for delusion.
Bi-bi-bi-bi-Billy.

The Eyelids of the Beholder

"That's totally brilliant! Amethyst said that?"

Billy and Candy had taken a bottle of tequila down to just a shallow puddle at the bottom. There were broken corn chips on the floor and a gob of avocado and salsa sauce on Billy's chin. He was too gone to be aware of it and Candy too amused to bother mentioning it. The three Xanax he had taken just before Candy arrived were just starting to kick in as well.

"What's so brilliant about it? It's one of those completely empty accusations that you can't defend against, because it doesn't exist in the real world. Not that it doesn't haunt me. It's like a fucking ghost which keeps moving the furniture around in my head every time I think about it."

"A little girl. Sure. I can see it. You *are* a playful creature. Maybe there *is* some Tinker Bell in the mix."

"Don't get crazy on me now, Candy. I'm in no condition for it."

"You're this experiment. God is running a double blind for a science fair."

"I'm definitely feeling like a victim of animal testing."

"A cat strapped to a neuro-grid, being pumped full of plastic lip filler or anti-fungal chemical douche. Or enough aspartame to make the Pacific Ocean taste like corn syrup."

"You know, Candy, being contrary is not the only possible response for every single situation. Irreverence for you is like some knee-jerk Planck's constant. Is this supposed to be funny?"

"I'm committed to believing that if I remember any of this when I'm straight, it'll make perfect sense. The bottom line, Billy, is I'm trying to help. It's not a joke."

"So help. And do it without all the mental masturbation."

"You can only be what you are. I don't know if you have a little girl living inside you or not. It's an interesting image. But it doesn't matter. I don't care. You shouldn't either."

"But I do care."

"It's all semantics. Having a little girl inside you doesn't makes you any less of a man."

"Right."

"Yes. Right. I am right. Come on, Billy. Pay attention. It creates a dualism. A complexity. Nothing's lost. It doesn't subtract anything, unless you let it."

"Why would I let that happen?"

"Because you are on your way to having a total meltdown? Because you're so fucking scared and intimidated you can't stop it from happening? You tell me. This is your self-impalement on the skewer of dread. Your chasing a tail you don't have. I know who the fuck you are. It's you that can't figure it out."

Billy just closed his eyes and polished off the tequila.

He gently glided into a dreamless meditation.

Translation: He was dead drunk.

But the mind never sleeps. The dull sloppy chewing of his alcohol and tranquilizer-doused subconscious kept its constant vigil on the cud of his conundrum. Sluggishly it all wormed its way through the second, third and fourth stomachs of his self-absorbed and self-absorbing ruminations.

What would come out the other end remained to be seen. But it was an easy guess.

Nevertheless, as they say, the devil is in the details.

Here is how it went — his cerebral gymnastics, that is.

There's no service manual, no set of directions for growing up. There's no road map for finding one's self. That's where mom and dad supposedly come in. Lacking parental guidance, everyone's on their own. People turn to friends, lovers, wives, gurus, counselors, therapists, priests, ministers, role models, friends, lovers, and so on. Most of these are just as confused or misdirected as everyone else.

It's a tragicomic story everywhere.

The lost leading the lost.

Everyone loses.

Billy faintly groaned.

Girls were always telling Billy how easy he was to be around, how sensitive he was, how unlike other men he was.

He should have never believed them. It bloated his ego and filled his head with nonsense. That just became the raw material for him to generate more nonsense.

Maybe he was different than other men. Maybe he was a sensitive kind of guy.

So what? What difference did it make?

It didn't save his marriage. It hadn't kept his parents from getting killed. It didn't stop the World Trade Center from being destroyed. It wasn't preventing the Earth from heating up and turning into a lifeless cinder. It wasn't even stopping Billy from being a magnet for the weirdness of the world.

If he was so sensitive, why couldn't he figure out the most elementary question in his relatively uncomplicated life: Who was Billy Green?

Billy moaned again and rolled onto his side in fetal position.

Amethyst had really spooked him by saying that he had a little girl inside of him. Candy was way too amused by it and thought it was a stroke of genius. What was so fucking brilliant and amusing about it? The idea? Or Amethyst telling Billy, and him ending up more bewildered than ever about everything?

The very idea seemed so absurd and surreal at the time, but frankly it continued to haunt him. It tortured him, had dug in and nagged and annoyed him like a piece of hot sticky shrapnel buried deep in his gut. He fought the idea with bitter resolve, thinking at the time that it must have been the drugs that had made him so vulnerable to what amounted to a flippant, spur-of-the-moment toss-off by a demented rocker chick. But the way it had bothered him, the intensity with which he had resisted, and been so put off by the idea, made him wonder now if there wasn't some bit of truth there after all.

Suddenly there was a bright explosion! Like the birth of a star.

His brain became a plasma of kaleidoscopic energy.

Billy jerked. It startled Candy. She slid over by him and put his head in her lap. His eyelids were fluttering.

The light was blinding. Brilliant. Radiant. Glaring. He felt like he was staring into an arc lamp, laying prone against the hot glass enclosure, the light and heat blowing through his transparent body like a solar wind.

OMG!

Candy was right. Amethyst was right. Everyone was right.

Except him.

The little girl was his guardian angel. His conscience. The little voice of truth. That pure voice which he and everyone else in this world yelled down out of convenience, selfishness, or pure stupidity.

Candy had channeled that voice. He had tried to yell her down too.

But she had made it crystal clear, as only she could ...

Women were his problem.
She was right.
What else had she said?
She also told him he needed a paradigm shift.
Alright. He could arrange that. A paradigm shift, eh?
Easily said.
Easily done.
How about this? ...
If women were his problem, then the solution was simple.
He'd change horses.
He'd jump ship.
He'd switch parties.
He'd join the other team.
Yes! He'd become a woman.
Now he was getting somewhere!
Ha! He'd finally gotten something right.
If Billy Green was such a total fuck-up as a man ...
Billy Green would live out the rest of his days on Earth as a female.

While he lay dead to the world on the plush white rug of his Upper East Side living room, and Candy caressed his temple and ran her delicate fingers gently across his cheek and through his hair, Billy's addled but still functioning brain had come up with a plan.

It would have to let Billy know.

If he ever sobered up.

A Jury of One

The next day, Billy woke up and with a Herculean effort managed to get up on all fours and crawl like a feeble lumbering Kodiak bear toward the bathroom, for an extremely urgent wiz. As he painfully made his way, he glanced at the clock. It was 2:35. That had to be afternoon, in light of the crisp blue sky he could see through the triple-pane window at the end of the living room.

His head hurt and he couldn't see through the haze to locate the fog that obscured the smoky cloud at the center of his skull. The win-a-stuffed-animal carnival sledgehammer had definitely rung the bell this time.

This required drastic action. After relieving himself — he wished afterwards he had had a stop watch, because he thought for sure the duration of his pee was in Guinness Book of World Records territory — he popped a couple Valium and an Adderall, then poured a tall glass of tequila sunrise mix, leftover from last night.

Even before the drugs had time to kick in, Billy noticed something. It was a sort of calm, a sense of relief. Behind the clanking throb of his headache, there seemed to be hovering inside an unfamiliar quietude. A shy new acquaintance. Maybe it was in there at the center of the smoky cloud.

He went to the balcony and looked out across Central Park. It was a stunningly beautiful day.

Slowly his head started to clear. He showered, got dressed, and went for the first of several long walks over the next few days.

It was a little nippy, but the cool air and clear post-winter skies, just made his brisk strolls through the park, and along the side streets of upper Manhattan, all the more exhilarating.

A whole new array of images were floating in on a high pressure front, sweeping aside the gray cloud cover and dank murkiness of his recent quandaries. Centered in the red rivulets of his bloodshot eyes were two brilliant star sapphires, the color of the sky, energetically darting side to side, looking out and looking in, signaling the arrival of a new day, a new season, and maybe even a new life.

Images …

Billy pictured his mom. But as she was when he was just a boy. He thought of his mom's friends, unable to remember their names but able to vividly see each of them sitting at the kitchen table, their stories written in their faces, their attitudes simulcast from head to toe. He pictured the gestapo nuns, Sister Grace, Mother Superior, the wretched Sister Bernadette. He warmed at the image of Sister Mary Felicia. Teaching. Talking. Laughing. The kiss. Then he briefly thought about crazy Jackie the Ripper. He pictured several high school girls. Lovely Roxanne Whittier. Crippled Marlene Goetz. The scholarly nympho, Darlene Thomas. The superwoman Theresa Karpinski. And the double-vision girls, Sally and Sandy Flasher. Cornell University's foxy five: Kristin, Angie, Erin, Tanya, Julianne. Oh yes! The stunning and alluring Julianne. Then … of course. Natalie. Natalie. Natalie. Natalie and Pam. Natalie and Annie Roberts. Natalie and Katie. Mmm. Katie. He pictured crazy Amethyst. Painfully, he visualized one-by-one the anonymous bakers dozen, including Frankenhooker. Then last but not least … Candy. Beautiful Candy. Eccentric Candy. Intelligent Candy. Brilliantly sarcastic Candy. Sexually explosive Candy.

These were the women of his life, casual and intimate — a few equally both casual and intimate — young and old, convivial and hostile, arrogant and humble, smart and not so smart, beautiful and ugly and everything in between. They were friends or foes, ports of call or passing ships in the night, misty dissolving impressions or deep and lasting memories.

Each one was a distinct individual. Some were unique and exceptional. A few were uniquely unexceptional. But they all shared a common essence — their femaleness. Whatever slight or enormous differences set them apart, their femininity united them.

As he visualized each of them, he tried to put some distance between himself and his personal interactions with them, between his personal feelings and whatever objective measure of them was possible. Then applying his most focused powers of concentration and limited male imagination, he wondered just what it felt like to be each one of them. What it felt like to live in their bodies, what the world looked like through their eyes, how it felt to move, to walk, to run, to dance, to speak, to shake hands, to pull a comb through their hair, to sip a cup of coffee, to smoke a cigarette. What it felt like when they laughed, cried, nodded and blinked, looked in the mirror, put on earrings, applied lipstick, pulled on their hosiery, rubbed cream on their cheeks, held a baby, stood at a grave. He crawled inside the grace and delicacy of their every movement, trying to translate the language of their bodies into the language of their hearts and the poetry of their minds.

It wasn't just an interesting exercise. It became a pleasant and comfortable one. He was surprised and heartened to find it came to him quite effortlessly. Almost as if he had foreknowledge of a letter and now just needed to open the envelope and confirm what he already knew.

He liked the way the world looked through their eyes. It was different. It was calming. There was a release and a relief. There was none of the anxiety, guilt, tension, pressure, urgency, and combative impulse, which had defined his every waking hour as a man.

Was it the mothering thing, the nurturing quietude of that half of the human race responsible for attentively guiding the entire human experiment along a sustainable path to eternal survival?

Was it the soft milky breast which fed the baby and beguiled the grown man to join her in perpetuating the species?

Was it the long arms of safeguarding love which brought the warrior to his heels and kept him from destroying everything in his path including himself?

How often he had heard feminists say that the world would be a completely different place — a much better place — if women ran things? Billy had to agree. War would probably be a thing of the past. The world's self-annihilating priorities would likely be turned upside down.

So it went for the next two weeks, as Billy warmed to his new awakening, slowly becoming friends with the strangest epiphany of his entire life. As he got increasingly comfortable, he gradually moved beyond the mystery, the fear, the intimidation, and the novelty, of what it must be like to live in this world as a woman — at least as much as he could without actually being one — and embraced the new possibilities for himself.

It was strange. He hadn't ever been one to spend time looking in the mirror. But now when he did, something was very different. His face was relaxed. He no longer had even a hint of that tough-guy mile-of-attitude scowl, or the mouth set in the macho fight-or-flight urge to growl. It was almost comical. His lips had more of a Mona Lisa smile. Or maybe it was the Virgin Mary.

Something was definitely happening. Maybe it was a paradigm shift.

Ha ha. That's very funny!

Understandably, he spoke to no one about any of this. It was all too new, too bizarre, too controversial, and frankly way too embarrassing. He still had enough of a grip on reality to understand that none of this would make any sense to anyone else, so there was no plausible reason to bring it up, much less try to explain it. At least until he got it all sorted out.

Where was this going? Was this really headed where it seemed?

Was he actually going to go through with this?

Where did this idea come from?

How did it take root?

Become a girl?

Holy shit!

This frivolous, peculiar, deviant, desperate, yet immensely alluring thought, now monopolized his every waking moment. There were so much to consider. To think and rethink. Evaluate. So many angles and perspectives.

Mostly Billy wondered how anyone who knew him, remotely knew him, barely heard of him, and even those who were outright strangers, were going to react if he crossed the gender line. If he took that "little girl" that was ostensibly inside of him, and installed her overtly and permanently on the outside.

Of course he wondered! He obsessed about it. This wasn't changing hair styles. Or buying new tennies. People were going to think he was totally crazy. Or perverted. Or desperate.

Hopefully his mom and dad, wherever they were, would be pre-occupied with the myriad of details encompassing their new lives in the eternal and infinite, and thus be looking the other way — whatever the other way was out there in the beyond.

Amethyst would probably publicly shrug it off, but either be laughing or pitying him on the inside. Anarchy had no rules and set no limits, making it pretty hard to predict her real reaction with any degree of certainty. At the same time, he had to believe she would still be there for him on some level. She had so far been a solid and supportive friend. She had in point of fact initiated this, whether at the time she was punking him or not.

The members of Amethyst's band were a mixed bag. Hypo, the leader of the group, was easy. He wouldn't care one way or another but would try to protect Billy when the other homophobes in Machines of Melanoma decided to kill him.

Natalie? Pam? Would he ever see them again? Probably not. But it could be interesting. Even so, he preferred not to think about it.

Miss Frankenhooker and the twelve or so other young fillies he had plugged over the past few weeks? Like it mattered? He couldn't even remember their names.

Was that it?

How pathetic. He hadn't exactly been a social magnet since arriving here.

But there was one last one he had to consider. One that was both difficult and painful.

Candy.

What had he called her? A hot-sex Rubric's cube?

That characterization was more ironic than clever. The kind of thing you say when you are so totally awed and so completely dumbfounded, you don't know what to say.

He couldn't figure her out at all. Or what would happen. She had been there with him and for him, ever since they first met. With perfect consistency, she handled him now the way she always had. She slapped him up one side and down the other with her sarcasm, probed and prodded him with her delicious humor, thought-provoking insights and sharp-witted scrutiny, entertained and cajoled him, mocked yet seemed to admire him, and last but not least had fucked his eyes out. For sure, the fucking-his-eyes-out part would stop after they chopped and channeled Billy into female form.

Would their friendship survive?

If it didn't, there was no doubt in his mind. It would be a real loss.

Then again, loss seemed to be the one thing he could count on these days. That seemed to be the way the deck was stacked. Every gain seemed to entail some major sacrifice.

It was not like he had the choice. It appeared to be an immutable law.

So then what? Candy or no Candy, what was next?

Maybe he'd have to start a whole new life — new friends, new hangouts, new everything. Perhaps he'd become a regular at Strange Love, or Tunnel of Love, or he'd have to open his own club called T-Girl Love or Post-Op Paradise.

So perhaps a clean slate. A completely fresh start. A new lease on life.

On the surface, this was a very appealing prospect.

Candy broke his reverie.

"Hey, Billy. You're awfully quiet."

"You've got it backwards. You're quiet for a change. So for once you happened to notice I am quiet most of the time."

"What's eating you?"

"Nothing. Nothing out of the ordinary."

"That's a scary thought."

He and Candy were on their way to something. What was it? A mystery event. The posters for whatever it was were everywhere.

?

Friday March 27th
8:30 pm
Trinity School
Main Ballroom
139 West 91st Street

Now really. How could he resist? Question marks were the snowflakes of his winter of discontent.

Conveniently, whatever this **?** might be was taking place right across Central Park from his luxury apartment. The taxi took only minutes to get there and drop them at the entrance gate of Trinity School in the Upper West Side.

For an event which was shrouded in such mystery, it certainly was well-attended. Either curiosity got the best of a lot of people or they knew something Billy didn't. Probably the latter. In any case, the place was packed.

When they walked into the huge ballroom, it was almost like walking into a planetarium. Except that instead of stars, the walls and ceilings were covered with four-inch squares of paper on which were printed a single question mark. The walls themselves were shrouded in black and the only light came from numerous black light fixtures. The effect was the infinite depth of space with question marks floating above and around them everywhere.

To put it mildly, it was an overpowering and surrealistic environment for Billy, Candy, and the hundreds of people milling around, gazing upwards in awe and anticipation.

As 8:30 pm approached, low ambient music started to build in volume and intensity. Slowly, hypnotic down-tempo rhythms filtered in — African drums, tablas, chimes, finger cymbals.

It had a familiar feel. Billy turned to Candy and whispered.

"Is this who I think it is?"

"Definitely not the Arctic Monkeys."

His answer came only a few minutes later.

At the stage end of the ballroom, the curtains swept apart. Massive banks of lights came on.

Apocalypso stood to one side at the top of a tall slender columnar pedestal. Seven musicians were arrayed on the opposite side, and were jamming away with subdued abandon.

Apocalypso was naked except for a loincloth. His eyes were closed and he had a slight smile. He stood perfectly erect but his hands and arms were spread slightly as he reached toward the audience in a beatific gesture of sharing. It could have only been by design that the first thing that came to mind looking at him was Jesus Christ on the cross.

An enormous white billboard took up the entire length of the wall behind him and the musicians. It was brilliantly lit by huge powerful arc lamps.

?

**AMERICA IS THE RICHEST COUNTRY IN THE WORLD.
WHY DO SO FEW HAVE SO MUCH?
WHY DO SO MANY HAVE SO LITTLE?**

When the full impact of the message had sufficiently wowed and wooed the audience, the music tempered and faded. A simple announcement came over the massive P.A. system.

> *Please each take one or more of the fliers from the walls.*
> *On the reverse side is a message of hope.*
> *Please give what you can.*
> *Blessings.*

The music started again, over which could be heard some sort of chant. It seemed to make no sense but Billy was still curious.

"Hey, Candy. What are they saying?"

"I was trying to figure that out. Maybe ... *Who's the cause sir, who's the cause sir, itty bitty head with a pig from Chaucer*. What do you think?"

"It sounds like a fight cheer from my high school in Detroit. *Ooh sa sa sa, ooh sa sa sa, hit 'em in the head with a big kielbasa*. We were very spiritual."

"I think maybe you're right. Hey! You never told me you were Polish."

Billy and Candy walked purposefully with the rest of the audience to the sides of the room. Each reached up and grabbed from the wall one of the fliers with a **?** on it.

On the back was a simple message:

We can right what is wrong.
To love is to change without fear.

Many people stayed for what was probably going to be a love-in rave on the order of what he and Candy experienced in Tribeca a year ago. He and Candy opted for a quiet evening alone, as opposed to the frenzied communal love fest getting underway. They headed for the exit.

As they walked out of the ballroom, they were approached by a number of young acolytes. Each was dressed in pure white monk robes cinched with a belt of machine gun bullets. They wore berets with the Ashram of the Urban Night logo.

Billy recognized one of them, in spite of the fact that a year's worth of growth had converted her previously shaved head into a shoulder-length pageboy. It was the young girl monk that had approached Billy the night of the first police raid.

She also remembered Billy.

"Glad to see you are still involved with our movement, sir."

"The only time anyone calls me 'sir' is when they're handcuffing me and putting me into the back seat of a squad car."

The girl looked puzzled but smiled.

"We would appreciate any support you can offer for our cause."

Billy wrote a check for $5,000 that night. It was the first of several generous contributions he made over the coming months to a cause he little understood, but somehow could now embrace with ease and confidence.

Another of his many prima facie contradictions?

The truth was much simpler. Billy was learning to live in the tight space between serendipity and impulse. He no longer felt the need to answer to anyone. Only himself. And he rarely asked questions.

He had internalized the message he needed to hear. The one on the back of the **?** leaflets.

He would right what was wrong.

He would love by embracing change without fear.

What could be simpler?

A thought brought a wry grin to the face of his private musings.

Maybe he was a girl after all. He was learning how to comfortably coexist with irrationality and inconsistency. He let his intuitions sweep aside the fog of his indecision and quandary.

He only needed some lipstick and he was there.

Ha ha! What a crazy fucker he had become!

Billy was quiet again, immersed in existential isolation for the taxi ride back to the East Side. Candy tuned into it and squeezed his hand.

"Still thinking about nothing out of the ordinary?"

"I guess. Can someone be overwhelmed and underwhelmed at the same time?"

"I hope so. That pretty much sums up my permanent state of being."

"I have so much to learn."

"And so little time."

"That's for sure."

Swarm Shoplifting

Billy and Candy never came close to agreeing on the legitimacy of Apocalypso, or whether his ideas had real potential to change things.

But neither did anyone else.

Of course, Candy was skeptical by nature, and Billy — punch-drunk from the blows he had taken over the past couple years, brain marinated by too much alcohol and too many drugs over a short time — was a house with all the doors and windows open. Receptive. Credulous. Easily impressed. Or maybe the right phrase was stupidly gullible.

While Billy seemed to miss or choose to overlook them, Apocalypso certainly did his share of highly dubious things, planting his own seeds of doubt. True, he was charismatic and seemingly visionary. But often he was eccentric to the point of distraction. Other times he was disarmingly predictable. Typical. Even pedestrian.

Candy went along with Billy just for laughs when he attended various Apocalypso events and gatherings. They certainly provided a lot of material for her stream of trenchant barbs and sarcastic commentary.

Interestingly, at one such occasion, it was Candy herself who was instrumental in Billy and Apocalypso becoming acquainted, beginning a relationship which would blossom into a distant but firm friendship over the next year.

The event was a community roundtable, an informal, open, town hall-style meeting for members of the Ashram of the Urban Night, and others sympathetic to its political agenda. This particular forum was being held to brainstorm about world peace and what individually could be done to move America and other truculent countries in a positive direction.

Billy, Candy, and Amethyst, who had decided at the last minute to come along, sat quietly in folding chairs toward the rear of the room.

A 30-something man with a burgeoning Karl Marx beard, wire-rim glasses, a wrinkled white dress shirt, threadbare camel sports jacket with worn leather elbow patches, black pants, white socks and brown penny loafers, stood at his seat. After he was handed a microphone, he began to speak. He sounded like he had a potato stuck in his throat or was the unfortunate victim of a tonsillectomy which had gone awry. He made everyone in the audience swallow.

"I say, as long as there is money to be made in weaponry, there will be war. People will be slaughtered to fatten the pocketbooks of the military industrialists."

He seemed to want to say more but changed his mind and sat back down.

A tall thin girl stood up to speak. She had wheat-blond hair done in dreadlocks, cinched with long strips of colored cloth, and was wearing tie-dyed pantaloons, an Indian wrap-around, and a long flowing purple scarf, adorned with peace symbols.

"Dude! That's so negative. If you send that kind of negative vibration into the world, then you're right. There will be no hope for peace. We have to believe deep in our hearts that peace is possible, and send positive vibrations out across the entire planet. It's the only way."

Most people in the room were too embarrassed to laugh. The notable and loud exception was Candy, who after a few seconds let out a big whoop before covering her mouth with both of her hands, which only muffled her unabated hysterical outburst.

After Candy let loose, more titters could be heard from the audience.

"What's so funny?" Miss Peace Hippie looked indignant.

Amethyst leaned over and whispered.

"If you put her brain in a seagull, it would fly backwards."

Another guy took the floor. He was dressed in camouflage, sported a Marine boot camp peach fuzz haircut, and looked one breath short of psychotic. But he was fairly articulate.

"Miss. You there who just got off the time machine from Haight-Ashbury 1968. Have you heard of Kim Jong il? Probably not. He's the maniacal dictator of North Korea who is trying to develop a nuclear weapon and a delivery system capable of dropping the big one on us. Do you think good vibes are a prudent defense against nuclear bombs?"

The hippie girl tilted her hips to put all her weight on one leg, then fluffed her tangled hair to admit more air to the region in and around her cranium. She brought forward both her hands, palms up in a gesture of compassionate supplication, then offered another bouquet of wisdom to the skinheaded, real politik soldier.

"You just keep thinking all those doomsday negative thoughts and it will happen. Because that is the reality you are creating. One full of death and destruction. And I hate to break it to you. But by thinking that way ..." She now pointed at him accusingly. "... it means you are on his side. That Kim dude."

The exasperation on military man's face was like a bad sunburn.

"I'm helping him by thinking bad thoughts? Lady! What fairy tale did you step out of?"

She was resolutely beyond being flustered, convinced she had the higher moral ground. Her innocent face beamed with the Dalai Lama's smile, but unfortunately lacked his intelligence and savoir faire. She now expanded on the ethical model she had lay the groundwork for.

"There are two forces in the world. The force of good, which is the light of the Universe, and the force of evil, which is the darkness. To drive away the darkness is simply a matter of bringing light into the world. Thinking negative thoughts keeps the world a dark and evil place. Thinking positive thoughts floods the world with light. Fills it with all of the potential good. So you need to choose. Whose side are you on?"

"No. I think you need to choose. Whether to live in some infantile fantasy world, or to join the rest of us here in the harsh acid bath of reality."

Someone shouted from the back of the room.

"Lady. Your lights may be on but nobody's home."

"How many hippie chicks does it take to screw in a light bulb?"

There were a few more titters and at least one loud guffaw. But hippie chick if anything seemed emboldened by the heckling. She just shook her head and looked in the direction the remarks came from and smirked condescendingly. She rolled her eyes, curled her tongue to the roof of her mouth, then glared at her opponents in utter disbelief at their ignorance.

Apocalypso had been the silent moderator until now. He stood up and came forward.

"For us to reach a collective understanding of how the world got to be in the shape its in, requires all of us to be open and receptive to the ideas of others. Personally attacking or ridiculing a person isn't going to get us there."

He walked over and put his arm around her.

"Astrid here has been attending my deep spiritual exploration workshops, and by working closely with me one-on-one, has achieved a very high level of metaphysical connectedness. Consequently, she is able to rise above the myriad of confusing and contradictory details of the mundane, and access certain larger truths."

Candy.

"Is one of those larger truths in your pants?"

Apocalypso's demeanor changed not one whit. The guy must be bulletproof. Great actor and consummate showman that he was, he betrayed no vulnerability or guilt — though he had been banging this young girl and drawing money out of her bank account for well over a year. He just looked at Candy and smiled, as if her remark could only come from some pathetic, unenlightened creature who was so incognizant and unevolved, she was only capable of pole dancer polemics and locker room humor.

Hippie chick immediately came to his defense.

"Now that is *really* negative. I wouldn't want your karma, that's for sure."

"And I wouldn't want his semen sloshing around in me. So I guess we're both where we want to be."

Apocalypso jumped back in to save face and hopefully assert some control over the tone and direction of the discussion.

"The monks of Tibet over hundreds of years of rigorous and disciplined asceticism and constant prayer, have sent out more good vibrations in the form of millions of mantras, than there are pebbles on the beach. These mantras are a call for compassion toward our fellow man, such that we may live in peace and harmony. Certainly no harm has come of this and they offer great inspiration to the rest of us who so desperately struggle to keep from sinking in the quicksand of our own ingenuity and becoming mired in the homicidal urges of our violent nature. But the admirable dedication of these monks hasn't been enough to keep the world from being at war with itself. As the two gentlemen pointed out, prayers and good feelings are no defense against the brutishness of some madmen in the world, nor will they deflect the course of the 20,000 plus nuclear weapons in the world. I'm of the mind that it is the confluence of both awarenesses that will prevent catastrophe, and eventually move mankind to a phase where the intentional destruction of human life becomes inconceivable."

He then turned the tables on the two who had nailed hippie chick, the Karl Marx guy and the psycho with the boot camp hairdo. Apocalypso asked them pointedly what their specific ideas were for preventing nuclear holocaust and establishing a reign of everlasting peace.

Of course they had none.

It was a cheap but effective shot. Both were humbled. Apocalypso's sweet young thing appeared to be somewhat vindicated and now carried away the master's implicit endorsement to continue babbling hopelessly naive nonsense.

For a while after this confrontation, the discussion seemed to wander without much focus. Apocalypso then closed the meeting with a simple prayer.

*"As we seek peace within ourselves, so must
we bring peace to the world."*

Refreshments were served — punch, cookies, cheese and crackers. Billy, Candy and Amethyst hung around a few more minutes to munch.

Amethyst made it clear she was not coming to any more of the ashram events.

"Sorry guys. This isn't for me. I'm just not feeling the love."

As she was finishing her remark, Apocalypso came up next to her, smiled graciously, then looked directly at Billy and Candy, who were in the midst of savoring shortbread cookies.

"Excuse me. I don't think we've met. You are?"

"Candy."

"You've got a great sense of humor, Candy. Right for the juggler. There's a place for you here, if you'd like to join our movement."

Apocalypso's cool caught Candy off guard. She would have expected him to try to rip her a new birth canal for her remarks. But here he was smiling, trying to recruit her.

"Do you have a swimming pool? I like to take a nice swim after clusterfucking the hearts and minds of my fellow comrades in training."

Apocalypso made a quick and not very discrete survey of Candy's physical assets.

"I don't suppose a hot tub would do. Not that we have one."

"You're a dreamer."

"Dreams are the wheat germ of heavenly bread."

"Do you always talk in stilted clichés?"

"Only on the third Saturday of the month."

It was the third Saturday of April.

He turned to Billy.

"You look familiar."

"I've been to a few of these things. Billy Green."

"Billy Green! Finally a face to go with the checks. You have been very generous with us."

"It seems like the right thing to do."

"If you're open to it, we should get together and talk. You're the biggest single contributor to the ashram, so you have a large financial stake in our success. I'd like to get your ideas. Your input."

"Right on, brother. I'll have my secretary call your secretary."

"Are you coming to The Donner Party?"

Billy was familiar with the inglorious occurrence of cannibalism known as the Donner Party which took place back in 1846. But he couldn't begin to imagine what the context was here. He looked uncomprehendingly at Apocalypso.

Candy jumped in.

"Are we talking about already dead people or are you slaughtering them fresh? I hate getting carved up and served to strangers."

Apocalypso seemed to be enjoying himself. He laughed a hearty laugh.

"It's a fundraiser. The Donner Party allusion is purely allegorical. No human hamburgers. You'll see. Come by. Both of you. It's next Wednesday. It's over on the West Side at the Desmond Tutu Center on 10th Avenue. There are fliers over there."

He pointed at a card table with various organizational pamphlets next to the door.

With that, he moved on to meet and greet the twenty or so others still lingering about, eating the munch and drinking the punch.

Amethyst was obviously getting impatient, so they called it a night.

Billy and Candy went to the Donner Party fundraiser the following week. Though Billy continued to generously support Apocalypso's activities, and sometime down the line would meet with him privately, this would be his last attendance at one of the public functions.

They arrived a little late and things were well under way. The place was packed out with New York's hipeoisie and neo-libs — a lot of new money, much of it credit card wealth.

This was a much classier function than any Billy had seen before. People were well-dressed, not expensively formal, but expensively casual. It was being held in a sizable facility that had splendid architecture and had been decked out to appeal to the upscale tastes of the potential benefactors.

Waiters circulated through the crowd with trays of cocktails, chilled rosé and white wine, and pricey imported beer. Everyone seem to be well on their way to feeling good. There was a general air of easy cheer and self-congratulatory camaraderie. The more than two hundred attendees, lubricated by the alcohol and filled with their own importance, stole glances at one another to see who was who at the event. They stood and milled around in front of a raised stage, and surrendered the minimum requisite attention to what was happening on the podium.

The MC was a John Lennon wannabe who must have had Plastic Ono Band posters all over his bedroom to make sure he got it right, before he ever left his cockroach-infested flat. As he stood at the podium which had been set up on a small stage at one end of the posh reception space, it looked like he was jacked up on something, maybe cocaine or speed or maybe just himself. His head kept bouncing up and down like a bearded dashboard happy face, as he reveled in his ten minutes of leading the revolution.

> *"Why, you ask. Why choose such an infamous and abhorrent historical incident as the theme for this fundraiser? What has the Donner Party got to do with the noble and necessary work of this ..."*

With a sweep of his hand he dramatically took in Apocalypso and his monk militia, who stood behind him on the podium.

> *"... admirable group of forward-thinking revolutionaries? Well, let me explain. It's actually quite simple. Capitalism is cannibalism."*

A muted cheer and sprinkling of applause briefly erupted.

> *"In its destructive, pointless and ultimately futile pursuit of more-better-faster, capitalism is eating the human race. It is eating the future. It is biting off, chewing up, and spitting out the old and infirm. It is feeding on the young, devouring their minds, fattening them up in so-called institutions of learning, which are nothing more than meat farms, so it can swallow them and their lives whole, slowly digest them as it moves them over the length of their life spans through the intestinal tract of consumerist slavery, then shit them out into numbered graves after an unsatisfying and fruitless 78.8 years of pursuing the non-existent American Dream."*

A few people cleared their throats. Most grimaced at the imagery. Lennon look-alike took this as a unanimous assent. Inspired by the imagined adoration of the crowd, he continued.

> *"And who are these capitalists? I'll tell you who. They are you and you ..."*

He jabbed both index fingers accusingly at the crowd.

> *"...and you and you and me. That's who. None of us want it this way. But we have been given no choice. Every other alternative, every other system — socialism, communism, agrarianism, socialist democracy — has been maligned. By default, and through no choice of our own, we are the capitalists and we*

*have been conscripted into the armies who devour and destroy
all that is good and hopeful and righteous. We are consuming
ourselves to death."*

Lennon-impersonator had mixed so many metaphors, and had so many distracting, off-putting mannerisms, people were — despite their best efforts to remain tuned in and on message — having trouble following him. He, on the other hand, was getting so worked up, he had spittle in the corners of his mouth and the lower half of his beard. He forged ahead.

*"Yes, it is all of us who perpetuate the feeding orgy, the outrage
of consumerist cannibalism."*

With this last pejorative it was becoming apparent that some in the audience frankly did not like what they were hearing. They didn't come here to be berated by some unwashed pseudo-insurrectionist about their shopping habits.

*"I say, STOP! Stop being part of the problem! Start being part of
the solution!"*

And?

*"You all have enough. We all have enough. You don't need any
more, especially if it is in reality just corporately raised meat,
packaged and tailored to make your gums water and your mind
think it's about happiness."*

Was this guy talking about everyone becoming vegetarians?

*"Say no to the false feast of profit. No more human meat for the
corporate grist mills."*

Throat clearing and a lot of shifting signaled the collective wish that he really should get to the point or shut up.

Bad Lennon-imitator mercifully was coming to the climax of the oration he had spent weeks honing to sophomoric imperfection.

*"Dig deep! Let's get this message out. Dig deep! We will
triumph and the human race will escape becoming more
hamburger for the corporate meat packing plants. Dig deep! I
say, dig deep! My friends, dig deep! Thank you!"*

Lennon-facsimile gave the V peace sign with both hands and backed away from the microphone, face beaming and hands still high in the air.

The audience, relieved that this histrionic ordeal was apparently over, responded with what to anyone who had just walked in would judge to be an enthusiastic round of applause and appreciative cheering. It was heavy-lifting to keep it going but worth the energy to keep him from coming back and saying any more, so it went on for almost a minute. Plus they did on some level support the message, even if they didn't resonate with this particular messenger.

While the audience clapped, post-Beatle Lennon-clone turned around and riding the adrenalin wave of what he imagined was an oratorical triumph, vigorously pumped the hands of and gave big show-biz hugs to Apocalypso and whoever else was within reach. They reciprocated with cool politeness, trying to hide their embarrassment at being on stage with such a pathetic spokesperson, for what they all believed was a momentous, history-altering cause.

Billy got it. The college of life, as well as university itself, had given him the necessary tools to easily cut through the layers of incoherence and rescue the kernel of cogency. Somewhere in the barrage of excess verbiage — the meat and gristle imagery he had just endured — was the *message*. They realistically could have dispensed with the speech entirely, because its essence was adequately and succinctly summed up in a huge banner that was stretched across the length of one wall of the room. The same motto was printed on thousands of bumper stickers available for the taking in boxes throughout the hall, assuming you had a bumper or some publicly visible flat place to stick it.

WE ARE CONSUMING OURSELVES INTO EXTINCTION!

To leave no stomach unturned, there was yet another whole level of on-message *visual* pugilism, driving home the evening's Donner Party theme.

All along the walls was a highly graphic installation of painted plaster sculptures which allegorically depicted the eating habits of corporate capitalism. Renoir Albertine Toulouse was first contacted to add his artistic vision to the cause, but he was too busy doing several major steel-and-copper abstracts and lobby reliefs for the G E Capital financial services headquarters in Stamford, CT, an assignment that would make him quite wealthy but from then on, a pariah of the left wing and the radical art chic. Second choice, and the artist whose works were on display this evening, was an upcoming highly controversial female artist, Isabel Frankot, who preferred just to be called Chaos. The press never got it right. She was Chaos Frankot and Isabel Chaos, but only rarely just Chaos. People already had so much chaos in their lives, there must have been an allergic aversion to the singular moniker.

Chaos had captured with little room for misinterpretation the message for the fundraiser. Skeletons dressed in business suits with labels like ...

Big Money

Corporate Capitalism

The Rich and Power-Mad Politicians

... were portrayed eating ordinary citizens of all ages. Tearing off their limbs, biting into their necks, ripping open their rib cages and sucking out their innards. All of the grotesqueness and gore that money could buy was there to goad the well-healed audience into parting with their greenbacks. It was *Night of the Living Dead* garnished with Tim Burton's *Nightmare Before Christmas*. There were even sound effects. Screaming and pleading. Gurgling of blood. Women yelling out, *"No! Don't take my baby!"* and men bellowing, *"If you kill me, who will feed my family?"*

It was sophomoric and laughable but no one was laughing. There seemed to be general agreement among those whose general agreement was solicited for such rising stars in the art world, that Chaos was the next big thing.

The man of the hour was about to give his speech. Shaking hands with everyone on his way to the microphone, then at the front of the stage, strutting like he was a rock star or the Pope, Apocalypso appeared to be in good spirits. He was smiling and waving like he was the substitute host for the Tonight Show, ready to give his opening monologue. Clearly he had come a long way from the rough-and-tumble school of the street, and had evolved dramatically over the past year-and-a-half from the solemn, self-effacing spiritual guru Billy had seen back then, to a high-powered, charismatic, rabble rousing icon, spit-shined with a patina of photo-op glimmer.

> *"Thank you for being here. Each and every one of you. I'm going to make this short and to the point. You put up the money and we'll take down the enemy. That's it. Around the room you will see a number of my donor party girls. That's 'donor', not 'Donner', so you don't have to worry about getting eaten."*

Lots of laughs for that one. Apocalypso was such a charmer.

> *"We take cash, real or counterfeit, pledges, even Visa and MasterCard."*

Hoots and hollers at the blatant capitulation to the system.

> *"Hey, folks. We do what we have to do. We're using their own weapons against them. Anyway, just walk up to one of these charming ladies, conveniently underdressed in red lingerie, and do your part. Like I said. You put up the money and we'll take down the enemy. Thanks again. Have a good time!"*

Waving and enjoying the enthusiastic applause, he stepped down from the dais and started to make the rounds. Apocalypso was a thorough and potent diplomat, personally letting each person he stopped and talked to, individually know how much he appreciated their attending tonight's fundraiser, and how valuable their support was to the cause.

It was definitely a high-roller affair. The checks poured in that night.

As soon as Apocalypso saw Billy, he brought a conversation he was having with a couple of East Hampton revolutionaries to a tidy ending, and rushed over. He stepped up to Billy with a Wall Street trader smile and his hand outstretched, poised for a firm and welcoming grip.

"Billy, good to see you. And Candy. Thanks for coming."

"I always love a good barbecue."

Billy reached into his pants pocket.

"I'm not one to beat around the bush. You'll get no flattery here. Your speech was fine. This fundraiser is crap. Here's a check for ten grand."

"Thanks again, Billy. Every little bit helps."

"Little bit?"

"Just an expression. Yes. Big bit. This is very generous of you. By the way, pardon me for asking, but I am still not entirely clear what it is you do for a living."

"Nothing except keeping my heart beating and my mind elsewhere. I guess you could say that I am a well-compensated failure. Except I'm as pissed-off as you are."

"I believe you. We all should be. So what are you pissed off about?"

"Everything is for sale. Consumerism has no conscience. Capitalism has no soul. Life sucks. It's every man for himself. Nobody's paying attention. Uncle Sam is Wall Street's lapdog. The rich are ruining the country. Kids are being educated to shop. God is dead."

"Except for that last item, we're all over it. Seriously, Billy. We're on this. It's all going to change."

"That remains to be seen. It won't be easy. Good luck, though."

"Keep the faith. Keep sending money."

They came late and left early. Candy had no complaints. It was what it was.

They marched out to hail a taxi.

Billy understood the need for these affairs. It was all about funding and visibility. But they were annoying. For the most part it was preaching to the choir.

Tonight was particularly bad. Tonight the choir was tone deaf-and-dumb. A bunch of rich, pseudo-progressives who would go home to their theater-size flat panel televisions, drink key lime martinis, check their stock portfolios on the internet, order new batches of fresh-cut flowers for their million-dollar condos, and sleep soundly in the knowledge they had thrown some money at changing the world.

Though he couldn't say it publicly — and didn't even share it with his closest confidants in the organization — Apocalypso now pretty much felt the same way. The fat cats were a necessary evil, a lucrative source of support, but only a steppingstone to more ultimate game-changing tactics. Just like he told the audience tonight. They would write the checks. Now he would change the world.

Or at least try.

Now he needed to figure out how to move it all forward. What was next?

For a long time, during what would be considered the nascent years of his ashram, he had dedicated himself to a hands-on, highly personal approach to building the organization, demonstrating his skills as an orator, organizer and spiritual leader, all in relatively intimate settings. Ad infinitum, he presented his ideas and slowly drew more people into the movement, inspiring them to contribute their time and money. The meditation sessions, mantra convocations, various metaphysical and political workshops, forums, town hall meetings, and entire range of fundraising events, had allowed him to build a sizable and loyal grass-roots following. With the resulting funding and a fair share of publicity, he was steadily able to spread his message to a curious and increasingly receptive broader audience.

But after more than two years, these small-scale events were becoming tedious.

Though he still did them — and certainly from the outside he looked like he was giving every public appearance his best — his heart really wasn't in it, and ultimately would not be where his real genius would show.

He wanted to move mountains, not just push around little piles of dirt.

With the confrontations he had had a year ago with the police and the poster campaign he had put together to harass and mock the public authorities, he had found the key.

Carefully orchestrated acts of outrage and street theater held the promise of reaching the many millions of people Apocalypso needed to reach, if he were to start making significant changes in both the public's consciousness and in the way things got done.

The initial stage of his new five-year plan he called Militant Meditation. This was just the first step on a path. Apocalypso knew exactly where that path would eventually lead.

Guerrilla warfare.

It would, however, be a different type of guerrilla warfare. No animals or humans would be harmed or killed. There would be no guns, grenades, rockets, or violent confrontations.

But it would ultimately be no less dramatic or spectacular.

It would grab the headlines, enrage the authorities, shake the pillars of power, and grab the imagination of the public. It would make good on Apocalypso's personal promise ...

"It's all going to change."

Almost immediately after the Donner Party, Billy started to see evidence of how the money accumulated at several recent fundraisers was going to be spent, and more importantly the new shape of Apocalypso's strategy.

The first sign was the introduction of hard-hitting, but simple and clear, issue posters.

The whole world — at least the majority of Americans — seemed to like their truths packaged in short sound-bites. Apocalypso's posters, printed in the thousands and plastered on every available vertical surface in all four boroughs, gave them exactly what they wanted.

They became the talk of the town. Beautifully designed with stark, eye-catching graphics. Amazing photos which without fail elicited some extreme reaction — laughter, tears, pity, rage. Aesthetically, they were as good as any of the print ads the top advertising agencies in America — most of them based right there in Manhattan — produced to sell the myriad of unessential products Americans were supposed to buy and buy, until they had emptied their wallets and savings accounts, and maxed their credit cards.

By contrast, Apocalypso's campaign didn't create false cravings for things, didn't wreak havoc with people's self-esteem, didn't promote the lie that the solution to all life's problems was to buy more stuff, didn't foist any products whatsoever on anyone, didn't cram anyone's brimming households with more useless junk, didn't inundate their over-medicated bodies with even more pharmaceuticals, and most importantly, didn't cost anyone a single dime.

Ideas are free.

The only thing it urged people to do was to think.

To question the status quo.

The first poster was a reiteration of the theme for the ? event Billy and Candy had attended at Trinity School at the end of March.

AMERICA IS THE RICHEST COUNTRY IN THE WORLD.
WHY DO SO FEW HAVE SO MUCH?
WHY DO SO MANY HAVE SO LITTLE?

Subsequent posters built on the controversy stirred by this initial shot.

Everything is for sale.

Consumerism has no conscience.

Capitalism has no soul.

A nation of zombies?

It's every man for himself.

God is dead. God bless America!

The government is Wall Street's lap dog.

Is your child learning how to think or how to shop?

They definitely had a very familiar ring to Billy. He had to smile as he saw them appear one-by-one over the next year. It felt good to be taken seriously.

The issue posters were actually just a set up. Each was designed to lay the groundwork for what was to follow.

These would be acts of civil disobedience and other high-visibility pranks — funny, weird, outrageous, both economic and political — which would unfold over the coming weeks and months.

For example, the first poster, referring to the extreme imbalance of wealth in the country, the scale of which had grown exponentially since the Reagan presidency, was followed by a sensational series of guerrilla warfare-style incidents over two weeks. It was effectively a loud public outcry and call to action, urging the marginalized have-nots to take what they thought they deserved from the rapacious haves.

It was called swarm shoplifting.

Swarm shoplifting consisted of a large number of people — a swarm — going into a store and on cue quickly filling their bags and pockets with everything in reach, then exiting en masse. The whole exercise usually unfolded in under a minute.

The sheer numbers of shoplifters, and their deftness, speed and efficiency, made it nearly impossible to defend against.

Apocalypso's troops — he called them the Klepto Kommandos — never raided local single-entrepreneur shops. They always hit corporate chain stores.

The first few, as much training runs for the bigger targets later, were small to medium size convenience stores like 7-11, CVS Pharmacy, Walgreens, and Mini Mart.

The drill was pretty much the same for the first several hits. Depending on the floor space of the store, ten to twenty-five "shoppers" slipped into the store as casually and inconspicuously as possible. Either when the second hand on the clock reached a designated time, or when a cue was given — whistling Madonna's hit song "Material Girl" was a popular choice — the Kommandos would go into action. Pulling plastic bags out of their hand bags or back packs, they would start stuffing them full of everything that would fit. Then thirty to sixty seconds later, they would all head for the door at once and make a clean getaway, dispersing in the street in every direction.

There were guards posted at these stores. But they were helpless to do anything. First of all, they were overwhelmed by the sheer number of shoplifters manning the invasion. Second, most of the guards were either old or fat, or old *and* fat, just trying to add a few pennies to their meager social security or pension checks. Or they were wimpy pencil-necks who were unqualified to get any other minimum wage job. In either case these guards were not exactly the stuff of heroes. Usually, none of the guards had ever had to do much more than prevent a teenager who was caught stealing beer or candy, from leaving the premises until the real police came. So they sure as hell weren't going to risk their neck in some pseudo-valiant, completely impossible stand-off with an efficient and ruthless army of professional thieves.

And what was the clerk behind the counter supposed to do, other than gawk in utter amazement at the quantity of stuff being hauled out the door? Was he supposed to pull out a gun and start shooting strangers over boxes of crackers, Q-tips, Bic pens, wine coolers, Pringles, microwaveable popcorn, tooth paste? No one had pulled a weapon or in any other way threatened him. He couldn't claim self-defense. If he blasted away over a few bags full of sundries, he would be sent away to the slammer on a life sentence for murder.

All of the stores had security cameras. But the Kommandos disguised themselves well, kept their faces turned away, and were in no danger of being identified.

On the other hand, the film footage of the raids played well on TV.

Really well.

It was a doozy of a story, the stuff of modern urban legends. Everyone who was anyone in terms of reporting news, was all over it. During the first week alone, there were nearly twenty such attacks. The nightly news had a heyday, playing the video tapes one after the other, and speculating as to why such a rash of broad-daylight robberies were cropping up. No one had much sympathy for the stores themselves and the whole thing played out as some sort of urban-life comedy piece, or contemporary Robin Hood street theater. In some twisted way, it was a public relations bonanza for the underdogs of the country.

Apocalypso couldn't have asked for better publicity. Not that anyone knew he was behind the raids. But it created excitement and anticipation for the next stage of the swarm shoplifting scheduled for the following week.

This round was for much much bigger stakes and targeted high-end chains of retail outlets.

They hit one each day starting on Monday. The Klepto Kommando squads numbered over forty for each of the first five strikes. Considering the size of the stores and the number of regular shoppers, they were easily dispersed and blended in well with the regular shoppers.

The raiding squads carefully went over the plan for each assault, synchronized their watches, then spread throughout the targeted buildings. Each commando carefully noted the time it took to get to and from whatever floor and department he or she was working. At a designated time, all would "shop" for at least one minute, the ones closer to the exit a little longer, then they would make their hasty retreat. They all had to arrive at the same exit door at the same time for their escape to be successful. Timing was critical, otherwise one or more might end up apprehended by the security guards. But as long as they all got there all at once, they could overwhelm the posted guard or customer greeter, and bolt into the street, bags brimming with overpriced but high quality paraphernalia.

The first five raids went without a hitch: Barney's New York, Macy's, Lord & Taylor, Bergdorf Goodman, and Sak's Fifth Avenue, in that order.

Even the densest security expert could figure out which store was next. It was obvious.

Bloomingdale's would be the crowning achievement on a week's worth of praiseworthy pilfering.

Security at Bloomingdale's over the weekend was extremely high. Even the police beefed up their patrol of the streets around the world-famous 3rd Avenue store.

Apocalypso was again one up on all of these so-called experts. For one thing, there were three members of the ashram working at Bloomingdale's at the time of the raid. This gave him access to the floor plans for the entire store, and sufficient logistical support on Saturday, the day the swarm would descend on the building.

A literal army of security staff, some in uniforms, some in plain clothes but as visible as they would have been wearing a park ranger suit and sitting on a horse, formed their own swarm. It congregated around the entrances to the building, the elevator doors and escalators, while a small mobile force wandered all through the store, either talking on hand-held walkie-talkies, headsets, or into their lapels.

They constantly reported suspicious activity, resulting in a lot of innocent people getting shaken down in the basement security offices. By the time the Klepto Kommandos showed up, things had not been going very well for the Bloomingdale's home team. Tempers were frayed.

Apocalypso anticipating Bloomingdale's intense level of preparation and accurately anticipating the strategies they would employ, had created a stripped-down, altered game plan that worked like a charm.

First, he only had fifteen actual commandos. But each of them teamed with some "innocent bystander" who would not participate in the actual theft. Usually it was an older person, also a member of the ashram, conservatively dressed, looking matronly or paternal, thus drawing the least amount of suspicion to the pair. He or she and the younger commando would stroll into the Bloomingdale's East 60th Street entrance, appearing generally upstanding and trustworthy. The older accomplices would later walk out of the store the same way they came in, maybe even with a small purchased item in hand or complimentary gift bag, appearing quite the same as they had when arriving — upstanding and trustworthy.

The shoplifters, however, would leave by a different door. In fact, it was the door to the loading dock. Two of the ashram's male members worked that area, loading and unloading delivery trucks, checking in shipments of the tons of stuff that arrived, for stocking the huge store with the items Bloomingdale's shoppers expected to find on the nine floors of racks, shelves, counters, and displays.

Secondly, only three floors of the vast complex were targeted. They would be the women's exclusive fashions and accessories on the 2nd Floor, the trendy New Arrival boutiques on the 4th Floor, and beauty products and jewelry on the Main Floor. This meant that in each of these locations five commandos would be in close proximity, allowing them collectively to create a lot of chaos and confusion and get the job done, before security staff showed up from the other six floors. By then, the shoplifters would have filled their bags and be long gone.

The third member of the ashram team working at Bloomingdales, was a maintenance man with keys to the entire facility. He would make sure that the doors leading to the main service hallway were unlocked until the commandos were through them, and on their way to the shipping and receiving area. He would then lock the doors behind them, providing a helpful delay in case the security people figured out where the shoplifters were heading for their escape.

At precisely 6:52 pm, when a number of the security staff were taking a short break to eat some much needed dinner, the swarm swarmed. By 6:55 pm, they were heading down the Employees Only service hall. By 7:00 pm they were in the white delivery truck which had been waiting for them in the Bloomingdale's vendors-only loading zone. At 7:01 the truck was pulling out into the heavy midtown traffic.

That evening the TV news talking heads reported that the take from Bloomingdale's was estimated to be almost two million dollars. Not bad for three minutes work.

The total losses for all of the swarm shoplifting over two weeks were roughly in excess of three million dollars. These were the best guesses anyone could make. Hard figures were impossible to come by, because some of the stores had backlogged inventory registers.

Of course, three million dollars was a drop in the bucket in the big picture. But its symbolic value was inestimable. Day after day news reports of this unprecedented shift of goods into the hands of a bunch of renegades made it look like a much bigger deal than the absolute dollar amount would suggest. No matter what monetary value you assigned to the losses, it was redistribution of wealth in its most direct and brutal form, right from the coffers of the corporations into the hands of the arguably needy. It was as much a political as an economic statement. It set a new tone for things to come.

The two-week swarm shoplifting campaign, climaxing with substantial losses to the most prestigious department stores in Manhattan, had a side effect which even Apocalypso himself didn't anticipate.

This was a wave of copycat crime over the following months, this by common citizens insisting on their own little piece of the pie. The perpetrators ranged from middle class housewives to indigents, well-dressed professionals to college students, waiters, bellhops, bartenders, clerks, ticket takers, office works, taxi drivers, maids and butlers, off-duty security guards, delivery boys, greeters, hostesses, street vendors, school teachers, at least one member of the clergy, two Broadway musical dancers, and even an undisclosed number of the staff working for the city's own government bureaus and service agencies.

They would walk in, take something they wanted, then just try to walk out and leave.

Unfortunately, all were duly apprehended and prosecuted, and many with perfectly clean criminal records until then, ended up with a misdemeanor staining their police reports.

During arrest and arraignment all made similar statements. They demanded what they believed was rightfully theirs, paraphrasing the issue posters that had appeared all over town: America is the richest country in the world. It was high time for the few to share the wealth with the many.

Apocalypso didn't invent swarm shoplifting. But he did turn it into a powerful symbol of what needed to and could be done to start tipping the balance sheet back in favor of the have-nots. It was an extraordinary political statement and dramatic coup.

He knew where America's soft spot was.

To deliver a severe blow to the establishment, you aimed for the wallet.

It was always the wallet.

And it was basic economics. As the bottom lines of the greedy corporations and their wealthy patrons went down, other bottom lines would go up.

Ultimately all of the booty from Apocalypso's swarm shoplifting ended up at soup kitchens and various other community service agencies, one which served the poor in Harlem, Spanish Harlem, the South Bronx, Jamaica Queens, and the disadvantaged areas of Brooklyn. It was a bonanza for people who had never seen, much less worn designer label clothing, used kitchenware which cost more than their base annual income, applied the same cosmetics as Jennifer Lopez and Angelina Jolie, or wore imported silk shirts in European cuts and sizes.

Swarm shoplifting was abruptly halted after the Bloomingdale's raid. Over thirty successful raids had been conducted. The phenomenon made international headlines. But it had run its course.

There would be much more along these same lines ahead.

Apocalypso was just getting warmed up.

The serious fun was yet to come.

The Circle Game

Astronomy and astrology. How often they were in the public mind confused or conflated.

At least among dilettantes and dimwits. That was Billy's take on it.

Whew! He had such a bad attitude these days.

Maybe he was paranoid. Or unnecessarily judgmental. But it seemed like everyone these days was on the take, on the make, or inherently fake.

Including himself.

Amethyst was sitting in front of a computer in her latest living-work space, a crudely and only partially finished loft in Hell's Kitchen she shared with her band leader, Hypo. She was quick to repeatedly remind everyone that theirs was a purely platonic relationship.

She typed away and stared at the screen like it was a gateway into the mind of God.

"What's your sign, Billy?"

"No fuel for the next 27 miles."

Candy came to the rescue.

"He's a Sagittarius. December 18th, 1982. Am I right?"

"My father always said it was a cold day in Hell."

"It would have been cold day in Detroit, for sure."

"Hell. Detroit. Same thing."

"Okay. Now I need your time of birth."

"Head or feet? I think I was a breach baby."

"You are such a pain in the ass! All of it. When did they hold you up by your toes, declare mission accomplished and give you the whack on the butt?"

"1:24 pm, if memory serves me. I remember being hungry and wondering if the cafeteria was still serving lunch."

Amethyst glanced back over her shoulder at Candy.

"How do you put up with this?"

"You get used to it."

Hypo was on the other side of the room with an acoustic guitar strumming some chords. Billy wandered over and sat down.

"New song?"

"New but not ours. We decided to do a cover. It's the thing these days. Pick a tune by some half-remembered icon from the 70s or 80s, and do your own version of it."

"So what is it? It sounds familiar."

"It's 'The Circle Game' by Joni Mitchell. Ever heard of her?"

"Not really."

"Here's the original version she recorded back in pre-historic times."

Hypo reached over and hit the play button on his boom box. Immediately a beautiful melodic finger-picked guitar floated out over the speakers, joined by a brittle but enchanting female voice.

"Doesn't quite sound like Machines of Melanoma material."

Hypo turned the song off.

"We're very adaptable. Anyway, I'm just getting the basic feel of the song down. The chords and stuff. We're going into the studio in a couple days to lay it down."

"Good luck, my friend. I can't wait to hear it."

Billy got up and started to head for the kitchen area, just a corner of what was raw warehouse space. The kitchen contained a refrigerator, a two-burner propane stove, and an industrial strength stainless steel sink. It was absolutely no-frills living here in Hell's Kitchen. Punk asceticism.

"Hey Am. Got anything to drink?"

"Carrot juice. Spirulina and wheat grass tea. Is that what you had in mind?"

"I was more thinking along the lines of a beer. Ice cold and detrimental to my health."

"Thank God for 7-11. There's one about five blocks north of here. Knock yourself out. Before you leave, though, I've gotta show you this."

"It better be good. I'm headed into severe withdrawal."

"I know you're a busy guy. So let me just tease you with a few dazzling highlights. You sir, are as follows: You are calm and deliberate, but very stubborn. You can't be bullied or pressured into anything. Sometimes you are lazy and lacking motivation. You get stuck and have trouble overcoming inertia. Often it takes a good push from the outside to get you moving on something. Though you are fun loving, spirited and energetic—"

Candy couldn't let that get by.

"Fun loving? Are we talking about the same Billy Green here?"

"But because your sun is in 26° Sagittarius, you typically tend to avoid intimate relationships. And with your rising sign in 12° Taurus, you tend to be self-indulgent. Then again, because your moon is in 3° Aquarius, you always solve problems — including deeply emotional ones — with your brains and intellect, not your feelings."

"Fascinating. Wonderful. I think I've heard enough."

Amethyst could not be shut down that easily. She was on a roll.

"No! No, Billy! Really. It gets better. Oh oh! This is fucked up."

"What a surprise."

"Your Saturn is in 1° Scorpio. You tend to release emotional energies only very reluctantly. You are sometimes overwhelmed by your fear of what horrible calamity might occur if you were to let go — your emotions are terribly complicated and intense. Meaning you sometimes succumb to negative and destructive forms of compulsive behavior."

"Like listening to this garbage?"

"Your time of birth puts Uranus in 6° Sagittarius."

"What about my anus?"

"This is very positive, Billy. Now listen carefully. You have the tendency to think that all ideas, customs and traditions from the past are outmoded and irrelevant. You are attracted to radically new ideas, philosophies and religions that will, hopefully, cause sweeping changes throughout the world."

All of a sudden, Billy stood up looking impatient, almost angry.

"Does it mention anything about me being a hapless loser? Or a sorry hypocrite? A total fuckup? A mutant dickhead who can't figure his ass from a hole in the ground?"

Candy who had been listening quietly with an amused fascination suddenly looked shocked. She realized Billy wasn't joking.

"What's gotten into you?"

"Mirror mirror on the wall. Say listen. I'm going to head back. Amethyst. Rocker chick extraordinaire. Friend of the frustrated and feckless. Maybe we can pick up where you left off next time I see you. Seriously. I'm not dissing you. I'm just not in the mood. I know you're trying to help. That's a good thing. I appreciate it. Hey, Hypo!" Billy glanced over and fingered him. "Good luck with the new song. I'm out of here."

He headed out the door, not even waiting to see if Candy wanted to come along. She stayed.

When she stopped by the townhouse the next day, she found Billy distant, quiet, remote. There was virtually no conversation. But there was no hostility either. Billy just seemed very pre-occupied. Not quite there. She gave him the space he needed.

Candy wasn't sure what to make of this most recent episode of alienation. She never knew how serious or life-threatening any of his mood swings were. She certainly had learned to never take it personally. At the same time, this round she was concerned enough to spend most of her free time over the next few days with him. There was something different this time round.

What Billy had failed to mention — what he could share with absolutely no one — was an incident which happened the day before he and Candy stopped by at Amethyst's warehouse space for his impromptu astrology reading.

He had been running a little low on weed, literally was down to seeds and stems, and was completely out of Ativan, as of late his anxiolytic, amnesic, sedative/hypnotic, anticonvulsant, muscle relaxant of choice. So it was time to make a trip down to Washington Square to see the man with a plan.

With all of the money Billy had in the bank, he could easily have had any of the best quality prescription and illegal drugs delivered to him personally at his Upper East Side residence by an off-duty airline pilot dressed as Mary Poppins, singing a medley of Broadway all-time favorites.

But that wouldn't have been any fun.

He liked the adventure, the daring, the edginess of going to his favorite dealer's street mall and scoring just as he always had, often doing repeat business with the handful of sleazy suppliers he had become acquainted with, since arriving in New York. It was stupid and risky, but consistent with the rest of the nonsensicality of his life.

Today's score was effortless. He spotted C-Note, a black dude from the Bronx who always had exactly what Billy needed. Billy copped and cruised, strolling casually back to the taxi he had wait for him, while he "took care of some business."

It was on the way back uptown when it happened.

They were heading north on 5th Avenue, and had just turned east on 57th.

When he saw them.

Natalie and Pam. Natalie and Pam and their two kids.

Natalie was carrying a baby, and Pam was walking hand-in-hand with a dark-skinned boy. That must be the little Costa Rican kid Natalie said they were adopting.

Billy started beating frenetically on the thick Plexiglass separator between him and the driver.

"Stop!! Stop!!"

The driver nearly jumped through the roof of the taxi in reaction to the sudden pounding. Flustered and concerned that he had a lunatic on his hands, he hit the accelerator, while quickly scanning the crowded mid-town streets for a beat cop or patrol car. Usually they were in abundance in this area of town.

"Please stop! I want to get out here."

Billy pulled a couple of twenties out of his wallet and waved them at the driver. The old man spotted them in the rear-view mirror and instantly hit the brakes. He wanted to get paid and get rid of Billy as quickly and expeditiously as possible.

Billy was out of the taxi and throwing the twenties at the driver before the car even had come to a complete stop. One of the twenties ended up on the street and the driver scrambled to recover it, as Billy went running frantically back in the direction they had just come from.

When he got to the intersection, he had run more than four blocks and was completely out of breath. Natalie and Pam no where in sight.

He slumped down on the sidewalk to rest and collect himself. Panting and frustrated.

What had he hoped to achieve? What was the point of running after them the way he did? What would he have said? He couldn't make any sense out of his own wild and impulsive reaction, but at the same time was thoroughly pissed off that they had gotten away.

He walked home from there, still on the lookout for any signs of them but increasingly aware that the odds of spotting them were slim and none.

By the time he had covered 35 blocks and stepped into the lobby of his building, he had become painfully aware of how much hurt, anger, resentment, jealousy, bitterness, and enmity, he was still harboring over the breakup with Natalie. He quickly concluded that something had to change. He had managed to repress it all, bury it deep inside, and make believe all of it was behind him. But it was obvious he had been kidding himself. It was still there, like a cancer eating him from the inside. He had not broken with this sordid, humiliating period of his life. It was what was holding him back, and he really needed to do something about it.

It was this random encounter that had been eating him during his last visit with Candy to Amethyst's pad, and ever since.

And the simple truth was, though he thought astrology was a big pile of kaka, a lot of what Amethyst said to him that day had gratingly and painfully hit the nail right on the head.

Sometimes you are lazy and lacking motivation.

Whew! He got tired just thinking about it.

You get stuck and have trouble overcoming inertia.

No shit, Sherlock!

You are sometimes overwhelmed by your fear of what horrible calamity might occur if you were to let go — your emotions are terribly complicated and intense. Meaning you sometimes succumb to negative and destructive forms of compulsive behavior.

Guilty as charged.

You are attracted to radically new ideas …

If you only knew!

At Candy's suggestion, she and Billy dropped by Amethyst's again a week later. Actually Amethyst had called her and begged them to come by as soon as possible.

She was stoked. They had just come from the final studio mixing session of "The Circle Game", the song Hypo was working on the last time they were there.

When Billy and Candy stepped in the door, it had just finished playing. Amethyst was running around, jumping up and down with excitement. They had never seen her so crazed — offstage anyway.

"Hypo! Dude! Play it again!"

She ran over and herded them right next to the boom box.

"Wait until you hear this, guys!"

They should have waited.

MOM's version of the Joni Mitchell folk classic sounded like a thousand rabid pit bulls unleashed on a classroom of school children, only through a cell phone with a bad connection. Again, Amethyst's vocal performance — and Billy thought she was an amazing singer from what he could tell when he actually could hear her — was buried back in the mix, playing fourth fiddle to the band, electronic hiss, and the street noise that leaked into the primitive studio they had used.

Amethyst jumped and danced and sang along like she was possessed. She careened around the entire open area of the loft until the song ended.

"Ohmigod! It's so fucking dope!"

She staggered back over to where Billy and Candy were sitting, drenched in sweat, panting.

"Whew! So guys. What did you think?"

Candy didn't know what to think. Or if she did, she kept it to herself.

Billy reached deep for something to say.

"Interesting. Is this a new direction for you?"

"Well, guitars still reign. But we are integrating some electronic elements. Loops and digital samples. We're not quite sure how this will work live. But you have to go with your artistic vision. You know?"

"To love is to change without fear."

Amethyst looked at him like he was stark raving mad.

"Billy. Sometimes you are one weird motherfucker. Anyway, I say we celebrate!"

The four of them — Billy, Candy, Amethyst, and Hypo — all agreed that this called for some serious splurging, so they headed for the legendary Landmark Tavern nearby on 11th Avenue.

Because he felt a little guilty about hating the new Machines of Melanoma production so much — even if he hadn't actually said so — and because by their standards he was disgustingly rich, Billy volunteered to pick up the entire tab for the late afternoon celebration.

The main dining room of the Landmark was ultra-formal, so they stayed in the bar. Soon the table was filled with Irish bangers and mash, shepherds pie, spicy chicken wings, and beer-battered fish and chips.

For drinks they kept their elbows on the table and worked both hands, tossing down shots of Glenkinchie single malt whiskey, chased with either Newcastle Brown Ale or Watneys Red Barrel Beer.

After their fourth round of drinks, Hypo's ballast tanks were overflowing.

"I need to pee worse than Amy Winehouse needs her teeth fixed."

He headed off to the plushest men's room he had ever been in, to succumb to Nature's call.

While the three of them were looking over the dessert menu, Amethyst suddenly turned to Billy as if she had just remembered something.

"Dude! We need to finish going over your charts. Honest! We just scratched the surface the other day."

"I think it infected."

"What the fuck are you talking about?"

"The scratch. You said we just—"

"Just hold on! The astrology thing has gotten a bad rap. There are so many fakes out there and all of these hucksters making big bucks on television and the internet, preying on people's gullibility and desperation. But that doesn't take anything away from the legitimate ones. The astrologers who know what they're doing."

"I know I know. Some people swear by it. And that's fine for them. I just think I have transcended the need. Lately I've been going over things. I've made a decision."

If Amethyst was put off, she didn't let on. She shrugged and smiled. Like it was his loss.

"No problem, Billy. No problem at all. Just having a little fun. You've made a decision. That's cool. You want to let your two biggest fans in on it. Or is it a big secret?"

"I ... I ... want to be like the two of you."

145

Amethyst rolled her eyes dramatically.

"I'm so flattered! What's the punch line?"

Candy smirked. She slipped into her chain-yanking mode.

"No. Wait. I can totally appreciate that. With Amethyst's musical genius, flare for spectacle, then my artistic talent and highly-developed diplomatic skills, I know exactly what you're saying. We do provide excellent role models."

"That's not quite what I meant."

Amethyst reached over and put her hands on his cheeks. She looked mockingly into his eyes like an overly-concerned mother. There was a hint of baby-talk in her voice.

"Well, then. What did little Billy mean?"

He stared back at her without blinking.

"I simply meant that I'm going to become a woman."

Amethyst: "Oh ... I see."

Candy: "Sure."

Amethyst: "Okay!"

Candy: "Makes total sense."

Amethyst: "Why not?"

Candy: "You're on to something. Great idea!"

A few moments passed. Billy just continued in turns to stare at them.

He didn't flinch. Didn't laugh. Didn't smile. Still didn't blink.

Hypo came back and couldn't help but to notice the stony silence.

"What's happening? Are you guys alright?"

No one answered. No one moved.

Then Candy and Amethyst realized in the exact same micro-second that Billy was absolutely dead serious and had the same singular reaction.

"WHAT?!"

Chapter Six

CH - CH - CH - CHANGES
Late Spring 2009

Dr. Gender Bender

Billy was surprised. He assumed there would be a long waiting list for a doctor with such an imposing reputation. But they slotted him in the very next day for what they called an initial screening interview.

Billy left early and got to the Upper Westside address they had given him on the phone, arriving a few minutes before his appointment time. It was 9:53 am, a sunny Tuesday morning with not a cloud in the sky. He felt okay, maybe a little nervous, as he approached the free-standing slate office building.

This must be the place. On a gold address plate to the left of the front door to the office, Billy read the ostentatious inscription . . .

> *Dr. Malcolm N. Bender, MD*
> *Specializing in Gender Reassignment Surgery*
> *By Appointment Only Please - No Solicitors*

The initial interview was rocky, to put it mildly. About halfway through, Billy thought that the phrase 'total disconnect' seemed to fit quite well. The good doctor skipped the social niceties and started right in on Billy.

"Mr. Green, why are you here?"

"Everyone . . . well not everyone. My girlfriend seems to think that women are my problem. So I just figured, if you can't lick 'em then join 'em."

"Your girlfriend won't let you give her oral sex?"

"I don't understand. I didn't say that."

"You said, if you can't lick 'em join 'em. If you can't lick 'em. Those are your words."

"It's just a figure of speech."

"And I was just joking. You don't seem to be in a very good mood. Are you always this morose, Mr. Green? Not that most men who come in here for gender reassignment counseling are exactly chipper. Most are nervous as hell. And they have issues."

"Look, I decided I want to be a woman. It's that simple. I don't need counseling or advice or anything else. Just get me started."

"This is not like buying a new shirt, Mr. Green. It's a long, sometimes distressing process. And it's totally irreversible. I need to establish that you're serious, that you fully understand the ramifications and risks. I need to be certain that you're doing this for the right reasons. Anything less would be irresponsible."

"Of course, I'm serious. What else do you need to know? Or what do I need to know?"

"You might be beaten to death by a mob of maniacal homophobes. Your family and friends might disown you. You'll have to squat to pee."

Billy hesitated. Should he just leave? Cut his losses. This guy appeared to be nuts.

"I am missing something here. Are you a real doctor? Do you have a degree?"

"I have several degrees, including a Bachelors in Biological Science, a double Masters in Abnormal Psych and Human Sexuality, an MD degree, and some course work in osteopathy. Of course, I also have advanced specialized training in reconstructive and cosmetic surgery. Lastly, I am a Microsoft Certified Technology Specialist and a Freemason."

"Impressive."

"I think the best way to approach this is to give you a special test I have developed. I call it the BMHGAT, which stands for the Bender Multiphasic and Holistic Gender Affectation Test. It will give me a reliable reading on your readiness for the requested procedure."

He reached across his desk and handed Billy a large pale green envelope with a string tie on the back. "Just bring this back when you have completed it. I'll take it from there. And Mr. Green?"

"Yes, doctor."

"Don't lick the envelope. Please use the attached tie string to seal the test questionnaire."

"Right. Don't lick the envelope."

On the way home, Billy pondered his interview with Bender. Without a doubt, the doctor was a strange duck. Something was not quite right with the man. On the other hand, while Googling him produced a whole range of commentary about his eccentricities and odd manners and mannerisms, no one faulted his performance as a surgeon. There were dozens of examples of his work, pictures which showed the spectacular gender transformations he had performed with his scalpel and exotic program of hormonal dousing. And though it wasn't a sex change procedure, Bender even claimed on his own website to have liposuctioned to rock star perfection, the unnamed lead singer of a world-renowned boy band. Bender apparently was a genius, and had earned the reputation as *the* master of gender-bending cosmetic surgery.

Billy decided he would stay the course for now, despite the gnawing doubts seeded by their initial meeting. He didn't have anything to lose at this point. He should at least seeing what the doctor might be all about. Of course, when the time came to pull out the surgical gear, it would be a different matter. Then he'd really have to decide if he had sufficient faith in Bender.

When he got home, he immediately took out the BMHGAT and was thrown for another loop. What a total whack job! Billy entertained the idea of suggesting to Bender, next time he saw him, that he change the name of his clinic to the Twilight Zone Cosmetic Surgery.

There were only nine questions to the test. It took him less than four minutes to complete.

Q. Finish this: A trannie walks into a bar ...

A. *The bartender asks: Is that a tampon in your pocket or are you just glad to see me?*

Q. Why do flies have wings?

A. *They don't. A fly is a baseball hit high into the air.*

Q. How old and who was your youngest sex partner?

A. *13 ... myself.*

Q. What is your favorite cooked food?

A. *Marijuana brownies.*

Q. Have you ever had sex with an animal?

A. *Don't know. It was late. I was drunk. Do Swarthmore girls have antlers?*

Q. Are you an 'in-ee' or an 'out-ee'?

A. *I pawned my bellybutton and gave the money to my grandmother to support her crack habit.*

Q. What problem do 8-year-old girls and boys have in common?

A. *Their spines break when you butt-fuck them.*

Q. Would you have sex with Mick Jagger?

A. *If he sang Ruby Tuesday I'd give him a blow job!*

Q. You are completely naked in Grand Central Station. What are you feeling?

A. *I'm going to have a helluva time getting into my apartment without my keys.*

He put the completed form in the green envelope, cut the string off and sealed it by licking it until his mouth was dry. Next day he dropped it off with the receptionist at Bender's clinic.

A week went by, then the good doctor's secretary called and set an appointment for them to go over the test results.

When he stepped into Dr. Bender's office, the surgeon was seated behind his desk, apparently going over Billy's test questionnaire. His face looked more gaunt than last time, his skin more sallow. Though his eyebrows were furrowed, his eyes had a dead impenetrable glaze. He spoke without looking up.

"Please have a seat."

Billy sat in one of two chairs directly in front of the doctor. Bender had some sort of optical apparatus strapped to his head and was wearing disposable latex gloves. Had he just come out of surgery? Or maybe they were shooting another *Re-Animator* sequel and he was the star.

"Does the sight of blood make you queasy, Mr. Green? It used to make me throw up."

"On your patients?"

"No. We kept a pail next to the surgical table. The nurses swapped it out as required."

"Nice. Thanks for sharing that with me."

"I have your test questionnaire, Mr. Green. It is right here in my hands. I am looking at your test questionnaire as we speak."

"Quite honestly, Dr. Bender, it wasn't what I expected. Kind of... unusual. Nice and short though. What exactly are you looking for?"

"Creativity. Confidence. Daring. Indifference or antipathy to convention. Flippancy. The-devil-made-me-do-it irreverence."

He continued to study the questionnaire like it was the court's final verdict at the Nuremburg trials. Billy couldn't read him. After an interminable minute or so, Dr. Bender suddenly became animated, almost enthusiastic.

"You passed with flying colors, Mr. Green. I see a strength of character here. Of course, there is an element of subjectivity on my end in interpreting the results. But I have developed a high-level of expertise in this, so the test is almost 100% predictive."

"That makes sense. It *is* your test."

"Exactly. So there is no one better positioned in this matter. You should know, Mr. Green, I have built in some subtle but very revealing contextual tripwires to nail down a person's true state of mind. These would escape the eye of the most perceptive layman, but they are there. Each question is multi-layered, an epistemological lens into the hidden architecture of the mind."

"Like the bellybutton question. I really wrestled with that one."

"I'm sure."

"And the trannie joke. That certainly set a solid tone. Great way to kick off something as important as this."

"Well then, let's just cut to the chase. In my professional opinion, you are ready. I think we can and should go forward with this."

He pulled the lenses of the optical headgear down over his eyes, got out a small note pad from the center drawer of his desk, and started writing furiously.

"These prescriptions are for your hormones. Start taking them immediately. There will be clear instructions on each bottle. Next I want you to see a colleague of mine, as soon as possible. Right off. No point in dragging this out. Sooner the better. Get it done and over with, I say. Her name is Dr. Veronica Hegel. She is a specialist in aesthetic procedures. Some surgical. Some not. Simple stuff. All out-patient. She will start the process of feminizing your face.

Obviously, she'll have a lot to do in that department. You don't exactly look like Audrey Hepburn."

He finished writing and handed five Rx sheets to Billy.

"Mr. Green. Have you thought of a name?"

"A name?

"Unless you're going to continue to call yourself Billy, which isn't attractive even as a man's name, and is truly an insult to the fairer sex as a girl's name, you might want to be thinking of a new name for yourself. Ursula. Bonnie. Something. And start having your friends call you by that. Immediately. No more Billy. It'll help you to start thinking of yourself in terms of the female you. I can do the stuff on the outside but you have to do the work on the inside. Not my department."

"Got it. I'll get right to work on that."

"Any other questions? If not, I will see you in three weeks. We'll do some blood tests to see how the hormones are taking hold, take a look at what sort of miracles Hegel has achieved, give you time to do some shopping, grow your hair, all that girlie girlie stuff that needs to be taken care of."

"Nicely put. You have a truly sensitive side. I like that."

The sarcasm was not lost on Bender. Bender's irritation was not lost on Billy. He got up to leave. At the door, he turned back around. The doctor was still glaring at him.

"By the way, Dr. Bender, I meant to ask what the 'N' stands for."

"I'm sorry, Mr. Green. The 'N'?"

"Yes. The 'N'. Your middle initial."

Bender hesitated briefly.

"Nostradamus."

"Perfect."

Andria's — For the New You!

It had only been a week since his initial consultation with Dr. Gender Bender. Nothing seemed to be happening as a result of the hormone therapy, but it was probably way too early to expect much. After all, it had taken 26 years to become a man. Hopefully, it wouldn't take 26 years for the estrogen cocktail to kick in.

There was still a lot of business to take care of. After staring blankly at a scrabble board for hours, then poring over baby-naming books in a Barnes & Noble for so long they asked him to leave, he still couldn't decide.

Billy had gone through them all. He had even bought *Best Baby Naming Book In The Whole World* online from Powell Books — he was too embarrassed to go into a bookstore again. Bridget. Sandy. Charmagne. Heather. Tess. Alice. Jo Jo. Kathy. Gina. Cassie. Marianne. Nancy. Judith. He had even considered Lola, but then remembered the Barry Manilow tune "At The Copa" and nixed it.

More than esthetic considerations, written or aural, it was a combination of punch-drunk weariness, after laboring over it for so long, combined with some fond memories of watching *Bewitched* reruns when he was a kid, that finalized his choice.

Samantha.

"I'm Samantha. Nice to meet you." He kept practicing in front of the bathroom mirror for what seemed like weeks — though in actuality it could only have been a couple days — but it just wasn't happening. It was contrived at best, ridiculous and comical at worst. He just couldn't seem to make it sound natural and genuine.

Finally, it dawned on him what the problem was. He still looked like a guy. How could anyone who looked a lot like Matt Damon and dressed like he was playing in a snooker tournament in the Bronx, convincingly tell someone that his name was Samantha — even if that someone was himself? *Especially* if that someone was himself, looking squarely back into the eyes of a pretty typical, boilerplate dude.

He needed to start looking like a chick if he was ever going to pull this off, even down to a simple and straightforward introduction.

"I'm Samantha. Nice to meet you."

The Upper East Side was blessed or cursed — depending how you looked at it — with a plethora of beauty aids supply stores and boutiques. These all sold the finest in cosmetics at a minimum of 800 times what it cost to manufacture. Elegant bottles and high-tech dispensers packaged in regal boxes and chic product-line kits, touted the potions, powders, liners, sticks, bases, tints, glosses, polishes, cleansers, creams, oils, on and on and on, as the beauteous and beatific beeline to perfection. Designer labels flaunted elitist names like Clé de Peau, Guerlain, Valmont, Estée Lauder, Borghese, Sisley-Paris, RéVive, Darphine, Ann Sui, Lancome and Dior.

This was beyond intimidating to Billy. It wasn't the money. It was the logistics. He had no idea where to begin. How exactly would he present his situation to the breathtakingly beautiful young sales girls who typically worked in these cosmetic boutiques?

> *Say, I'm just getting started on this sex change — see I'm a guy but soon I'm going to be a girl just like you — and I wondered if you could help me spend $3000 on a bunch of stuff I don't even know how to use or for that matter have any idea what all this stuff is for or why I would want it — though I guess I need it. Whaddya think? Hmmm?*

No, for this first round, he decided on both economy and anonymity. Billy popped into a Dollar Store on the very southern boundary of Harlem, fifteen minutes later left toting two bags bulging with everything he thought he required, and a lot he didn't.

For the next several hours, Billy — or more obligingly Samantha — tried to master an art form which took millennia to evolve and usually took a young teenage girl many anxiety-filled years to perfect. He repeatedly congratulated himself for including in his manic spending spree at the Dollar Store copious amounts of makeup remover. Over the course of at least a dozen attempts at creating an understated but beautiful Samantha face, no matter what combination or order of the cosmetics he tried, he always ended up a tragicomic mess. The result each and every time was the same. He looked like Divine, the raunchy star of *Pink Flamingos* — on a bad day.

This was not working. He slathered on one last round of makeup remover, then rinsed and toweled his now puffy, raw skin, and sat down with a 40-ounce bottle of Miller Lite to regroup.

What to do?

He picked out a Cosmopolitan magazine he had randomly thrown into his waste basket for empty beverage containers. The feature stories were *12 Ways To Please Your Man and Have Him Eating Out of Your Hand*, and an interview with Madonna about her recent spiritual retreat to a monastery in India and her conversion to Zoroastrianism. He casually flipped the pages until he noticed an article on a new trend, the sprouting of total makeover salons. These were for the most part regular beauty salons that had dramatically added to their standard menu of services, so that in addition to hair and nails, a woman could get advanced skin care treatments — non-surgical "facelifts", derm abrasion, special herbal and chemical peels — and valuable advice from a professional in-house image consultant on makeup, and the latest techniques and products. A lady could walk in a Plane Jane and walk out a Kate Beckinsale. At least that was the theory.

This was the solution to his problem!

Next morning he taxied across Central Park into the Upper West Side. He kept his eyes peeled. When they rounded one corner, he spotted what he was positive he was looking for.

"Here. Right here. This is perfect." The meter only said $5.40 but Billy threw a twenty at the driver and jumped out.

A new canvas awning hung over the deep-set French windows of a vine-covered brick building. There were flowering plants across the entire store front, with a bronze copy of August Rodin's *The Kiss* and trellises with climbing Clematis on either side of the entrance. Above the awning was a huge sign…

G R A N D O P E N I N G !!
Andria's — For the new you!

He held the door for a 40-something woman unseasonably dressed in a fur stole, who was made up as if she were hosting a formal reception for the Royal Family of Lichtenstein.

"Why thank you, young man."

He then stepped into his first beauty salon.

"May I help you?"

"Yes, I want a complete make-over."

"Hair, nails?"

"Everything. Don't ask any questions. Just make me beautiful. Jessica Alba beautiful."

"No problem, sweetie. I'm Andria."

She said the first syllable like 'awe', drawn out for effect.

"We do this all the time. You're gonna stop the trains, the planes, and fill the window panes. They won't be able to get enough of the new you! I'm not sure about Jessica Alba, though. With your jaw line, we might want to think in terms of Hillary Swank beautiful."

With the dumb luck of a saint and a fool, Billy had chosen well. Over the past twenty years, even starting before that, the Upper West Side had been developed and gentrified, and was now Gay Central Station for the city. Its restaurants, clubs and parlors reflected the vibrant aesthetics and refined taste of its gay, lesbian and transgender residents.

Andria's was on 72nd Street around the corner from Amsterdam in a beautiful ground floor suite whose potted plants, ceiling fans and tapestries challenged the decor of the best restaurants in town.

Even before they instituted the "new you" complete makeover, Andria's had been providing some of the best glamour cuts, manicures and pedicures, facials and waxes, to bring out and enhance the feminine beauty of its highly loyal clientele, whether they were male or female. It was very popular among the transgender crowd, transsexuals and transvestites alike.

Billy's transformation was business as usual for this particular salon.

When he left after nearly five hours of styling, primping, trimming, depilating, coloring, curling, waxing, scrubbing, defoliating, and of course, applying full-on makeup worthy of a princess, he felt like a new man. Correction. New woman! Because from all outward appearances, no one would suspect he was a man, not without looking under his tail.

Ladies and gentlemen, may I present to you …

Miss Samantha Green.

When a Stranger Calls

"I'm very sorry. I must have the wrong address. Do you know where Billy Green lives? That's B - I - L - L - Y—"

"You think you're so funny. Candy. Remember. You're supposed to call me Samantha."

"I remember. But it's not easy. You're going to have to do something about the clothes."

"The clothes."

"You look like someone took a longshoreman and sewed on Hillary Swank's head."

"It's funny you'd say that. Hillary Swank, eh?"

"Whatever. You get my point. I guess I need to show you a few things. Girl tricks."

"Like what."

"Like what. Like what." She grabbed her breasts. "I know you know about these, Billy."

"Samantha."

"Samantha. Christ! I'll never get used to this. Anyway, there was a time when I knew about them too — tits I mean — but didn't have them. Just like you. But there are workarounds. That's how you get through the first five years of puberty."

"How am I supposed to know all of this? I'm just getting started. This face and hairdo aren't even a day old."

"But you still want me and everyone else to call you Samantha, and think of you as a woman. I'm telling you, it's not easy. The way you're dressed. Your flat chest. You've still got six inches of tube steak hanging between your legs. Believe me. It's not at all easy."

"Seven."

"Seven? Seven what?"

"Seven inches."

"See what I mean. You're even still worried about how big your penis is. As a girl I can honestly say I have never spent a single moment my entire life worrying about how big my penis is. It's not exactly what girls do."

"Point taken. Maybe it's gonna take a while. Just give me some time."

"Give you some time? Like I'm in on this with you? Are you completely out of your discombobulated skull? I'm not your rooting section here. This is completely your deal. I think it's really *really* weird."

"Gee Candy, thanks for being there for me. And here I thought I could count on you, to maybe be a little supportive."

"Supportive."

"If you wanted to be a man, I wouldn't try to stop you."

"Remember when I told you that your problem was women? That it all came down to that?"

"Yeah, I remember. It was a real kick in the jewels. But I admit now, you were right."

"No, actually I wasn't right."

"Don't complicate things. I've moved on. I'm happy being Samantha now. Or at least becoming Samantha."

"But you haven't moved on. And your problem is not 'women'. It's one particular woman."

"Fuck! You never let up. Where are you going with this?"

"Look at yourself."

"I do. Every day in the mirror. How does my makeup look?"

"It's a gruesome start. Believe me, I like you a lot better as a man. But you look ... you look alright. Decent anyway."

"You were saying? One particular woman. Not that I want to hear this."

"Yes, Billy. One particular woman. And that one particular woman is your lezzie wife. What was her name? Natalie?"

"Now you are treading *very* dangerous ground, Candy. That's a minefield. Do not enter."

"Don't you see what you're doing? Trying to become a woman. You are either trying to become her or ..."

Candy paused. She was a little afraid of how Billy would react to this.

Then she forged ahead.

"*Or* … you are trying to win her back."

"Stop! Right now! You're way *way* out of line. Come on! Get her back?"

"Yes. As a woman. She likes women, right?"

"That is the all-time dumbest thing you have *ever* said, Candace Susan Kalkin. You've really hit bottom now. And here I thought you were a *genius*."

"I am not to be judged. IQ can be fudged. I am just being honest with you."

Billy turned his back to her. He started waving good-bye theatrically.

"So long! Nice seeing you! You were leaving, right?"

"I just arrived. But have it your way." Candy stood up abruptly and headed toward the door. She stopped and looked back over her shoulder.

"Hey, Billy. I still love you."

He whipped around and looked angry.

"You don't understand. I need you to hate me."

Candy took it like a bullet. Tears welled in her eyes.

"Why? Why did you say that?"

"I guess it sounded good."

"Not to me."

Billy could see she was trying not to cry. He walked over, put his finger under her chin, and raised her head so that he was looking squarely in her eyes.

"Candy. I'm sorry … about everything."

She forced a laugh, an unconvincing burble, then broke into an ironic grin and put her hands on his shoulders.

"Hey, Samantha girl! Maybe I'll see you at Victoria's Secret tomorrow. There's a big sale on garter belts and cotton thongs."

Candy lowered her hands, sniffed slightly, then smiled, reached up and playfully touched the tip of his nose with her long graceful finger.

"Au revoir, mon petite bon bon."

"Boom boom, gutes Fräulein."

Mr. Bill

Dr. Bender's secretary had set Billy's first appointment with Dr. Veronica Hegel, the facial aesthetics specialist, apparently a cosmetic surgeon in her own right. It was three days after his consultation with Bender. Then some sort of emergency with one of her patients necessitated moving his appointment to the following week. Billy avoided even thinking about what the problem with the other patient was all about. Her face fell off? Tits exploded?

Off he went. Across town to an Upper West Side office tucked away in a predominantly residential area on 97th Street near West End Avenue. It was a converted brownstone.

The reception and waiting area was no-frills — rustic and simple — and very clean. There were four vintage stuffed chairs, a couple antique tables, one supporting a garish porcelain vase containing dried and artificial flowers, the other with popular magazines laid out in a neat and orderly fashion.

Pretty typical.

What was not were the two other patients there when Billy arrived. He was immediately assailed with some serious second thoughts, and his first impulse was to turn right back around and run.

One patient, who appeared to be in her late 40s or early 50s, glanced furtively at him as soon as he walked in. He checked in with the receptionist, a mousy girl with orthodontic braces and dull unstyled hair pulled back in a matted ponytail. When he turned around to take his seat, the lady was staring at him over the top of a large paperback book, which she held upside down. Or maybe just the cover was upside down. When she caught his eyes, she quickly went back to pretending to read. She apparently had had a few too many facelifts. Her face was frozen in a look of terrified surprise. With her sandwich-baggie skin stretched taut like the head of a tom tom, and her fixed expression of fight-or-flight stupefaction, Billy thought she could have easily been one of the Martians in Tim Burton's movie *Mars Attacks*. He couldn't look at her without cringing.

The other person was a younger male, probably in his 30s. Billy learned later he was a minor celebrity, an icon among the increasing number of people for whom cosmetic surgery had become a religion, the new enlightened path to self-fulfillment.

This was none other than Steve Erhardt — aka the Living Ken Doll.

Putting 'before' and 'after' pictures of Ken Doll side-by-side was mind boggling. It was as if Philip Seymour Hoffman had somehow transmuted into Jude Law. Except that the 'after' picture hinted that some peculiar process was in play here, some mix of witch's brew and voodoo mechanics, an irregular meddling and extreme tinkering with the natural order.

Even so, unlike the world's most famous African-American pop star and accused pedophile, this guy still looked human. In some strange eclectic way. Looking at him was like looking at one of those Photoshop composites, where each feature was borrowed from a different face — eyes from here, nose from there, mouth from someone else, each ear on loan from yet another contributor. Maybe he should have been called the Living Picasso.

Which is not to say he was grotesque or repulsive. In fact, in some obtuse way he was quite beautiful. Very feminine but on the whole attractive. There was a uniqueness to the entirety of his face and an individual beauty to each of his carefully chosen features. He had the kind of comeliness that is common among the girls of Japanese anime. The kind of appeal that George Lucas might conjure for an alluring alien fatale in one of his Star Wars movies.

Billy finally stopped stealing glances at Ken Doll and tried to grasp his situation. But before he got close to deciding if he should cut his losses and run, or just stay, he heard his name called and he was escorted into the dimly-lit private office of Dr. Veronica Hegel.

She was German to the core — focused, robotic, abrupt, efficient, laconic, blunt, humorless. She had the personality of an ATM machine and the social graces of Klaus Barbi. Billy wondered if she might be related to Kurt Blome or one of the other quack Nazi scientists who had experimented on live human beings. For five minutes, completely devoid of niceties, she reviewed the basics of his personal information and medical history. For the entire interview, she had only one out-of-the-box editorial comment.

"Have you ever had any sexually transmitted diseases, Miss Green?"

"No."

"Hmm. Really?"

There it was. *Hmm. Really?*

Form filled in and complete, she took him into her outpatient treatment room, which looked a lot like a dentist's work space. There was the reclining chair, overhead lamp, and swiveling tray for surgical instruments. What was not typically seen in a dentist's office was an imposing digital camera on a tripod, and a large flat panel screen. Billy would later see that this was for taking stills of his face, then applying a "feminizing" program using some proprietary morphing software. With this, Dr. Hegel could explore the different ways she might approach her work, and decide which techniques would result in the most flattering and natural female version of Billy, aka Samantha Green.

He was given a mild relaxant and injected, when it was required, with tiny syringes of local anesthetics.

There was no conversation the entire time, no assurances, no queries as to how he was doing, nothing but curt instructions to her two assistants, who rotated in and out of the room through the long procedure.

Finally she was done.

"This will be all for today. I have completed my work. You are to come again in two weeks. Make an appointment with my assistant." Out she went, back into her private office.

Billy was exhausted. Four hours of pinching, pulling, and needles. His face hurt like hell. His eyes burned from the intense glare of the surgical lamp. He had a throbbing headache. His lips burned from numerous injections of some kind.

He had intended to go to Stanley's over on Columbus Avenue for some 8-ball and a beer, but took a taxi directly home instead.

As he walked through the door, Candy's face was the perfect seesaw of shock and disbelief.

"Billy! What happened to you? You look like Mr. Bill."

"Who's Mr. Bill?"

"God, Billy. You are so hopelessly ignorant. In the not-so-distant past, I'll have you know, Mr. Bill was a cultural icon."

"So what's your point?"

"Your lips. You look like a fish."

"Mr. Bill was a fish?"

"No, I was changing the comparison to something I thought you could grasp. So why do your lips look like tubes of cookie dough? Did you get in a fight with a boxing kangaroo?"

"How did you guess? It *was* a kangaroo. I tried to kiss her but she was with someone else. What? You don't like this? It's supposed to enhance my sexual appeal. The mouth is the foyer to a person's erotic temple. The lips are portals of passion."

"Yours look like potholes of putrescence. Whatever. The way I see it, lips are just sphincters that can eat potato chips."

"Candy, don't ever bother to take acid. Believe me, you don't need it."

She walked over behind Billy, wrapped her arms around him in an unyielding clinch, and stuck her tongue deep in his ear. He squirmed and twisted in the pleasurably wet discomfort of her slurping and tonguing, struggling frantically trying to break loose. He laughed and yelled at the same time.

"Stop! Stop! You're a lunatic!"

"More than you'll ever know."

She took off her clothes. Then his.

His headache was gone in less than three minutes.

Billy suddenly became very serious.

"Candy. You keep forgetting."

"Forgetting what?"

"You're supposed to call me Samantha."

"Samantha. This is very weird."

"You're telling me."

Guerilla Warfare

First there was militant meditation.

Then there was militant mischief.

Now there was militant mayhem.

For a week straight, cats were jumping out of windows and off balconies. Billy first heard about it watching the nightly news. Then he had first hand experience one afternoon, standing on his balcony with a joint in one hand and a finger nail file in the other. He had intended to take in the breathtaking view of Central Park from his condo, and to touch up his new acrylic nails, two of which had small chips on the tips. As soon as he leaned against the guard railing, a blue Siamese went sailing on down right before his eyes. If he had reached out in that moment, he could have caught it and probably been scratched to death.

It was the same story all over Manhattan. From high rises everywhere, cats — usually Egyptian Maus, Angoras, various Siamese, Asheras, British Shorthairs, Persians, Russian Blues, Birmans and other exotic breeds typically owned by the rich and famous — were packing it in and committing suicide. Local newscasters would open their programs saying things like ...

> *"It has been reported that so far today, eleven more cats*
> *have jumped to their deaths in the recent ongoing*
> *and inexplicable rash of feline suicides."*

This bit of quirky and disturbing news was just the beginning of a puzzling assortment of bizarre, surreal, but seemingly unrelated happenings.

At first, these incidents — what could have been just pranks or silly bits of vandalism — made it onto page two or three of the papers, and got only passing *hey-get-a-load-of-this* mention on broadcast news shows. Life-in-the-Big-Apple stories with a twist of monkey business …

People on their way through Washington Square arrived early one day to find the fountain piled high with over two hundred wheelchairs. Some thought it was an art project.

Another day all of the parking meters in a twelve-city-block area in Hells Kitchen jammed. None of the coinage could be recovered and all of the meters ultimately had to be replaced. This resulted in several weeks of free parking, until the City finally got around to installing new ones.

One morning over half of New York City's 4,373 buses wouldn't start. The subways were completely jammed and taxis overtaxed. Half of the population of the Big Apple was late for work that day.

Then bizarre signs of what was characterized even in the conservative press as possible supernatural instability, metaphysical turbulence, collective chaos, the early-warning signs of social anarchy, and finally, the remote possibility of political terrorism, starting cropping up all around.

Precisely at 10:00 am on an otherwise unremarkable Monday, the screen workspaces disappeared off the monitors of every single Citibank computer, replaced with a picture of John Lennon. The caption below it read …

Imagine there's no future.

It took two days and the bank's best IT specialists and network admin guys to get the workstations functioning again.

That same week, on Saturday sometime after midnight, over 800 dogs showed up in Battery Park. They were a feisty bunch with serious territorial issues, who fought and barked and snarled at one another in a huge cacophonous street fight, before fanning out to terrorize the rest of the city. Several even made it as far as Rockefeller Center before being subdued by a small army of animal control officers from the NYC Department of Health, reinforced with extra recruits pulled from the police and fire departments.

The next Tuesday, a crew from the Department of Parks reported for groundskeeping duties and found both the pond and the lake in Central Park dyed bright red. They were so intensely red that a space shuttle mission reported being able to see the crimson patches from Earth orbit.

After a brief lull, the cat suicides started up again. This time the numbers were outrageous. One day alone, over fifty impaled themselves on the pavement below many of the most exclusive townhouses in New York's Upper East Side. It became national news.

The following weekend, all of the manhole covers in a sixty-seven square block section of the Upper East Side turned up missing. As rats emerged from the sewers and ran wild for the two weeks it took to fix the problem, fear of ankle bites and the spread of rabies and other diseases, panicked everyone from doormen to taxi drivers to the privileged denizens of the area. Contingency planning had not anticipated the simultaneous need for over a thousand manhole covers of various sizes.

Frankly, the rats were pretty happy about the dead cats falling from heaven.

But the humans were not so appreciative.

To put it mildly, there was a lot of tension in the air. While the first few incidences merely provided amusing stories for the final segment of the daily news programs — intended to balance with a closing smile the preceding grizzly accounts of murders, fires, rapes, political scandals, and showbiz gossip — as the weird reports kept coming and coming, they started to not seem so amusing anymore. People began to see the predictability, comfort and relative safety of their routines crumble and disintegrate. The basic comity of their lives was now under assault by bizarre, seemingly random acts of sabotage, divine intervention, or malicious misconduct.

Initial curiosity turned to anxiety which quickly escalated into outright fear.

Public reassurances by the police, mayor and other city officials did little to dampen the paranoia that was building, and did a lot to undermine their own credibility and what shred of confidence the public might have in them.

Privately these same officials were frustrated and angry that their best minds, investigative machinery, and spin doctors, couldn't seem to get a leg up on whoever was responsible for the mischief and chaos.

The feeding frenzy by the media, always hungry for something sensational to top yesterday's outrageous stories, kept stirring the pot, and appetites for the latest news of the debacles remained high.

The less reputable but more entertaining rags, like the Post and Daily News, ramped up talk about paranormal forces, possible space aliens that had assumed human form, and offered pious speculation about the beginning of the End Days as prophesied in Revelations.

More sensible commentators rightly attributed what was happening to human misconduct and characterized it as some sort of low grade terrorism, either by random, unaffiliated troublemakers, or — and this had the authorities concerned and anxious — by some single army of provocateurs who had yet to make their agenda and demands public.

A lot of speculation and finger-pointing went on.

Interestingly, no one got it right.

No one took seriously the two-bit ersatz guru from the East Village.

Which was perfect.

He wanted to keep them guessing.

Chapter Seven

MESSAGES FROM THE OTHER SIDE
Early Summer 2009

Hormones

Billy sat in the center of his living room. Around him were three boxes of Kleenex and countless wads of used tissues. He heard the door open.

Candy looked like she had just come from a Renaissance Faire.

"That's a new look for you, Candy."

"I've been online taking a virtual tour of the Louvre. How are you, Billy?"

"I'm so horny I can taste virgin blood."

"Wonderfully stated. What did you say you studied at Boomfuk U? Poetry? Linguistics?"

"I'm a little busy right now. Is this business or pleasure?"

"With you, Billy, it's always pleasure. You take me to the top of the mountain. It's always a Martin Luther King moment. I have a dream! Did you say something about virgin blood?"

"These hormones are really really messing with me, Candy. I feel like crying all the time. And I have a perpetual hard-on. You're a woman. Is this normal?"

"Do I have a perpetual hard-on? Think about it, Billy."

"Come on, Candy. You know what I mean. The crying. Christ, no matter what I think about. I was watching a Mr. Bean video last night. I bawled my eyes out."

"You should be bawling. Fucking Mr. Bean? Mourn the death of good taste. Your brain must be turning to clam chowder. I think I better go. Is encephalitis contagious?"

"Help me, Candy."

She did.

It was over in less than three-and-a-half minutes.

Billy ... uh Samantha ... felt better. He was so happy he cried.

Sushi for Beginners

Billy had one final pre-op interview with Dr. Bender.

"Well, Ms. Green."

"You can just call me Samantha, doctor."

"As I started to say, this is it. I see you are progressing admirably. You are, as people of your age group are wont to say, a real fox. Dr. Hegel has done her job. You have done yours. Do you have any questions?"

"Yes. I have been reading some stuff on the internet. But I am still not clear. Will I be able to enjoy sex? I mean ... will I be able to have an orgasm?"

"That's a good question, Ms. Green. And a common one. There are no guarantees, of course. But we have been experiencing a 87.6% success rate in that area. Without going into to much detail, I will say that the relevant tissue of your penis will be meticulously transferred to the upper edges of the vaginal lips we will be constructing for you. Barring unforeseen complications, after a nominal period of adjustment and healing, that area should be available and sensitive to the normal stimulation of a penis inserted for sexual intercourse. Or any other stimulation aptly applied to that region. Your own fingers. A cucumber. A vibrator. The short answer is that you should be able to get off."

"Thanks for both the long and the short answer, doctor. I feel truly warm and bubbly about the whole thing now. Especially the image of you rearranging my chunks of flesh like a sushi chef."

"Your sarcasm is your most unattractive feature, Ms. Green. That makeup doesn't begin to disguise your irritating attitude. Having said that, and having answered your question, let's proceed to the final step. We're experiencing a high demand for my services these days. I think it might be the popularity of *The L Word* on TV. Nevertheless, we're looking at about six weeks before I can fit you in. Does that work for you?"

"I don't see that I have a choice. So I guess it does. Sometime around six weeks from now. Slash. Bleed. Stitch."

Bender exerted a huge degree of self-control, barely managing to disregard Billy's flippant characterization. Tension deepened the cavernous sockets of his steely-blank eyes.

"Right. Just see my secretary and she will pin down a mutually workable date and take care of the other details. See you on the operating table, Ms. Green. Have a nice day."

"Namaste."

Billy filled out about 10,000 forms and set the date.

The final action item in Billy's irreversible gender reassignment was set for July 22, 2009.

Mad as Hell

It wasn't just Billy who was looking for a big change.

Change was in the air and on the lips of everyone in New York who could talk.

On the lips of everyone in the country.

Something had to change.

It was like Howard Beal said in the movie *Network*. People were mad as hell and weren't going to take it anymore.

For the common citizen, it was the same every month. Everything was so damn expensive. The only way to balance the budget was to take out another advance against whichever credit cards had not been maxed out. Or by arranging a second or third mortgage against their houses and condos, or a collateral loan against their cars. Obviously it had to eventually come to a screeching halt.

Something had to change.

While 99% of the people were busting their butts to just make ends meet, splashed across the front pages of every daily newspaper and internet news site, were scandals about the rich and powerful filling their pockets with billions in salaries and bonuses, via short sells, buyouts, takeovers, liquidations, and all sorts of incomprehensible exotic weapons of financial destruction, all while bringing down banks, ruining cornerstone corporations, bankrupting the nation as a whole, draining the savings and retirement funds of the common citizen, and turning America into a Third World economy.

Something had to change.

The talking heads talked and shouted, speculated and commented, trying to make sense and dinner time entertainment out of the whole mess. They only added to the confusion, the proliferation of worthless conjecture, the disingenuous speculation about what needed to be done.

Something had to change.

The politicians — though they themselves were in the 1% who were on the receiving end of the plunder — expressed their words of concern and caring, reiterated their commitment to get to the bottom of it all and fix the problems, reaffirmed their solidarity with the people who were being dragged under, and like the captain of the Titanic, reassured everyone that the ship wouldn't go down. Then they went back to the hallowed halls of whatever legislative bodies they had been sent to by a gullible and trusting electorate, to pass more laws which would protect their bulging coffers, and guarantee that the money would keep on flowing their way.

Something had to change.

Lost in the media torrent and whirlwind were many unheralded voices, voices of people who lacking corporate media clout, political position, or the window dressing of commonly lauded credentials, would never be noticed, much less judged on the merit of their ideas. Some of these voices came from academicians, who lacked the gamesmanship and political savvy to attract the media spotlight, or by their nature were not interested in 15 minutes of fame. Some of these voices came from individuals who chose to remain on the outside. Individuals whose essential commitment to truth, whose firmly-held beliefs and values barred them from ever wanting to become insiders.

Apocalypso epitomized this last group of outsiders.

And to make sure his message got out there, he had his own set of unique outsider tactics.

> *"See, it's like this, my friends. I'm a straight-shooter and I'm a straight-talker. I might have my head in the clouds but I got my feet on the ground. And come election day, most people ain't gonna vote for some freaky, dread-locked, whack son-of-a-bitch like me. The other reason they ain't gonna vote for me is 'cause I ain't running for anything. Even if I got in, it wouldn't make a bit of a difference 'cuz things are set to run the way they are. And the people sitting in the thrones of power ain't gonna tinker around with a system that keeps them rolling in the cold green.*

So you ain't gonna vote for me. But you <u>will</u> listen to me. Because I am a straight-shooter and a straight-talker and what I'm sayin' is coming right out of your own mouth. You may not know it yet but that's the fact. I'm thinking the thoughts you're thinking, and sayin' the words that you want to be sayin'. All I can say is, stay tuned. There's more to come. Keep the faith. This is your man, Apocalypso, talkin' atcha from an undisclosed location right here in greatest city in the whole wide world. Like I said, good people, <u>stay tuned</u>!"

Actually, no one had to stay tuned at all.

No one could miss his next stunt.

How did he do it?

That was the question on the lips of everyone who heard it.

How the hell did he pull this off?

Some asked with respectful admiration. Some asked with vindictive rage.

It seems that everyone who made a telephone call and was put on hold anywhere in the city — all four boroughs — between 10 am and 4 pm on Thursday July 10th, or between 9 am and 2 pm Tuesday July 15th, heard Apocalypso's straight-shooter straight-talker message followed by the Beatles singing, "All You Need Is Love".

Apocalypso's people had cracked the security wall for all of the phone systems for the entire region, aired his personal promissory note, and brought the nostalgic bliss of a 60s love-power anthem to over three million people.

It was the talk of the town, the state, the nation.

Jay Leno and David Letterman each did two monologues around it. Larry King interviewed two highly suspect, barely believable characters who claimed to be Apocalypso's high school principal and gym teacher. News reporters, commentators, political experts, security experts, media experts, psychiatric experts, all speculated and analyzed. No one could explain how it happened and what it meant. Fox TV even assembled a panel of psychics to divine what might be coming.

All of this attention pretty much guaranteed people would continue to honor Apocalypso's request.

They were staying tuned.

There's more to come.

There was something about his simple, matter-of-fact statement that no one could take lightly, especially in view of all of the bizarre stuff that had already happened over the past couple of months — the hara-kiri cats, parking meters, buses, the 800 dogs, missing manhole covers, the red lakes of Central Park.

Speculation as to what might be coming next, ranged from apocalyptic predictions — an easy call in view of his name — to spiritual manifestations, which included the Second Coming of Christ, the reincarnation of the Buddha, the Rapture, even Mohammad riding down Broadway on a white horse.

The Department of Homeland Security announced it was putting the nation on high alert, code red, for an unspecified length of time. The National Guard was mobilized in several metropolitan areas. Uniformed soldiers could be seen in all sorts of public places — bus and train stations, airline terminals, post offices and other government buildings, churches and synagogues, stadiums and concert venues, movie theaters, shopping malls.

Special guards were posted at Disneyland and Disney World, though from the extremely careful scrutiny the young rent-a-cops gave them, an observer would conclude that the suspected threat was being secreted into Mickey's magic kingdom by one of the hundreds of young girls who paraded through the parks in shorts and halter tops.

No one knew what was coming. But expectations were building.

Apocalypso was in no hurry. He would wait another week before he would deliver.

Some would be disappointed.

Some would be amazed.

Some would just laugh.

For Billy it turned out to be a life-defining event.

City Lights

Between 8 and 10 pm, one after another, whole blocks the length of Manhattan lost power.

It was the strangest blackout to ever hit the city. No one could make sense out of it. Why it was happening, what was causing it, why it just affected the blocks it did.

The first ones to put it together was an United Airlines crew.

"You won't believe what I'm seeing!"

They were on the approach to JFK on a United Airlines flight from Los Angeles. His copilot spotted it first from his side of the cockpit, and now the pilot was reporting to the control tower what he was looking at.

"Of course I'm sure. This isn't a UFO. It's written in big block letters from one end to the other. C-A-N-C-E-R, with a question mark at the end."

Electricity was completely restored before midnight, but it made the late night edition of the news. Every station were taking their news helicopters high over New York to provide live shots and film footage to be re-broadcast later.

Cancer?

What did it mean?

The next day all sorts of theories were flying. One bubble-headed female newscaster, who never did anything without checking her daily horoscope, speculated that since it was July, the cancer referred to the astrological sign. Not that her hypothesis clarified anything.

Over the coming months, Apocalypso removed any doubt as to who was responsible for the spectacle or what it meant. Starting almost the next day, he embarked on his *Cancer?* poster and ad campaign. Thousands of huge posters were pasted all over Manhattan, and ads were taken out in the daily and weekly papers, every other week with a new target.

They were simple and devastating. Each poster featured some prominent corporation, usually the facade of their corporate headquarters, with the *Cancer?* written boldly at an angle across the middle. There were photographs of the New York Stock Exchange, Goldman Sachs, AIG, Merrill Lynch, Shearson Leymann, Exxon-Mobil, Citibank, Chase Manhattan, Bank of America, Walmart, Microsoft, GlaxoSmithKline Pharmaceuticals, Philip Morris Tobacco, the New York Federal Reserve, McDonald's, Pizza Hut, Nike, and the Gap. Nike and Gap layouts included inset photos of dark-skin Asian children making shoes and clothes — pre- and early-adolescent corporate slaves, with drawn, starved faces and sallow complexions, looking exhausted and sickly.

Lastly, there was a poster targeting Starbucks, certainly a predatory corporation if there ever was one, but one he also had a personal grudge against. One of their stores had refused him service because he wasn't wearing a shirt, though he had on a full leather vest that gave a mere glimpse of his hairy chest.

The tobacco company ads also included the Surgeon General's Warning:

Smoking may be hazardous for your health.

The Walmart poster had a warning in the same format:

Shopping at Walmart may be hazardous to your community.

And for the petroleum companies:

Petroleum products may be hazardous to the planet.

He made his point, disturbing and profound.

Corporations were the scourge of America and the world.

Despite the directness and the *prima facie* appeal of his campaign, it was a hard sell. The truth was a bitter medicine for most people to swallow.

But Apocalypso had everyone's attention.

They were certainly staying tuned.

Careful What You Wish For

Two men stood over Billy. They were dressed in hospital whites.

"You won't remember any of this. Tomorrow, you'll wake up a new man."

The anesthesiologist smirked as he exchanged glances with his assistant.

"Maybe that wasn't the best choice of words, Ms. Green. But you get my meaning."

As Billy started to drift off, he suddenly felt a rush in his loins. Real or not, he felt like he was getting an enormous erection. Simultaneously his head was filled with the image of his rock-hard member pulsing, throbbing, about to plunge into the heavenly space between Candy's outstretched legs.

Like being struck by a bolt of lightning, suddenly he realized something. He wanted to scream it to the whole world.

I love my penis! I love being a man!

In view of the urgency of his current situation, the whole rest of the world would have to wait. What was incumbent on him now was to posthaste let the two men standing over him know. Tell the two smart-mouth guys who were watching him drift off under the influence of the sedative, that the operation was off. They had to stop everything! He had changed his mind!

Billy tried to lift his hand to grab their attention, as he put every ounce of his lungpower behind the words he was trying to form. His arm felt like it weighed a ton. His lips were rubbery and his throat completely uncooperative. It was like he was trapped in a giant jello mold, which completely reduced his mobility to nothing and rendered him mute and paralyzed. The thickening jello was pushing the receding faces of the anesthesiologist and assistant into a congealing glutinous blur. Billy attempted with all of his strength to shout. Not only could he not hear his own voice, but all of the sound of the room was silenced as well. He could barely make out the faces of the two men, but they seemed to be chatting away in a distant out-of-focus silent movie, and now the projector bulb was quickly fading, fading. Then it was out. Complete darkness. Absolute silence.

"He's gone nighty night."

"Look at that face. He looks scared shitless."

"I would be too if they were cutting off my dick."

Slowly, ever so slowly, the room came into focus. Billy felt like he was floating in a dream.

He wasn't. Not quite.

Rather, he was floating in the post-operative euphoria of the latest generation of general anesthetics. They were designed to completely block the immediate experience of pain, avoid the backlash of nausea which had accompanied prior formulae, totally erase all memory of the surgical procedures and attendant discomfort.

Gradually, he became aware of his surroundings. There was the blinking and quiet beeping of various medical monitoring equipment on his left. Above his head he could see a clear plastic bag suspended, with a long thin tube which terminated in his left arm.

Ohmigod! He suddenly understood. This was the morning after. He had just come out from under whatever they used to knock him out last night.

He panicked. No! No! He wanted no part of this!

He started to reach his right hand down between his legs. Just as he did a nurse came in.

"Well. Look who's awake. Good morning! That anesthetic shit they use is certainly powerful stuff."

She was black and beautiful. Billy could tell she loved dispensing with the formal airs they had taught her, and relished displaying her street credentials in the stuffy setting of the hospital.

"So how are you feeling ... hmm, what am I supposed to call you?" Glancing at his chart. "It says here you are officially William Green, but I'm to call you 'Samantha'. What's this? You in here for a changeover? Gonna become a pretty lady like yours truly?"

"I … uh … what happened?"

Unable to wait another moment to find out, he reached down and grabbed himself.

Much to his shock — much to his relief! — there were no bandages.

"My dick! My penis! My beautiful, wonderful friend! You're still here!"

He laughed and cried and giggled and yelled all at the same time.

"Whoa! Whoa! Slow down, Samantha!"

"Billy. Just call me Billy. Please! Ohmigod! What happened?" He stopped carrying on just long enough to look at her nametag. "Shannelle. Please tell me what happened!"

"They had to postpone the surgery. There was a massive power outage last night. It was some crazy political stunt—"

"What?!"

"Just minutes before you were wheeled into the operating room, everything went out. They have power back-ups for the lights and all, but they definitely couldn't be cuttin' you up with the electricity gone. I'm here to reschedule. We can't get—"

"Reschedule? No way. No fucking way! I'm not doing it. I'm outta here."

He started to sit up. His left arm was strapped down and still had monitoring sensors and the IV drip apparatus attached.

"Slow down. Just slow down! You're checking out?"

"Out and as far away from this butcher shop as I can get."

She called for assistance. In just a few minutes, his arm was free. He jumped out of bed. Though he was still a little disoriented from the sedative and harsh dose of surgical anesthetic they had loaded him up with the night before, Billy leaped into the air, rushed at Shannelle and gave her a big kiss.

She managed to break his grip on her and push him back onto the bed, but not before feeling the poke of his erection against her body.

She winked at him.

"Too bad I'm on duty and such a dedicated professional."

"Shannelle, I… I love you."

"I'll get your clothes so you can get dressed. You'll have some forms to fill out, *Mr.* Green."

It was all Billy could do to contain his excitement. He bounced on the bed, waved his hands in the air, kept fist-pumping.

"Yes! Yes!"

Shannelle returned with Billy's clothes. She looked down at his crotch and could not help but notice through the flimsy hospital gown that Billy's erection hadn't subsided one bit.

"Billy. I think you've made the right decision."

"I know I have. Are you married?"

Chapter Eight

THE PURSUIT OF HAPPINESS
Late 2009 – Early 2010

A Very Merry Unbirthday

Billy had always hated cats.

Actually, that wasn't quite true. He assumed he hated cats. He never had one. Never wanted to have one. Always ignored them. They ignored him.

It probably wasn't hate at all. Just some sort of mutual disregard. A genetic pact between him and an entire species which established some huge swath of neutral territory between them, a de-militarized zone, an honored sector of non-engagement into which neither ventured.

Even during the cat suicide affair, which had sent cat lovers nationwide into convulsions of sympathetic mourning, Billy had a characteristically cynical reaction to the carnage.

"If these cats were intended to survive this, God would have given them wings."

"Billy. Get real. You don't believe in God."

"The more relevant point is that God doesn't believe in cats."

Five months after his aborted sex-change operation, Candy walked into the townhouse with a cardboard pet carrier in one hand, and in the other, a huge plastic bag, heavy and full.

Billy was sitting in his favorite soft leather reclining lounge chair, listening to Jason Mraz on his iPod. When he saw her, he pulled the headphones out of his ears.

She put the plastic bag down, walked over to him, placed the pet carrier in his lap, then broke into her own antic version of "A Very Merry Unbirthday" from *Alice In Wonderland*.

"Is this what I think it is?"

"I never know what you're thinking. Only what you should be."

He opened the carrier.

A soft furry face peaked over the edge. Then the seven-week-old kitten, jumped out and landed directly on Billy's chest. She tentatively pushed forward with her nose, sniffing the air between them, then took a few short steps forward and gave Billy a single lick on the end of his nose. It was love at first sight.

Over time, the two of them became practically inseparable. He gave her at least 20 names, then finally settled on Suzanne Antoinette Creamcheese — Creamcheese for short.

One time Creamcheese settled into the small of Billy's back while he missionaried Candy. Granted, it was a very short ride. But both girls seemed to enjoy it immensely. Candy yelped and whelped and gasped in a melodious expression of intense pleasure. Creamcheese purred in comfortable delight.

By February, Creamcheese was in the full bloom of her adolescent insanity. Billy sat with Candy at the kitchen counter eating. They both watched as the frisky kitty raced from one end of the townhouse to the other, suddenly stopping and arching her back at some invisible opponent, then resuming the imaginary chase with her hallucinated playmate. She went racing into the bedroom, and they heard the clatter of something as it fell to the floor.

"I have to tell you, Candy. You made a huge mistake here."

She just looked at him amused on the surface but inside still guarded against one of his mood reversals, or tumbles into the black chaos of despair, though such incidents were much less frequent now.

"And how's that?"

"What song were you singing when you landed this creature on me?"

"A carefully selected masterpiece from a collection of my longtime favorites."

"Yes. And that was?"

"Quite appropriate. It captured a mood. The zeitgeist."

"You're avoiding the question."

"You know very well. It was 'A Very Merry Unbirthday'."

"Exactly. You were wrong. That day *was* my birthday."

Candy just smiled.

"Creamcheese is still here, isn't she? Is today your birthday?"

"You're always one step ahead of me."

"Always will be."

Arrested and Arraigned

It was just a matter of time.

You can't stand every day in the middle of a driving range and not get hit by a golf ball.

Apocalypso was arrested and being held for arraignment pending the rulings of a grand jury investigation into his activities as a political organizer and suspected terrorist.

The procedural details and legal basis for his arrest were pretty questionable. A first-year law student could easily make a convincing case that his rights had been grossly violated.

But this was the Decade of Terrorist Paranoia, one which was characterized by public trembling, fear mongering, witch-hunts, and a laundry list of embarrassing historical precedents in the spirit of the McCarthy hearings and Sacco and Vanzetti, driven by eight years of Bush-and-company thuggery, megalomania and visions of world conquest, yielding the napalm-squirting flame throwers of Patriot Acts I and II, which they and enforcement agencies happily used to torch both common sense and the U. S. Constitution.

If someone was perceived as a potential threat to the homeland ... well, best lock 'em up.

Any excuse would do.

Of course, just listening to any of Apocalypso's public speeches, attending the workshops at his Ashram Boot Camp, reading the political tirades posted on his website, or merely noting the inflammatory and confrontational tone of the thousands of issue posters which appeared on any available flat vertical surface in New York City, put him at the center of the center of any law enforcement bulls eye. He was easy pickings and a high-value target for an easy public relations victory, available to any local or national team of terrorism-fighting G-men who nabbed the surly troublemaker.

In spite of this, the actual hard evidence — the stuff connecting him to specific acts of terrorism which would hold up in a court of law — was pretty slim.

Sure. A lot of weird stuff had been happening. Some scary stuff. Big bold headline stuff.

But other than his highly audible loud trumpeting of the value of doing some serious political ass-kicking, and the need for both waking and shaking up the somnabulistic American public, hopefully in the process getting the attention of the power brokers who were running the country into the ground, there was nothing which made a direct or indirect connection between him and the things he was being accused of.

But in the Decade of Terrorist Paranoia, one technique had been polished to a fearsome high gloss. That was a sinister new brand of guilt by association.

Not association with other allegedly sinister characters or organizations.

But association with allegedly sinister ideas which were contrary to a new simplistic definition of patriotism, and a new mutated depiction of the American Way.

Being in the same room was enough. Having the wrong thoughts pass through your head was enough. Political jokes were no joking matter.

Big Brother was watching.

Your own sister might be watching.

Check books out of the library mentioning so-called un-American ideas?

You were suspect.

Hold up a sign at a political rally challenging any administration policy?

You were suspect.

If you didn't accept George W's ungrammatical, embarrassingly ignorant, and transparently deceptive utterances as divinely-inspired pearls of wisdom?

You were suspect.

If you didn't hate the French and insisted on eating *French* fries?

You were suspect.

Question the presence of weapons of mass destruction in Iraq?

You were suspect.

Question the political shrewdness of randomly bombing the shit out of and killing the innocent citizens of other countries?

You were suspect.

Question the right of the questioners to question you?

You were suspect.

For the eight years of the Bush administration, this vast poisonous web of suspicion snared some pretty strange catch.

Restrictions were imposed on non-government service organizations like the International Red Cross and Doctors Without Borders, when they were merely trying to provide financial relief and on-the-ground assistance to the victims of the 2004 tsunami in southern Thailand, making it impossible to properly function when their help was most needed.

Registered charitable organizations like Kindhearts in Toledo, Ohio were raided, completely shut down, had their business records seized, their financial assets frozen.

Senator Edward Kennedy was even refused boarding a plane to Washington DC because he was informed that his name was on the Department of Homeland Security terrorist list.

The Homeland Security gestapo nutcases even targeted CODEPINK.

CODEPINK weren't fanatical minions of Osama bin Laden's terrorist squads with plastic explosives strapped to their chests. They were a bunch of septuagenarian and octogenarian ladies dressed in shocking pink from head to toe, exercising probably for their last time, their Constitutional right of free speech before dropping into 8 x 6 holes in the ground.

Under the new Obama administration, things were only marginally better. At a national level, many of the obvious abuses were allegedly being reigned in. Later it would be discovered they were only being better hidden.

At a local level, most of the fever-pitch of persecution was still burning hot. There was too much political capital and headline-grabbing to be gained from high-visibility discovery and capture of "potential terrorists" for it to completely abate. This would go on for many years to come. Sanity and common decency is easily lost — and regained only after a protracted uphill struggle.

The best and most direct way to nail a supposed terrorist was a brutal trial in the court of public opinion. This was the real razor-sharp edge on the gleaming sword of anti-terrorism. Just alternate the person's name with a list of possible acts of anti-Americanism and sabotage, or unpatriotic thinking and suspicious behavior, and down the person went.

When Apocalypso was hauled in, the media — guided and egged on by the authorities — had a field day. Actually it had a field couple-of-days. Then it moved on and Apocalypso's hazardous potential and public notoriety was confined to two adjacent cells in a holding tank under NYPD headquarters.

For those two days of trial by public vilification, it went something like this:

Apocalypso ... SUSPECTED TERRORIST! ... Apocalypso ... TERRORIST CELL LEADER! ... Apocalypso ... POWER OUTAGES! ... Apocalypso ... SABOTAGE! ... Apocalypso ... DESTRUCTION OF PUBLIC PROPERTY ... Apocalypso ... TAMPERED PARKING METERS ... Apocalypso ... CIA WATCH LIST ... Apocalypso ... CITY BUS CATASTROPHE ... Apocalypso ... ANTI-AMERICAN GRAFFITI ... Apocalypso ... CAT SUICIDES ...

Cat suicides! Whoa! Now that's really scary!

What was truly embarrassing, and would only come to light months later was this.

The only evidence connecting him to any of the damning allegations trumpeted in his kangaroo trial by the media, was some gourmet kitty food found on the premises of his ashram at the time of his arrest.

This was the same cat food which many of the rich denizens of New York, whose cats had mysteriously jumped from balconies to their death, had reported receiving in the mail prior to the tragic leap. The labels said ...

HARRY CARRY CAT FOOD™
A Gourmet Blend
Contains a highly refined extract
of the herb *apocalyptus upyurbutthoal*
Patent Pending (2008)
Harry Carry Corp, LLC

It was the fine print at the bottom which made the incriminating, if comical, connection.

But even that was pretty tenuous at best. No scientific evidence had yet come forth establishing that ingredients in the cat food samples were responsible for the mass feline exodus into the afterlife. Nor was there any proof that Apocalypso or the members of his staff, in spite of their well-known twisted sense of humor, had produced and mailed the cat food. When questioned, one of Apocalypso's close associates merely said, "We love Harry Carry Cat Food here. We buy it by the case and feed it to the local strays all of the time. On one occasion, an intern accidentally put it on crackers for one of our fundraisers, and it was a huge hit. People couldn't get enough of it."

So effectively, Apocalypso was now under tight security — in jail without bail — a national security risk, a suspected terrorist, a clear and present danger to the local community, all for having several cans of a kitty food which may have caused the rich cats of a bunch of fat cats to jump off of the balconies of prestigious high-rises in Manhattan.

Lock him up!

Whew! What a relief.

America could sleep soundly tonight.

I Swallowed Elton John's Sperm

Candy came into the room stretching and yawning, to where Billy sat on the floor watching television — some wake-up America news-and-talk show.

"Whatcha watching?"

Billy looked over at her. How could anyone just crawl out of bed in the morning and look so absolutely fresh and beautiful? Billy didn't think he hit his stride until at least four in the afternoon. Even then he often thought he just got passing marks. She was always an A+.

"Some psychologist with a new book called, *The Seven Billion Person Question: Who Am I?* Actually he's pretty fascinating. A unique perspective. A rather different take on things."

Candy sat down next to Billy and put her arm around him.

"He sure eats well. Is he German?"

"Yes. I have to say, I'm impressed."

"By how much he eats?"

"You know that's my main criterion for judging the worth of a man's words. How they sound through a mouthful of cheese pizza or wiener schnitzel on rye."

The interview was wrapping up. The show's co-host performed the usual courtesies with a twinkle in her eye and a television smile, amplified by the glare of her geometrically perfect, cosmetically-bleached teeth.

> *"We want to thank you, Dr. Freundlich, for taking the time to share your insightful, fascinating views on the identity crisis that seems to be the new pandemic of the affluent countries, both here in America and abroad. This morning, we've been talking to Dr. Christian Freundlich. His latest book is currently available in bookstores everywhere. It's called 'The Seven Billion Person Question: Who Am I?' I am sure you will enjoy it as much as I did, and find it an amazing powerhouse of important survival tips, and surprisingly, a truly fun read."*

> *"Thanks for having me, Robin. It's been my pleasure."*

Candy got up to go the kitchen.

"Another in a seemingly endless parade of blowhards. Want some coffee, Mr. Green?"

"Sure. Like tar, please. I need a strong jump start."

As the coffee grinder whined in the background, he thought about what he had just seen. Billy actually was impressed. So impressed, as a matter of fact, that by the end of the day he tracked Dr. Freundlich down and made an appointment with his secretary to see him.

Freundlich's calendar was filling up fast. They still managed to fit Billy in the following week on a Thursday afternoon.

Freundlich didn't have a regular base of patients, as was typical of the majority of shrinks in New York. He was more of a consulting psychologist than a psychiatrist. He didn't 'do therapy', but offered what he called empowerment sessions. And he guaranteed results in one, or at most two sessions. He'd have to guarantee something at $600 per hour.

Of course, with a new book out, one that already was on the New York Times bestsellers list for non-fiction, Freundlich would have a good run and be a very busy man — at least until someone else with the title of Dr. came along, bumped him off the Top 10, and became the new darling of the swelling ranks of damaged people, desperate for self-discovery and self-help advice.

Candy was her usual skeptical self.

"I thought he looked cannibalistic."

"I promise, if I walk in and there is a human-sized barbecue pit in his office, I'll turn around and walk right back out."

"I was speaking figuratively."

"Tell you what. If you buy his book, I'll get him to autograph it."

"You'd do that for me? Billy ... *you da man!*"

He finished his coffee and took his cup back to the kitchen.

Billy noticed a pile of mail that had been accumulating for several days. On top was a flier that had been posted to them by Amethyst. It pictured her laying in a coffin with her mouth wide open, as if she were screaming. There was an atomic mushroom cloud coming from the porthole of her dayglow yellow lips, with the details of her upcoming gig written on it.

That weekend, at a special Sunday night showcase at the Hammerstein Ballroom on West 34th, Amethyst's band, the Machines of Melanoma, were going to debut their new single. Obviously this was something Billy and Candy wouldn't want to miss.

This appearance was quite a leap for the band in terms of their professional development. Usually they played small to medium-size clubs, questionable dives tucked away in the more sordid areas of town. The Hammerstein was a renovated vintage opera house located mid-town, which frequently hosted national acts and only the most select local bands. Billy and Candy were of course thrilled that Amethyst's career as a pop star icon, which had for several years seemed to be permanently stalled, had apparently made a dramatic leap forward. Understandably, they were very curious how it had happened.

Shortly after they arrived, Amethyst found them. This was a small miracle in itself, in that the club was enormous and was packed to the walls with glitz, glam and punk posers, as well as hard-core personal fans, who were there to experience 125 decibels of continuous fuzz-bomb guitars and guttural screaming from five different bands.

"We're on in two hours. Next to last."

"That's top billing, eh?"

"I guess. Did you see the posters out front? I look pretty fucking scary, eh? It's so exciting. We're all stoked."

"So how did this happen? It's kind of sudden."

"New manager. I fuck his eyes out and he beats the pavement. It's a lovely arrangement. Actually, I like the dude. He'll be here later. You can check him out."

Amethyst continued making the rounds, saying hi to her friends and fans, rallying the troops, doing what she did best, the kind of self-promotion where people got pumped up by being someone the outrageous Amethyst Reigns personally knew, an upcoming star who breezed by to ply her zany charm. Others would watch enviously as they waited their turn for an edge of the limelight should she happened to come near by, or would try to figure out how they could attract her direct attention, hence be pulled into her revered circle of adoring sycophants.

She was a star both on and off stage — even if she was just walking into a convenience store or carrying out her trash. When she was in full make-up and wearing her brazen MOM stage wear, heads turned and eyes almost fell out of sockets. She was singularly responsible for a lot of next-day neck cramps.

The first three bands came and went. Nothing special as far as Billy was concerned. Candy seemed to be in her own zone, quietly sipping on a series of lime bitters, gin and soda. Conversation was out of the question. The roar of the bands made it impossible to talk, and the effect of the music was that of a well-aimed anesthetic dart to the frontal lobes of the cerebral cortex.

Finally, Machines of Melanoma hit the stage.

The energy level and the excitement of the crowd jumped into the next orbit. It was obvious that in terms of the crowd, if MOM didn't have a clear majority, they had a sizable plurality. They definitely had the most vocal fans.

Billy and Candy had seen Machines of Melanoma countless times. They loved Amethyst, even if they couldn't particularly relate to her music. Amethyst wasn't one of those needy, insecure artists who required everyone's approval. She had spared them having to come up with disingenuous diplomatic comments, by rarely asking them what they thought of her music. Don't ask don't tell. She was glad to have them as friends and appreciated their attendance and support, regardless of all else.

Billy and Candy almost knew the MOM set as well as the band. Had either of them had any musical talent, they could have sat in for any of the four musicians, if anyone had called in sick.

Though it wasn't their cup of tea, they both agreed that there was something unique about the songs, even the band's performance of them. So they sat there, casually nodding and smiling, tapping their fingers and feet, as they heard one familiar MOM tune after the other.

Then came the big moment of the evening. The show-closing debut of their new single.

Amethyst alternately pranced and slithered from one side of the stage to the other, like a hungry caged Bengal tiger. Cunning. Majestic. Carnivorous.

"Sex is dead, motherfuckers. Sex is dead. This is the end of the human race. And you know what? It makes me so fucking hot just to think about it. Here's our new single, you pathetic nihilistic losers!"

Except for a small core of sweaty moshers at the front of the stage who maintained their night-of-the-living-dead postures and inert cool, the crowd went completely berserk as MOM blasted into the feature song of the evening, a brand new number which Candy and Billy had, of course, never heard.

The song opened with a wild neo-psychedelic intro. Soaring, echoing guitar lines. A whole new musical dimension and level of musicality, which Billy and Candy had never heard from the band before. Unfortunately, after an abrupt dissipating of the beautiful guitar lines, the ethereal musical bed was replaced by the building thump-thump artillery rumble of bass and drums. That exploded into the more standard MOM wall of throbbing dissonance and discord, as Amethyst then launched into the first verse.

The lyrics were incomprehensible. But the visuals were great. MOM definitely knew how to put on a spectacular teeth-gritting show. Leaping scissor-kicks. Thrashing head-banging. Gravity-defying back-bends. Faces contorted in mock-epileptic paroxysms of pain.

Amethyst herself was in goddess-of-anarchy top form, even if her singing couldn't triumph over the clamorous roar of the band. Watching her created the disconcerting impression her microphone had been turned off.

After sixteen bars of Amethyst's miming the words of the verse, the chorus kicked in.

The band reached a whole new level of cacophonous distortion, the drums sounding like a rapid succession of high-speed car crashes, the bass creating a pulsing rumble that landed on the chest like a prize-fighter's punishing jabs, the guitars machine-gunning the air into slices of eardrum shattering shards of harmonic shrapnel. Miraculously Billy and Candy could now hear the lyrics …

> I swallowed Elton John's sperm
> I gotta say it kind of made my stomach churn
> It chapped my lips and made my tonsils burn
> Yeah baby I swallowed Elton John's sperm

The band and Amethyst then muscled their way through the next verse, but again the lyrics were buried in the muck of two slashing guitars which seemed at war with one another, and were further muffled by the muddy quicksand of what sounded like a continuous bass solo bearing no relation to the song.

Billy and Candy looked at each other and shrugged.

Then came a chorus, the lyrics of which they understood all too well. Then another verse which was indecipherable. Finally for the clinching blaze of glory, that catchy chorus again repeated three times over.

Billy noted that by the last reprise of the chorus, people were singing along. Well, more like shouting along. But that they had picked up on it so quickly on a first hearing, and were apparently so enamored with it that they joined in singing, caught him off guard.

It shouldn't have. Though neither he or Candy had any way of knowing for sure, the place was *packed* with diehard MOM fans. They would have gone with anything the band wanted. Amethyst could have led them en masse to jump off the Brooklyn Bridge or run naked through the Lincoln Tunnel at rush hour.

To climax their set, Machines of Melanoma tried to put a huge rave-up flourish on the end of the song. But they were already maxed out, so it kind of went nowhere. The crowd still went nuts. There was a full two-minute ovation consisting of screaming, slamming, stage diving and pugilistic exchanges. Amethyst did her part with her signature move of going to the front edge of the stage, pulling guys' heads between her legs up into her skirt, and rubbing her silk-thonged crotch against their sweaty faces.

All in all, it was a performance that made believers of the most intractable hold-outs. And confirmed in the minds of established fans that they were in the presence of greatness.

Maybe this was it! Machines of Melanoma were finally on the road to the big time.

The final band's set was mercifully short. From the start, it was obvious that the lead singer — a kid that was barely twenty but whose youthful appearance had been all but destroyed by life in the rock 'n roll fast lane — was incoherently drunk. On the first song alone, there were two false starts as he failed to come in singing where he clearly was supposed to. They did manage to get through the next two songs by having the bass player sing along, to fill in the gaps left by the lead singer as he faded in and out of consciousness. At first the crowd seemed impressed by the mere act of him remaining vertical. But boos and catcalls started to creep in. When the lead singer noticed them, he'd flip off the crowd and shout obscenities back. Even these simple expletives proved too challenging to him, sounding more like he was in the advance stages of cerebral palsy. The young band's brief appearance at the world-renowned Hammerstein Ballroom ended a few bars into their fifth song, when the lead singer turned around to be sick and vomited on the bass player's pants and shoes, then collapsed in his own fetid puke. The rest of the band put away their instruments and just walked off in disgust, leaving their star front man laying in the puddle of stomach juices, Jim Beam, and a partially digested submarine sandwich.

Billy and Candy caught up with Amethyst at the stage door and the three of them went out to catch a bite and a drink.

A strange thing happened while they were leaving the service alley behind the Hammerstein. The two girls were chatting away, as Billy followed a few yards behind. Seemingly out of nowhere, a motorcyclist apparently trying to circumvent a cluster of taxis ready to transport some of the people still streaming out of the ballroom, shot up on the sidewalk directly toward Billy. His reflexes were good and he managed to get out of the way in time, but in the process he slammed his face into a lamp post. There was no blood but he had definitely taken a serious blow to his left eye. He staggered, then went partially down on one knee to steady himself. Candy was the first to rush over to him.

"Are you alright, Billy? Whoa! You're going to have a real shiner! It's already darkening."

"I'll be fine. No problem. Just a light tap on the cheek."

In a few moments, the three of them were again on their way.

They caught the A-train to the West Village and sat down in an all-night deli specializing in Greek food and Turkish coffee — Athena's Tender Pebble.

Billy was characteristically quiet around the two girls. It was usually entertaining enough just to sit back and listen. Having just been clobbered in the eye didn't exactly contribute to making him talkative.

"Where's your new manager qua boyfriend?"

"He said he'd try to make it later. Of course, I didn't tell him where we were going and he didn't ask."

"He sounds like an organizational genius."

"He has too many deficiencies to enumerate in a single evening. But he pulls a rabbit out of his hat every once in a while. Like the Hammerstein."

"And what is his take on the new song?"

"He claims it has hit potential and can get it on the radio."

"You believe him?"

"Of course not. I don't believe anyone in this fucked-up business anymore. But he thinks it represents a good direction. He's always saying, 'Amy' — for some reason he calls me Amy — 'Keep them coming. More songs like *Sperm* and it's to the top of the charts.' What am I supposed to say to that?"

"I've got to be honest with you. I'm having trouble picturing you accepting the statue for Best Pop Single of the Year at the next Grammy Awards ceremonies, while Kings of Leon and Kanye West politely applaud, and Chris Martin from Coldplay sits glumly, wondering why he didn't think of writing a song called 'I Swallowed Elton John's Sperm'."

They could always count on Candy.

"And you Billy? Can you see that happening?"

"I'd say you've got an uphill battle. Actually … straight up."

Amethyst put her head on the table and looked like she was weeping inconsolably. Then she suddenly reared up and laughed as hard as they had ever seen her laugh before.

"I love you guys!"

Men Who Love Too Much

By the time the day came around for his appointment with Dr. Freundlich, Billy was beginning to think it was a really lousy idea. But what the hell. What's $600 to meet a TV celebrity?

The doctor was more imposing in person than he was on television. He had been seated during the TV interview, which gave no clue of his 6' 8" height and the jaw-dropping size of his frame. He was more than a very big belly. He was a very big man.

"Please sit here. Relax. My assistant will now put in place a couple of sensors on your fingers, and a blood pressure monitoring band around your arm. These are connected to the flat panel display on my desk. I have found that the basic vitals of the human body are key indicators as to what is going on in your mind, as our session unfolds and develops."

Good to his word, an athletic Nordic girl in her 20s with a nurse's cap on for effect, but otherwise dressed in fashionable office wear, slipped four electrical sensors on the fingers of his right hand, and wrapped the real-time blood pressure monitoring apparatus on his left arm. Billy got a nice view of her breasts along the way and wondered if not wearing a bra was part of her job description.

Dr. Freundlich occupied himself by looking through some papers, until the devices were set and activated. He glanced at his flat-panel display.

"Ach! Everything seems to be working. Thank you, Annina."

"Yore velcome, Doktore."

Quite an accent. Another kraut. Dr. Freundlich continued to arrange the papers and from a quick glimpse, Billy could see that what he was looking at was the lengthy questionnaire that had taken Billy hours to complete in preparation for this session.

Freundlich finally looked up and smiled.

"How did you get the black eye?"

"I bumped into a lamp post."

"Right. I used to love boxing. Tyson? Badass son-of-a-bitch. But what a great boxer. When he was just starting out anyway. You couldn't have gotten that by throwing a left hook. I'd say it was either a right hook or a roundhouse. Definitely a right, though. And the difference between a world-class boxer and everyone else is never dropping the left. Even when throwing a blockbuster. I've seen both men go down because the guy who should've won dropped his left."

"I walked into a lamp post. And I'm not here for boxing tips, thank you very much."

"Of course not. That was free advice. You can take it to the bank. Or the gym. I see you have been off hormones for four months. Any regrets?"

"Any regrets? Sure. I regret that my parents both died in a freak jeep accident. I regret that we've had an imbecile in the White House for eight years. I regret—"

"About not going through with the sex change?"

"I'm a man. M-A-N."

"Spencer Davis Group. They had a song out that went like that. I think it was 1967."

"I can see why you get the big bucks."

Dr. Freundlich laughed. More like a neigh than the husky bellowing Billy would have expected to come from such a barrel-chested man.

"Sarcasm. I love sarcasm. But it's symptomatic, you know. Let's talk about you, Mr. Green. The reason you filled out such a lengthy pre-counseling questionnaire is that I don't want to waste our time here on background. Yes, I do get the big bucks. So let's get down to business, eh?"

"I'm all for it."

"At one time, you were very serious about being surgically and hormonally transgendered. You said that you didn't change your mind until you were on the operating table. That's about as close as you can get. I will grant you that there now exists a new openness about gender roles, gender reassignment, and even commingling sexual identities — meaning the commonplace exchange between the sexes in matters of fashion, persona, role models, and even behavior. But the actual number of people who go as far as you did to implement a gender change is relatively small. The percentage annually is .0004% of the world's population. About one out of every quarter million people worldwide. Those are the most recent statistics."

"Are you going somewhere with this?"

After a discernable furrowing of his pipe-like Aryan brow, Dr. Freundlich's face widened into a smile of breathtaking proportions. He could have been running for high office.

"Of course I am, Mr. Green. Of course. Simply put, the choice you made, though aborted at the last possible moment, is symptomatic of something. That's what we're here to find out. Because that issue or that set of issues may not have gone away."

"Does it ever go away?"

"I like to think so. I have staked my reputation on it. I have devoted the entirety of my professional career to, whenever possible, making it go away."

"I am ready for my cerebral enema."

"You might at least open yourself up to the process, by dropping your smart ass attitude."

"I grew up in Detroit. In Detroit, this is not considered an attitude. It's called survival."

Dr. Freundlich put his reading glasses back on and again glanced down at the questionnaire, several times turning it sideways to read some notes he had apparently made.

"Your father hated and abused you. Your mother worshipped and nurtured you. School was a war zone you survived by being smart and competent academically. Cornell. Great school. Married very young. Your wife turned out to be a lesbian, so that didn't work out. No kids. Parents died in a safari accident. You now live in New York with your girlfriend. But along the way, especially the last few years, you have been making quite a frantic attempt at putting your sense of self in order. This is quite a story. But it's all over the map. There's no real discernable progression. Then finally, you get it in your head that you want to be a woman, so you arrange for hormones, surgery, the works. Finally, at the last minute you back out. Interesting."

"But would it make a good movie of the week?"

"I appreciate the nuances in all of this. But you already know the story. And I think I do too. I'm just throwing out the thumbnail tour here to lay the framework for an expedient session."

"I personally think it's been very expedient. But have we gotten anywhere yet? Or are we still window-shopping? Did I touch on that in the questionnaire? I'm a very expedient window-shopper."

"It comes down to this, Mr. Green. You mentioned growing up in Detroit. And survival. You unwittingly made an extremely valuable point. Survival."

"I'll take that as your unwittingly paying me a valuable compliment."

"Mr. Green, there are approaching 7 billion people in the world. Each one of us confronts this. Each one of us has nearly 7 billion potential enemies. Thus each one of us must effectively be a fortress. We must stand guard over our individual destinies, our integrity, our wholeness, our personal identities. You made a courageous assault on your own identity, thinking at some point that you needed to tear down some walls and rebuild them from scratch. This was a fundamental rethink on your part, going to the core of your being, then making that choice. However it played out — and I do believe you are solidly committed now to remaining a male — the important thing is that the fortress that is you, Mr. Green, be secure. It must be guarded at all costs for you to remain functional and survive. Back to that indeed. Survival."

"With all due respect, Dr. Freundlich, I can certainly follow what you're saying. But you know that as much as I respect good writing, I've never been too keen on poetry. It is pretty to listen to, has some nice fleeting images, playful juggling of words and juxtaposition of ideas. All very nice."

"But?"

"But I've never learned a damn thing from a poem. I'm hearing what you're saying but what am I supposed to take away here? What's the lesson?"

There was a momentary crack in the smiling iron mask of the good doctor.

"If you let me finish ..."

"Of course. You're the doctor. I'm the patient. And I can see you're getting impatient."

"We're just two human beings—"

"On the third rock from the sun."

"The fortress only has so many soldiers. The common error, driven I believe by the desperation of loneliness, the intimidation of a species which has become hyped up on its own superiority, and the anonymity of living among 7 billion kindred spirits, is sending too many soldiers out into the field, and not keeping enough inside the fortress to guard the most sacred territory of all — the unique and hallowed ground which for each of us is the center of the Universe."

"I'm right with you. You've got a great analogy going. I'm in perfect sync."

"I should hope so."

"But I'm still waiting. Do we have enough time for you to tell me what the key to all this is? Or do I have to come back after a word from our sponsors?"

"Mr. Green. Unlike many of my unscrupulous colleagues in the field of self-induced human evolution, I don't need your money. You are, of course, welcome to come back. But I intend for you to leave today with exactly what you need to build a perfect Billy Green."

"Ready when you are."

"The soldiers are the love we put out there. We send them on different missions. Exploratory. Expeditionary. Reconnaissance. Conquest. It doesn't matter why they're sent. The crucial thing is that you never send too many. You have to keep a sufficient number inside the walls to guard the fortress."

"Don't put out too much love."

"Since the 60s — obviously long before you were born but a very exciting, experimental, optimistic period I personally remember well — a misconception has achieved widespread currency. This is the myth is that we all need to pour as much love into the world as possible. And everything will get better. More love. More better. Individuals like yourself have become the victims of this naive and onerous fallacy. It's of course good to love, Mr. Green. But it is self-sabotaging to love too much. You have to hold some back. How much to hold back varies from person to person. But the universal truth is that when you put it all outside yourself, there's none left for you. People lose their sense of worth. They lose a sense of what it is about themselves that is good and unique. I often see people who love everyone else but loathe themselves."

"I put out too much love?"

"You, Mr. Green, are ... a man who loves too much."

"And now? What now?"

"That's all you need to know. Put that to work for you. There's no set of mantras or special secret techniques. There's no road map or guide book. Just do it. Tomorrow, you get up and look in the mirror and say what needs to be said. Just say it loud and proud."

"And that is?"

"Just say, 'Good morning, Billy. Yesterday you were the man who loved too much. That was then. This is now. Have a nice day.' Or something along those lines."

"That's it?"

"That's it."

Right on cue, Annina came in and quickly removed the sensors. Really *really* nice breasts.

Dr. Freundlich stood up, came around from his side of the desk, approached Billy and gave him a giant ribcage-crushing bear hug. Then he put his hairy Visigothic arm around Billy's shoulders and escorted him to the door. As tall as Billy was, he felt like a dwarf next to the massive superstar psychologist.

"Good luck, Mr. Green."

Billy wrote a check for $600 and left.

The counseling session had gone exactly 59 minutes and 47 seconds.

Vertical Tongues of Fire

The pronouncement left little to the imagination.

THE SKY WILL BLAZE WITH VERTICAL TONGUES OF FIRE!

And just as Apocalypso had predicted via internet postings, fliers, posters, even using skywriting planes on three consecutive days over Manhattan, fires were breaking out one by one in the most exclusive high-rise residential buildings in the Upper East Side.

One building each day for eleven days straight.

Eleven buildings.

So far.

Amazingly, there had been no fatalities and only a couple slight injuries. One older resident sprained his ankle leaving his building in a panic. Another cut her hand breaking a window to scream for someone to rescue her, though she was in no immediate danger.

The best minds of the city's arson investigation unit were put on the case. No one could figure out how whoever was doing this, was pulling it off. It was so methodical. Organized. Planned and executed with such perfect order and timing.

The conclusion that there were a lot of "insiders" involved was unavoidable. These were people who worked in the buildings and knew all of the critical details of their layout, their architectural and structural characteristics. But even this wasn't much help.

The pattern was identical with all eleven fires set to date.

A modest fire would break out in some unoccupied area of the building — storage lofts or mechanical rooms. The fire department would safely get the people out of the building. Then while the firefighters would try to isolate and put out the modest fire, the whole rest of the building would floor-by-floor ignite in a conflagration which would eventually reduce the whole thing to a big pile of ashes and structural rubble.

It was stunning to watch. Breathtaking in its incendiary beauty. Awe-inspiring in the precision and totality of its destruction.

Miraculously, not even any firefighters had been seriously injured to date.

As with all of his previous attempts to protest the status quo, Apocalypso made his case to the public, leaving no room for doubt as to his intentions and political agenda. Before anonymously turning some of the most luxurious buildings in the richest part of Manhattan into Roman candles, he pointed the finger at the affluent class and accused them in no uncertain terms of bankrupting the country purely for their own enrichment, and of perpetrating a class war on the middle and lower classes. If they weren't going to, for example, address homelessness, they should themselves be made homeless. If the haves weren't willing to share their material possessions with the have-nots, someone should turn them into have-nots by incinerating their stuff.

For once the privileged class would know what it felt like to be on the wrong end of the stick. Apocalypso was sure this was the best way to re-educate America's wildly prosperous well-to-do, and publicly point the way to a more egalitarian future.

Plain and simple. Building by building, he would level the playing field.

He would destroy those things which both symbolically and in actuality epitomized the enormous gap between the rich and the poor, a gap that seemed to be increasing exponentially each day, as new scams surfaced to rob the personal savings of the majority of decent Americans, and even loot the U.S. Treasury itself.

After all their money had gone up in smoke, the rich would finally know what it felt like to be broke.

It was an interesting theory.

Not very realistic. Impossible to fully implement.

But interesting.

What was incomprehensible was how the fires were handled by the media. How the dark dirty secret — the motivation behind them and the parties responsible — was totally closeted by the press.

Everyone knew why and what was going on.

How could they not? Apocalypso had mounted a publicity campaign leading up to the string of high-profile fires which would be the envy of the best public relations firms on Avenue of the Americas. He made sure everyone knew the why and what.

But someone, or several of the someones who were so utterly humiliated by not being able to stop this home-grown Osama bin Laden, must have put on a lot of pressure to cap the real story. Instead of just stating the obvious, talking heads both on the air and in print, gave wholly laughable characterizations of what was turning out to be the largest single terrorist act in America since the 9/11 attack on the World Trade Center.

> *For the third evening in a row, a prestigious Upper East Side residential tower was completely destroyed in a spectacular fire which lit up the evening sky and could be seen from miles anywhere in mid-Manhattan and beyond. Police and fire detectives are saying it could be coincidence but are now leaning towards thinking it's arson. No one that I've talked to will go on record to speculate what could be the motive behind such destructive acts. The three buildings are owned by three completely different, unrelated companies, which would seem to rule out a disgruntled employee or tenant. One gentleman, who spoke on the condition of anonymity, said to me and I quote, "There's never exactly been a shortage of crazy people in this [expletive deleted] town."*

It was truly bizarre that no official statement, no news reporting analysis, no commentator on-the-ground or in-the-studio, no media icon or government figurehead, made the immediate and obvious connection between Apocalypso, with his publicly stated and broadly advertised doctrine of insurrection by theft and demolition, and the spectacular fires. He had in no uncertain terms *predicted* the torching of the buildings. Though he personally was still in jail without bail — itself a laughable distortion of habeas corpus which had drawn only cursory coverage in the press — Apocalypso's PR team had delineated in black-and-white and a rich palette of eye-catching color, the rationale for attacking the rich on their territory. Every posting, poster, and public statement had for all intents and purposes been signed: *Yours truly - Apocalypso.*

The only plausible rationalizations for this blackout were that first, after he had humiliated the city's best legal team in court and gotten all serious charges dropped, the powers that be didn't want to bring attention to him again, and add to his credibility and celebrity in the public eye. Martyrs make big headlines.

Second, a big hullabaloo had surrounded his incarceration and arraignment, and the claim blown up hugely out of proportion, that this enormous threat to the public safety — technically at this point that he might cause more cats to fall from the sky — had been neutralized and now everyone could sleep soundly. To suggest that he might have somehow coordinated arson on the scale being seen on every television in America, day after day on the news, would be tantamount to admitting that they hadn't done their job at all. That he had from his jail cell, escalated from suicide cat terrorism to flambéing hundred-million dollar chunks of New York real estate.

By the seventh and eighth building, the story hadn't changed much. Except a new tone of panic seemed to saturate the reporting, especially the television coverage.

You can see down across the street right in front of the Helmsley Wickerton, there are three private armed guards posted at the front entrance. Owners of many such properties have gone great lengths to boost security. Tenants have been instructed to report any suspicious activity. Now interestingly enough, in terms of the fire we are covering as I speak, and you can see it now for yourselves as we pan back to what looks like a gigantic spear of flame and smoke reaching up into the sky — I mean, would you look at that! This is unbelievable! That whole building is one huge torch starting from the ground going all the way up beyond the top floor. Anyway, I talked to the additional security guards and the regular doorman, who by the way has worked here for over twenty years. And none of them reported anything out of the ordinary. Not a thing. So if it's arson, they must be invisible because no suspicious people were seen coming or going from the building. This is Samantha Fox reporting live from the Majesty Tower fire on 73rd Street, Upper East Side Manhattan. Back to you Tim.

By the tenth and eleventh fire, there was still no public mention of Apocalypso by name in connection with the conflagration. It was obviously a stonewall.

Authorities are now all but certain that these fires are the direct result of arson, individual acts of sabotage. Just yesterday, combing through the rubble of the fifth building to have burned to the ground — that was the Westfield Arms on 81st Street this past Thursday — the charred remains of a highly sophisticated timing device were found, apparently for activating an incendiary bomb. Based on this discovery, some investigators have gone so far as to say that they suspect these horribly destructive acts are part of an organized attack by domestic or foreign terrorists, though they still have no leads as to who the perpetrators are, or what their motives might be.

Now people were getting scared. All day lines of taxis and limos could be seen lining the streets, waiting to ferry away the wealthy residents of the Upper East Side to safer havens.

Billy wasn't worried, however. Not for his or Candy's safety, or about his building.

Apocalypso promised Billy that his place would not be targeted.

There was a simple and straightforward reason for this consideration. Billy had been and continued to make significant contributions to Apocalypso's political machine and citizen's militia. Billy had never been particularly "political", certainly never politically active. But both through Candy and on his own, he had recently developed some strong opinions on the state of the country and didn't at all like what he saw. Things were really bad. The Bush idiot state. The war in Iraq. The crashing economy. The fear. The hate. It all had to change.

Apocalypso was hardly the master statesman of the revolutionary left. But he was out there saying things that needed to be said. Doing what he thought was right to wake people up before it was too late.

Billy could see the value in that.

And though Billy was now too embarrassed to bring it up — especially to the man himself — Apocalypso had inadvertently saved Billy from making the biggest mistake of his life, that being his sex change. But for the power cut which resulted from one of Apocalypso's political stunts earlier this year, on July 22nd the day of his surgery, he would now be a she.

Billy felt he owed him big time.

So he put some money where Apocalypso's mouth was.

Apocalypso appreciated Billy's support. Every "little bit" counted.

Thus, at least in part funded by Billy's magnanimity, hell was now breaking out in Manhattan. One towering inferno after the other.

But since there were plenty of buildings to choose from, he could spare Billy's and Candy's.

Or at least save it for last.

Moreover, though they had their differences of opinion on many things — more about tactics than philosophy — Apocalypso definitely liked Billy. He had been up to Billy's rich guy digs several times, saw how modest the furnishings were, talked politics, ate the food, drank the wine, had a few laughs. Billy definitely wasn't one of the exploitive fat cats who usually lived in the Upper East Side. Moreover, though Billy just laughed it off, it seemed from the way Apocalypso looked at Candy, he probably wanted to sleep with her.

He was a guy, after all.

Guys will be guys.

Guys will be boys.

Boys like to play with matches.

Boys like to fuck girls.

It's all so simple.

There's No Place Like Home

It is just after midnight.

Creamcheese sleeps in a curled ball, on her own pillow in one corner of the living room.

The warm, luminescent light from a burning building only a block away backlights the room with a pleasant, flickering glow. Smoke billows and dances into the sky, a silent, celestial wallpaper for a contemporary urban landscape, the cotton stuffing of surrealistic daydreams and Kafkaesque nightmares.

In their plush Upper Eastside townhouse, Billy and Candy are watching the *Wizard of Oz* on his enormous flat panel HD television screen.

It could have been a Norman Rockwell painting. But it wasn't. Not by a long shot. The tips of Candy's nipples are visible through a white Ashram of the

Urban Night t-shirt. She wears a ripped denim mini-skirt, yellow knee sox. With delicate focus she is sipping through a purple plastic straw a blend of grenadine, Stolichnaya vodka, and skim milk. From the demure expression on her face, she could be a callow10-year-old girl drinking a jello, ice cream and marshmallow float, sidled up to her dozing grandmother. But no. Rather she is a fully-grown, lithe, skimpily dressed, erotically-charged neo-hippie, anchored by random events and enigmatic choices to a man for whom every moment is just another uncharted minefield fraught with the potential for humiliation and catastrophe.

Billy's impassive expression, liquefied and softened by 40 ounces of Miller Lite Beer, is a fragile portrait of composed panic, underachiever boredom, and midnight ennui. He is the Billy we only think we know.

A Billy with an impenetrable mask and exposed heart of exile, of existential solitary confinement.

Billy from Detroit, Michigan.

It is the final scene of the movie. Dorothy has awakened back in Kansas. Revelation is in the air.

> Dorothy: *But it wasn't a dream. It was a place. And you and you and you ... and you were there! But you couldn't have been, could you?*
>
> Aunt Em: *Oh, we dream lots of silly things when we —*
>
> Dorothy: *No, Aunt Em. This was a real, truly live place. And I remember that some of it wasn't very nice. But most of it was beautiful. But just the same, all I kept saying to everybody was 'I want to go home'. And they sent me home.*
>
> *(Chorus of patronizing chuckles)*
>
> Dorothy: *Doesn't anybody believe me?*
>
> Father: *Of course, we believe you, Dorothy.*
>
> Dorothy: *Oh, but anyway, Toto, we're home! Home! And this is my room, and you're all here. And I'm not going to leave here ever ever again, because I love you all. And ... Auntie Em. There's no place like home.*

Appearing on the screen in a beautiful cursive font.

The End

Billy shakes his head and tries to get up. Candy rolls over on top of him.

"Candy. I can't believe you made me watch this."

She undoes his pants, and like peeling a banana has them off him and in a heap on the floor.

"Believe it."

Her skirt and panties are now gone. His member instantly stands duty-ready at attention.

She mounts him and starts to writhe in obvious pleasure, the slow-motion whipsaw of a child on a pink plastic mechanical horse, the kind outside of a supermarket. This one didn't need a quarter.

She came.

He came.

It was over in less than three minutes.

Epilogue

Till Death Do Us Part
Early 2010

Dear Dr. Freundlich,

I've been thinking a lot about what you said to me.

You were wrong. About me in particular, but also about everyone in general. <u>Very</u> wrong.

A person can't love too much.

Sure, sometimes you love the wrong person. Or the other person doesn't reciprocate. So you might decide he or she doesn't deserve all of that love you're pouring out.

But love too much?

I don't think so.

It's a fuck of a lot better to love too much than too hate even a little bit. And it's a fuck of a lot better to love even a little than to be indifferent.

Life is unfair. But averaged out, it's equally unfair to everyone.

So a person might not think they're getting their fair share, but so what if someone's got a little piece of your action? Or you have a piece of theirs. It's love we're talking about. Not internal organs.

And that's why it's perfectly okay, maybe better than okay, maybe even <u>commendable</u>, to love too much.' Cause that extra bit, the "too much" part, is somebody's piece of the action. And love is a good thing. It feels good on both ends and in general makes the world a little more tolerable. Sometimes it even makes the world a much better place.

And let me say one more thing that I just thought of.

The way you said I _loved_ _too_ _much_? How could I love too much? I didn't even know how to love. You can't do too much of a thing you don't really know how to do.

Yesterday I didn't know how to love either. And I had to learn it again today, this morning sitting across the breakfast table from Candy. Tomorrow I'll learn it again.

Loving is something you can't know. You never really get it down. Every day you have to try to master it again.

Again and again and again . . . every day _learning_ _to_ _love_.

And that's the beauty of it. That's what makes it so special. That's where the fun is too! Always _learning_.

Suit yourself. But if I were you, I wouldn't be peddling that weird love-too-much philosophy of yours anymore. Even if you need the money. Just come up with something else. The world is full of people hungry for some light to fill the dark voids in their lives. You're a smart guy. Figure it out. And spread more love, not less.

You'll see. It'll feel good.

Take it from someone who's been there.

There and there and God knows where.

By the way, Candy says 'hi'. Of course, she's being sarcastic, since she doesn't know you and thinks your an unscrupulous predator and an amoral opportunist — I think those were her choice of words. But you seem to be partial to sarcasm. So I guess her wholly ironic greeting might make your day.

Candy is absolutely phenomenal in every way.

She's someone I definitely couldn't love too much.

She's the one who helped me figure this all out.

The guy with a black eye,
Billy Green

More Books by John Rachel

If you liked this book, you might want to check out these other novels by this author and political blogger.

"An Unlikely Truth"

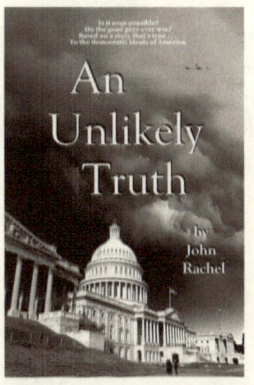

In this political drama, a bright, young, idealistic, Green Party candidate in his bid for the congressional seat of a very conservative district in Ohio, teams with a beautiful, fiery African-American intern to combat the slick deceptions and ruthless tactics of a sweet-talking right wing incumbent.

Amazon (Kindle): amzn.to/1jetpiY
Amazon (Print): amzn.to/1lddvsp
Barnes & Noble: bit.ly/1l5FmuG
Apple iBook: bit.ly/1gT2O7w
Smashwords: bit.ly/1fIU3Mq

• •

"Blinders Keepers"

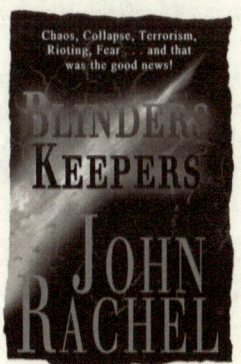

In this dark comedy, a young man who escapes his hopelessly hayseed home town in Missouri is mistakenly labeled a terrorist and must survive a manhunt by government security agencies, while the President of an America in chaos and collapse perpetrates an end-of-the-world hoax, attempting to reclaim control and get himself re-elected.

Amazon (Kindle): amzn.to/122cnyF
Barnes & Noble: bit.ly/17MtgjE
Apple iBook: bit.ly/11WqJiv
Smashwords: bit.ly/190zmgs
Kobo: bit.ly/18wHki2

• •

"11 - 11 - 11"

Noah was turning 23 and desperate to get out of town. Pulnick, Missouri had always been bland and soporific, but now it was now being invaded by white supremacist meth heads, plagued by an unprecedented crime wave, exploited by spiritualists and local politicos, and driven to hysteria by paranoid rumors that the world would end on November 11th.

Amazon (Kindle): amzn.to/1sEWaf0
Barnes & Noble: bit.ly/1nlgS2Z
Apple iBook: bit.ly/1z8TCKS
Smashwords: bit.ly/1paiJ6j
Kobo: bit.ly/T7181J

• •

"12 - 12 - 12"

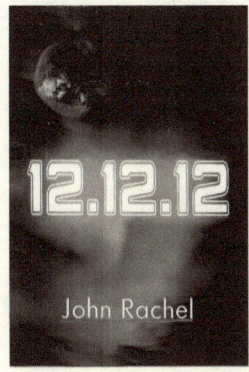

Welcome to the parallel universe of "12-12-12". This not what actually happens during 2012. But what unfolds is not more implausible. Nor is it less implausible. It is dark satire, a portrayal of reality with healthy doses of surreality and comedy, spawned by the tragic absurdity of our times. One reviewer calls it "laugh-out-loud brain food for hungry minds."

Amazon (Kindle): <u>amzn.to/1DaFrDL</u>
Barnes & Noble: <u>bit.ly/1w5Yw5D</u>
Apple iBook: <u>bit.ly/1sJasMO</u>
Smashwords: <u>bit.ly/1o9GaSg</u>
Kobo: <u>lnk.ms/c1CWm</u>

● ●

"Candidate Contracts: Taking Back Our Democracy"

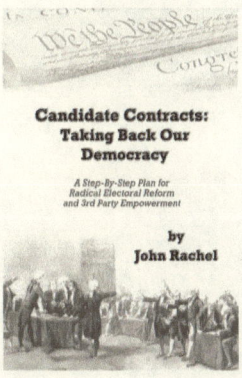

This political manifesto offers a detailed, step-by-step plan for cleaning up the corruption in Washington DC, replacing the current crop of pay-for-play, toadie politicians with progressive, independent, minor-party candidates, who will be bound by legal contract when elected, to faithfully serve the interests of the voting public. This is about restoring true democracy to America.

• •

Coming Soon

"Petrocelli"

"Love Connection"

"The Last Giraffe"

"Sex, Lies and Coffee Beans"

"Happy Happy Dreaming Girl"

"The Naked American"

"St. Jerome's Home For The Sexually Insane"

About the Author

John Rachel has a B.A. in Philosophy, has traveled extensively, been a songwriter and music producer, and is a bipolar humanist. He has spent his life trying to resolve the intrinsic clash between the metaphysical purity of Buddhism and the overwhelming appeal of narcissism.

In October of 2008, while visiting Japan, he completed his first novel, *From Thailand With Love*. It's a thriller about the trafficking of adolescent Asian girls for prostitution in America. Unfortunately, it was hijacked by an unscrupulous New York publisher and never released in its entirety.

In November of 2009, he completed his second novel, *The Man Who Loved Too Much*, written over ten months, as he lived in and traveled through Japan, China, Nepal, India Thailand, and Malaysia. It follows the convoluted life of a young man from age 4 to 28, as he tries to find his place in the world. The story is set in Detroit, upstate New York, and New York City. At 800+ pages, it is an epic. This encyclopedia of white trash pulp fiction plotlines has been split into three volumes, the novel you have just read being the last book of the series.

While writing his third and fourth novels in 2010 and 2011 — *11-11-11* and *12-12-12* — which track two years in the life of a young man, a hapless victim born in a hopelessly hayseed town in Bible-belt Missouri, the author hopped around between Japan, Taiwan, Indonesia, South Korea and the Philippines. Those two efforts evolved into the short and snappy adventure, *Blinders Keepers*, both as a novel and a screenplay. Combining plot elements from *11-11-11* and *12-12-12*, *Blinders Keepers* is social-political satire in the tradition of Jonathan Swift, Kurt Vonnegut and Joseph Heller, but revved up and spit-shined to take on the historical new levels of absurdity and dysfunction of the 21st Century. *Blinders Keepers* was published as a novel in 2013, after which the author bounced between Japan, South Korea, the U.S., and nine countries in Europe.

He then became somewhat rooted in a small traditional farming village in Japan near Osaka. It was there, immediately after poking himself in the forehead with chopsticks, that he was inspired to plant soybeans and sweet potatoes in his small but promising vegetable garden, and to write *An Unlikely Truth*, published March of 2014. In this political drama, a bright, young, idealistic, Green Party candidate, in his bid for the congressional seat of a very conservative district in Ohio, teams with a beautiful, fiery African-American intern to combat the slick deceptions and ruthless tactics of a sweet-talking right wing incumbent.

A non-fiction distillation of the political strategy embedded in *An Unlikely Truth* appeared in June 2015 as *Candidate Contracts: Taking Back Our Democracy*. This paradigm-shifting manifesto offers a detailed, step-by-step plan for cleaning up the corruption in Washington DC, replacing the current crop of pay-for-play politicians with progressive, independent, minor-party candidates, who will be bound by legal contract when elected, to faithfully serve the interests of the voting public. Author Rachel expects the impact of this work will result in his being put on international no-fly lists and perhaps his becoming a target for drone assassination.

With the publication of the *The Man Who Loved Too Much* trilogy, he now has two more novels in the pipeline: *Love Connection*, a drug-trafficking love story set in Japan, and *The Last Giraffe*, an anthropological drama involving both the worship and devouring of giraffes. It unfolds in sub-Saharan Africa.

Also in the works is a creative non-fiction work, *The Naked American*. It is allegedly an account of author Rachel's travels since leaving America August 2006, but more likely the product of the voices in his head which have plagued him since puberty. Several prominent publishers have declared that they will do everything in their power to make sure this book never sees the light of day.

The author's last permanent residence in America was Portland, Oregon where he had a state-of-the-art ProTools recording studio, music production house, a radio promotion and music publishing company. He recorded and produced several artists in the Pacific Northwest, releasing and promoting their music on radio across America and overseas. John Rachel now lives in a quiet, traditional, rural Japanese community, where he sets his non-existent watch by the thrice-daily ringing of sonorous temple bells, at a local Shinto shrine.

• • •

You can follow John Rachel's adventures
and developing world view at:
http://jdrachel.com

• • •

Since the open mind recognizes no borders, you are also
invited to join us in the ongoing dialogue about
the writing arts here:
http://literaryvagabond.com

Legal Notices and Disclaimers:

The Man Who Loved Too Much is a series of original novels (a trilogy) which is protected under international copyright law and registered with the U. S. Library of Congress © John D Rachel 2014.

The Man Who Loved Too Much, Book 3: Oxymoron is entirely a work of fiction. Names, characters, places, brands, media, and incidents are either the product of the author's imagination or are used fictitiously. Any references to celebrities and nationally-known figures and their roles in the story are likewise fictional. No participation by such individuals in the writing of this novel or their endorsement of its point of view and message is claimed or otherwise implied.

The author acknowledges the trademarked status and trademark owners of various products referenced in this work of fiction, which have been used without permission. The publication/use of these trademarks is not authorized, associated with, or sponsored by the trademark owners, but appear as common features in the story as they are common features in modern everyday life. No product endorsements are meant or implied by their use.

Reference to Steve Erhardt — a real person aka the Living Ken Doll — is purely a fictional prerogative and is done without the knowledge and consent of aforesaid. No malign or mockery intended. Steve Erhardt is a controversial public figure, who if anything I respect for his boldness and courage in the art of remaking himself into a preferred likeness. I'd be on the next surgical bed but I just can't afford it. But if this trilogy sells well, you never know. Maybe my next book will be by John Rachel, aka The Living Hemingway Doll.

The author quoted song lyrics as part of the story: "Blowin' in the Wind", Copyright 1962 Special Rider Music (SESAC) written and performed by Bob Dylan; "Lola" Copyright 1970 by ABKCO Music Inc, written by Ray Davies, performed by The Kinks.

Dialogue was quoted from the closing scene of the classic *The Wizard of Oz*; directed by Victor Fleming; starring Judy Garland, Frank Morgan, Ray Bolger, Bert Lahr, Jack Haley, Billie Burke; Copyright 1939 distributed by Metro Golden Mayer.

Eight adapted excerpts from *The Man Who Loved Too Much, Book 3: Oxymoron* have appeared as short stories in online and print publications: "Dr. Gender Bender" appeared in the San Francisco humor Magazine, Hobo Pancakes, May 2010; "Spider Man" was published in the New York-base magazine, Full of Crow, April 2010; "The Tea Lady of Kashmir" was published online at Troubador 21 (USA), May 2010; "Little Tantrums" and "Queen for a Day" were published in the American print magazine, Audience, June 2010; "Apocalypso" appeared Million Stories (USA), July 2010; "Guerilla Warfare" was published in the Australia print magazine, The Mutant Life, July 2010; and "I Swallowed Elton John's Sperm" appeared Million Stories (USA), May 2012.